The Lusitania. The biggest, fastest, grandest, best known vessel on the North Atlantic run.
'The *Lusitania* . . .' breathed Stancombe, turning the word over in his mind and remembering that time, it must be six years ago, when he had trodden her decks. Stancombe remembered his first sight of that giant black hull, nearly 800 hundred feet long, towering above the Liverpool quay. He had been told that the distance from the water-line to the tip of the aerials was 165 feet and he could believe it. He remembered too how dwarfed he had felt by the four immense red and black smokestacks and the six decks. The first class, with its lounge, music-room, smoke-room, writing-room and library, and its great domed dining-room taking up two whole decks, must be like the Ritz. But the *Lusitania* was special in another way. She was the first liner to be driven by steam turbines. They were the engines that had given her her great speed and wrested the blue riband of the Atlantic from the Germans.
'Do I understand, sir,' said Stancombe at last, 'that you intend to attack the *Lusitania*!?'

Attack the *Lusitania*!

RAYMOND HITCHCOCK

SPHERE BOOKS LIMITED
30–32 Gray's Inn Road, London WC1X 8JL

First published in Great Britain by Michael Joseph Ltd 1979
Copyright © Raymond Hitchcock 1979
Published by Sphere Books Ltd 1981

TRADE
MARK

Set in Lasercomp Plantin

Printed and bound in Great Britain by
Collins, Glasgow

FOR LAL AND FLEUR,
who have suffered me so nobly

AUTHOR'S NOTE

I would particularly like to acknowledge the help received in reading Colin Simpson's *Lusitania*; the Hoehlings' *The Last Voyage of the Lusitania*; by talking with Commander Geoffrey Greenhalgh, RN (Retired) – who also read the manuscript; the patient ex-submariners of the Submarine Museum, HMS *Dolphin*; and Keiran Dempsey of Belgooly, County Cork.

I

It was to have been all over by Christmas. No one on either side had expected it to last more than three months at the most. The boys were to have been back in time for plum pudding and bitter or sauerkraut and schnapps, depending on which side of the North Sea they lived. But it had all gone wrong and no one knew why. Instead of victory, there was an unbroken line of trenches from the Alps to the sea; millions were already changing their natural habitat for that of the mole. Instead of decision there was deadlock. Manoeuvre seemed to have vanished for ever.

In England, as long ago as November, the Cabinet had conceded that their hopes and belief in a short war had proved false, and in Germany the sense of frustration was even more acute, for they at least had come near to victory. But for Sir John French's 'Contemptible Little Army', the Schlieffen Plan might just have worked. No wonder that leaders and led alike were mystified by events, and that lacking any experiences of a large-scale continental war with the new weapons, the aeroplane, machine-gun and submarine, neither generals nor admirals knew where to turn, or from which muse to pluck inspiration.

Mystification might have been universal, but on neither side was anyone more mystified than George V, who at that moment, by the grace of God, was sovereign not only of Great Britain and Ireland, but of those vast tracks of land called the British Empire. Enthused with a sense of calling and duty, feeling himself to be truly the father of that polyglot multitude and in some vague way responsible for them,

1

yet baffled by events and disinclined to see in his Prime Minister, Asquith, the whole truth and nothing but the truth, he sought other, deeper sources of information and explanation. Hence the discreet dinner that February evening at White's.

Of the four men present, but for the chance of birth all except two might have been thankful to have any gainful employment, and perhaps their highest hopes would have been to find a safe niche in the warrens of the City. In which case instead of sipping their 1865 Grande Champagne brandy — carefully chosen as the King's birth year — in the warmth and elegance of that private room, four hours ago they would have been scuttling across the wind-swept wastes of Waterloo Bridge, clutching their bowlers against the icy eastern blast that had ruffled the murky waters of the Thames all that day. But Fortune had smiled on them, and now as a consequence they were, in varying degrees, bewildered partners in the decision-making strata of Imperial Britain.

For the King, there was one man missing from the table who he would dearly loved to have had present. Douglas Haig. Of all his soldiers and sailors he liked Haig the best. Ever since Haig had been his ADC they had got on together. Like the King himself, Haig was simple, dependable and, of course, dull. But Haig, whose conventional military mind had forecast the cavalry as the dominant arm in any future war; the artillery as useful only against raw troops; and who had yet to pronounce, in the face of the most horrifying evidence to the contrary, that the machine-gun was a much overrated weapon, could not be spared. He was in France commanding the newly formed First Army.

The King might have asked that Kitchener be invited, for with Asquith deeming it beneath himself to actually meddle with the conflict, the conduct of the fighting was virtually in the hands of two men, Kitchener and Churchill. One ran the land war, the other the sea war. But Kitchener, in spite of the massive sway he still held, had not been invited. Although the Field-Marshal was becoming more mono-syllabic and unintelligible with each succeeding day, the King still found him too clever by half. After all, not only had Kitchener startled the Cabinet by saying that the war would now last three years and not three months, but for all his autocratic faults he did have a strategic vision, something very rare at the top. So there was no one to speak for the Army.

The isolation the King felt by the absence of Haig was partly compensated for by the presence of his cousin by marriage, Prince Louis of Battenberg. The King always felt more comfortable with one of his extensive family present, and in this case there was an added bond. Until his resignation on the grounds of his German parentage four months ago, Prince Louis had been First Sea Lord. But it wasn't just the absence of Haig that Prince Louis compensated for, it was also the presence of the two youngest at that dinner table, the First Lord and the relatively unknown Captain RN who sat beside him. Not that the King disliked Winston Churchill or Gavin Tweedman; it was more that he didn't quite know what to make of them. Both men had ideas and when you were conducting a life-and-death struggle as this was turning out to be, ideas could be damned dangerous.

They had examined the war like Hatton Garden merchants about to tender for the Koh-i-noor. Here and there the King had even expressed a guarded opinion. They had added up the casualties in France and made them 111,000 in seven months, the destruction of half the British Regular Army. They had discussed too that potential Government destroyer, the shell shortage, and Lord Northcliffe's threat to make it public through his paper, the *Daily Mail*. From the mud, blood and muddle of Flanders, they had moved through the perpetual problem of Ireland, and the military disasters in Russia, to the comparatively cleaner sweeps of the oceans. But here too there were deep anxieties. Churchill had put it most succinctly.

'The deadlock is not just on the land, sir, it is on the oceans too. We have to a very large extent planned for a war that is just not happening. For big gun versus big gun, in which, as you know, the Royal Navy has a calculated superiority. The truth is, the German High Seas Fleet remains in its fortified harbours and we have no idea how to get it out!'

And there for a while they dwelt on the grey waters. When they discussed, as they inevitably would, the loss of the three old cruisers, *Hogue*, *Aboukir* and *Cressy*, sunk together by the U-9, Prince Louis remembered it as the catalyst for his own departure from office. When they got to the mining of the super-dreadnought *Audacious*, Churchill brushed away a tear. Launched barely two and a half years ago, the ship had never even had the chance to fire one of those great 13.5-inch guns in anger. When they retold the story of Jellicoe taking the whole Grand Fleet to sea on the reported sighting of a single periscope in Scapa Flow, which had anyway turned out to be false, Tweedman put their thoughts into words.

'A war of submarine and mine in which a thousand-pound munition can destroy the work of three years and sink a two-million-pound battleship.'

'Like the long bow,' said Churchill solemnly, 'the leveller of that proudest of warriors, the armoured knight.'

'And this time, First Lord,' said Tweedman, 'it is we who are the armoured knights!'

At this retort Churchill scowled behind a haze of cigar smoke. The King lit another cigarette and stared at Tweedman as if, under the royal gaze, the Captain might change into something else. Perhaps a fellow bottle to that excellent 1865 Grande Champagne that had put its fruity spell over them all. Under such scrutiny, Tweedman did what he always did in moments of stress, and sometimes even joy. He knocked the bowl of his pipe five times against his wooden leg. The muted clicks, like a stump being driven into the ground with the handle of a bat, startled the room and reminded the King of the stories he had heard of this irregular but intrepid sailor, the most apocryphal of which was that his left leg still lay in the brambles beyond the Members' Hill at Brooklands.

It was more than just Tweedman's penchant for fast cars — he was one of the few to have lapped Brooklands at over 120 miles per hour, achieved in a big chain-driven Isotta-Fraschini — that made the King wary. Tweedman was the Director of Naval Intelligence and the King, a true-bred operational officer, had a natural distrust for the

4

Intelligence branch. The Captain's crackpot schemes for furthering the war effort, and the odd people, even writers and women of doubtful morals, he was reputed to use as agents, did nothing to inspire confidence in this most conventional of monarchs.

For Tweedman, that brief interlude after he had tapped his leg had a quite different significance. He had been far more aware of his chief's displeasure than of his sovereign's distrust, and when the First Lord rather huffily pointed out that armoured knights still had their place on the battlefield and that being mobile could at least turn a flank, Tweedman corrected matters in the most obvious way. They had not discussed the forthcoming Dardanelles venture, for the divisions of opinion were considerable. Now Tweedman took up the First Lord's point about mobility and gave him the perfect cue.

'The First Lord is quite right. Of course the armoured knight still has a place on the battlefield, and if this Dardanelles operation works as it should and we turn the Germans' south-eastern flank, then it will be more than just a case of "Tomorrow is Saint Crispian!"'

At this, the First Lord's eyes opened and all his giant reservoirs of patriotic emotion overflowed. So did his oratory. Within seconds he had completely altered the mood of the table, firing the little group with his own optimism, while never for one moment mentioning his own misgivings that the nominal military commitment was far too small.

When Churchill had finished, the King tapped the table.

'Gentlemen,' he said, scanning each face in turn, 'I thought for one moment we were all going home in the belief that the year held nothing for us. That all 1915 had to offer was darkness. But now we are reminded of a ray of hope, Winston's Dardanelles venture. We must pray for God's unstinted blessing upon it. On the other hand,' went on the King, believing it his duty to add at least a note of caution, 'should our prayers not be answered, we need only hold on one more year until Kitchener's new armies are ready, then General Haig or Sir John French . . .' The King tailed off, not quite sure of the next strategic move.

'The Dardanelles are one thing, sir,' said Tweedman,

rather too off-handedly, 'but as for the Western Front, I'd rather put my money on a knackered horse or a damned good miracle!'

The King's eyes narrowed. Never one to like frivolities, blasphemies or *lèse-majesté*, this sounded ominously like a bit of each. He stared at Tweedman so that Tweedman was driven to tap his pipe upon his wooden leg a second time.

'A knackered horse or a damned good miracle, Captain?'

'Oh, not your water into wine or anything like that, sir,' said Tweedman, still a little too flippantly. 'No, I was thinking more of a deliberate diplomatic miracle.'

'Pray explain yourself!' said Churchill curtly.

'If this war is really going to last three years as Kitchener believes, then we may well need a new ally.'

The King blinked. 'A new ally?'

'The weak link is Russia, sir. I don't see them lasting three years, not after General Samsonov's defeat at Tannenberg and the news we are now getting of the destruction of their Tenth Army in the Augustow Forest.'

'The Austrians . . .' began the King, but Tweedman interrupted.

'The Germans soon plugged that gap, sir.'

There was a moment of silence. The King, shaken from the feeling of well-being he had so enjoyed, leant across the table and asked in a cold guttural voice:

'What ally have you in mind, Captain Tweedman?'

'Why there is only one, sir,' said Tweedman cheerfully, 'the United States!'

2

It was three-thirty in the afternoon when Tweedman got back to his desk in the Admiralty. He had lunched at Simpson's with his opposite number in MI5, Mark Beresford, and they had swopped information over an underdone sirloin and a bottle of Chapelle-Madeleine. Now, before picking up the afternoon signals, Tweedman made a note of all that had been said. He was well pleased and his pleasure did not stem from memories of either the food or wine.

As always on these occasions, Tweedman felt that he had gained that little bit more from the exchanges than had Beresford. This is what had pleased him. He had no wish to score off the head of MI5, it was simply that the Naval Intelligence Department, with himself at the helm, was on the way up fast. MI5 on the other hand, efficient though it was – and after all, by the second day of the war it had pulled in every German spy in the country – had much smaller horizons. Inevitably, with NID now operating in almost every major country in the world, its outlook was getting more and more strategic. And that suited Gavin Tweedman's vision perfectly.

Take today for instance. They had talked yet again about the great spy round-up of 4/5 August, for there were still stories coming in and interrogations going on. They had talked too of the tiny trickle of replacements the Germans were now beginning to send across, mainly amongst the Belgian refugees. And Tweedman had deliberately turned the conversation towards Ireland and inquired about events there, particularly the links between German agents and the

Sinn Feiners. But never once did he talk about his future plans, and the most he gave away were details of Room 40's code-break that had led to the successful action at the Dogger Bank.

Satisfied, Tweedman began the afternoon's signals. Stancombe, his chief clerk, entering silently to place a file in front of Tweedman, took him to be completely absorbed in what he was looking at, but he was not. Tweedman was working out, as he had been working out ever since last Friday's dinner at White's, throughout the weekend and at today's lunch, his deliberate diplomatic miracle. The first three signals he passed almost without noticing, the fourth caught his eye. It was further details of last night's torpedoing of the steamer *Dulwich* in the English Channel. The next one, the one just brought in by Stancombe in a folder marked MOST SECRET, made him sit upright. It was an intercept from Room 40 of a message to the German High Seas Fleet:

> For urgent political reasons, send orders by wireless to U-boats already despatched not to attack, for the present, ships flying a neutral flag, unless recognized with certainty to be enemies. As indicated in the announcement on 2 February, HM The Emperor has commanded that the U-boat campaign against neutrals to destroy commerce, as indicated in the announcement of 4 February, is not to be begun on 18 February, but only when orders to do so are received from the All Highest.

Tweedman knew the German Declaration of 4 February by heart. The waters around Great Britain and Ireland, including the whole of the English Channel, were to become a war zone. In addition, neutral ships, because of the misuse of neutral flags by the British, were to be at risk. Tweedman knew too of the American reply. Indeed, he had known of it before the Germans, for one of the cipher clerks in the American Embassy in London was on his payroll. It was a strongly worded protest, dated 12 February. It must have been this that had led to the postponement now in his hand. He pressed the buzzer on his desk.

*

Stancombe had been Tweedman's chief clerk for five years. Tweedman had chosen him from amongst the ranks of the Admiralty civilians because he was almost the only one known not to be hostile to the then embryonic NID. He had also chosen him for his extreme reticence, his anonymous face and his invulnerability to surprise. Tweedman not only completely trusted Stancombe, but was by now heavily reliant upon him. Everything, from letters to his bank manager in Pall Mall to instructions to an agent in Constantinople, passed through Stancombe's hands, and more often than not it was now Stancombe who heard the first whisper of a projected operation. Tweedman now found it far easier to pose his unorthodox thoughts direct to this poker-faced man from a terraced house in Chiswick than to those who, like himself, had been through the conventional conditioning of Dartmouth. Indeed, Stancombe now knew more about Tweedman than any other living person, including Tweedman's wife.

What Stancombe thought of Tweedman no one knew, for Stancombe never talked. He would come out of Tweedman's room to his own small corner and scratch away with a pen, or thump with two fingers on the typewriter. No one ever seemed to see what he wrote. Even Mrs Stancombe thought her husband was a shipping clerk in the City. Nowhere could the Director of Naval Intelligence have found a more perfect foil and confidant.

When Stancombe answered the summons, Tweedman pointed to the file. 'You've read this?'

'Yes, sir. I'm afraid the translation leaves much to be desired, but the message is clear. The Kaiser does not wish to upset the Americans.'

Tweedman tapped his leg. The idea forming in his head seemed so preposterous that at first he wasn't sure whether he could even mention it to this robot of a man.

'Remember me telling you about the need for a deliberate diplomatic miracle?'

'Yes, sir.'

'It might cost some lives; after all, very little is achieved in this world without someone getting hurt. But on the other hand, properly carried out, it could save thousands of others, perhaps even millions.' As he spoke, Tweedman glanced at the photograph that stood in its silver frame, the only one on his desk. Major Jack Tweedman MC, killed in action on 30 October 1914 on the Zandvoorde Ridge, had often been seen at the Admiralty.

'Russia won't last another year,' said Tweedman quietly. 'Morale in their army is ebbing away, discipline crumbling. I told His Majesty on Friday that we would soon need another ally. He didn't like it, of course, he's very fond of his cousin the Tsar.'

'And the First Lord, sir?' inquired Stancombe politely.

'He's already striding through the Dardanelles with Johnny Turk on his knees,' said Tweedman, not unkindly, 'or leading the Armies in France to glorious victory.' Suddenly he looked up, straight into Stancombe's eyes, 'Not a word of this is to go down on paper, understand? *Not a single word!*'

Such was the atmosphere that Stancombe did a very rare thing. He just nodded.

'Tell me,' said Tweedman, 'how would *you* go about getting another ally?'

'The United States, sir?' asked Stancombe.

'Who else?'

Stancombe's face assumed an air of great concentration. Tweedman prompted him.

'Would you perhaps arrange the assassination of the President?'

Stancombe shook his head. 'I'm not one for personal violence, sir. I find it hard to even put salt on the slugs in my garden. No, I would let it be known, most discreetly, through the relevant diplomatic channels, that the German Government was seeking an alliance with Mexico and that in the event of hostilities between Germany and the United States, Mexican co-operation would be rewarded with the territories of one or two of the Southern States − say, New Mexico and Arizona.'

Tweedman lay back in his chair and burst into laughter.

'Oh, I like that, Stancombe, I like it very much! And I must remember it. It might well come in useful one day.' Suddenly his manner changed, 'No,' he said with great

10

firmness, 'your scheme might be all right in a year or two, but it is not opportune. The mood of the moment is all sea and America's eyes are on ships. The current words are torpedo and mine.'

Tweedman paused, stared defiantly at Stancombe as if challenging him to disagree, then turned the next signal over like a gambler turning a card. It happened to be an ace. Captain Dow, Master of the *Lusitania*, was reporting that he had received the Admiralty warning of U-boats in the Irish Sea, hoisted the American flag as instructed and increased speed right up to the Mersey Bar.

Tweedman stared at the report for half a minute, then breathed one short sentence.

'My God, the *Lusitania!*'

He had been thinking of a much smaller ship. The White Star liner *Arabic* perhaps, of just under 16,000 tons. She did the Atlantic crossing regularly and carried Americans. But the *Lusitania*! God, that would do it! Bring the Yanks sailing over!

Tweedman slowly raised his head. Stancombe had not moved.

'I want details of the *Lusitania*'s next three eastbound sailings.'

'The *Lusitania*, sir?' said Stancombe, this time unable to conceal his reaction.

Tweedman nodded. 'With the *Aquitania* and *Mauritania* off at the moment, she's the biggest, fastest, grandest, best-known vessel left on the North Atlantic run. Besides, she is *ours*. We, the British taxpayer helped pay for her.'

'The *Lusitania* . . .' breathed Stancombe, turning the word over in his mind and remembering that time, it must be six years ago, when he had trodden her decks. His sister and her husband had been emigrating to the United States. Stancombe remembered his first sight of that giant black hull, nearly 800 hundred feet long, towering above the Liverpool quay. He had been told that the distance from the water-line to the tip of the aerials was 165 feet and he could believe it. He remembered too how dwarfed he had felt by the four immense red and black smokestacks and the six decks. Although his sister and her husband had been

11

travelling second class and had an inside cabin on E deck, at the very stern of the vessel and directly over the four great screws, he had still been impressed with the quality of the passenger accommodation and the elegance of the public rooms. The first class, with its lounge, music-room, smoke-room, writing-room and library, and its great domed dining-room taking up two whole decks, must be like the Ritz. But the *Lusitania* was special in another way. She was the first liner to be driven by steam turbines. They were the engines that had given her her great speed and wrested the blue riband of the Atlantic from the Germans.

'Do I understand, sir,' said Stancombe at last, 'that you intend to attack the *Lusitania!*?'

'Means something, doesn't it?' said Tweedman, his excitement growing. 'One of the "Incomparables", blue riband holder, a fast, sleek, greyhound of a liner, famous the world over, with every luxury except a damned swimming-pool! Indeed, Stancombe, a name to savour.' He leant forward in his chair, 'And doesn't she have 400 Americans on board at this moment?'

'About that, sir . . .'

'And I also want a British submarine captain. Someone who, for one reason or another, will do as we want!'

By now Henry Stancombe felt distinctly worried. He normally followed his eccentric chief with ease. Indeed, seeing most of the signals and letters first, he was sometimes even ahead of him. This afternoon, however, he was not only behind, he was also very disturbed. Although it was only February, could the Director of Naval Intelligence be suffering from some form of early spring fever?

'Forgive me, sir,' inquired Stancombe, 'but are you quite sure you are justified in acting as an *agent provocateur* in this matter?'

'An *agent provocateur*, Stancombe, is one employed to flush out the enemy by tempting them to overt action. I am not doing *that*.'

'No, sir,' said Stancombe, 'but if I understand it correctly, you are proposing that *we* should attack a British ship.'

'Stancombe,' said Tweedman, as if talking to a small boy,

12

'26 October, last year. That French steamer, the *Amiral Ganteaume*, with Belgian refugees aboard, torpedoed in the Channel by Schneider in the U-24. Only forty lost, but remember the outcry in the States?'

Stancombe nodded.

'Last week,' went on Tweedman, 'Washington sent that protest to Berlin. As a result of this U-boat war, atrocities in Belgium, all these stupid stories of nuns being raped and babies bayoneted, America is tottering on the brink. You've seen the reports from our agents there. Anti-German feeling is ready to bubble right over. All we want is one more little push. Something that would involve plenty of Uncle Sam's nationals, and important ones at that. One more act of German arrogance, one more example of their complete disregard of the rules of war.' Before Stancombe could speak, if indeed he had intended to, Tweedman added, 'But it must be something memorable and dramatic. And the Yanks must feel that they are part of it. Now get me those details on the *Lusitania*, and find me that submarine captain!'

'Captain Tweedman, sir,' said Stancombe in uncharacteristic desperation, 'there are not that many submarine captains, and as for one prepared to attack the *Lusitania* . . .'

'We don't have to tell him at this stage what he has to do.'

'But at some stage, sir, he will have to know.'

'Psychology, Stancombe. Let us wait until we know the person. He may be the perfect subject for blackmail.'

Surprising even himself, Stancombe showed distinct displeasure.

'You don't approve?' asked Tweedman.

'I've never mixed with the underworld, sir, so blackmail is not something I am well acquainted with.'

'A homosexual?' said Tweedman quietly.

Stancombe shifted uneasily.

'Or one with a German mistress?'

'Even so . . .' began Stancombe and shook his head.

'You still think they wouldn't do it?'

'Would you, sir?'

'Good God, of course I would, with what's at stake! 500,000

British lives saved in exchange for one . . . one outrage!'

'If you put it that way, sir . . .'

'I do put it that way. Now find me a commanding officer for a submarine!'

But Stancombe had one more worry:

'May I ask, sir, how you propose to get rid of the evidence . . . afterwards?'

Tweedman did not answer at once, but limped to the window. He stood there looking down for a while, then spoke without turning round. 'There's a girl down there in the Horse Guards handing out white feathers. Now she is typical of the multitude in this country who do not seem to realize that war today is frightful. She has just pressed a feather on to a young man who has walked through the arch and who I happen to know, since I heard him telling his friends in the "Clarence" last week, has joined "The Artists' Rifles" and is awaiting his papers.'

Tweedman walked back to his desk and looked down at the oval photo. His brother's regiment, 'The Blues', had been used as infantry to plug the gap in the line.

'In three months' time, our young man will be in a wet, stinking, rat-infested trench,' said Tweedman quietly. 'If he puts his head up, a sniper will send a bullet through his brain. If he keeps his head down, since we still have not started the production of a steel helmet, it is liable to be horribly lacerated by overhead shrapnel bursts, that is if he is not blown to pieces by shellfire or trench mortars. If he gets out and drags himself across the mud, he is liable to be mown down by a machine-gun or bayoneted. If he obeys his natural instincts and turns back, he will be shot by his own officer or a firing squad. And his own artillery will be quite unable to support him since our production of high-explosive shells is 700 a day against the German quarter of a million. The trench warfare that has now developed in France is as crazy and obscene a way of fighting as was ever devised, and I am exceedingly glad that I went to Dartmouth and not Sandhurst. I would have hated the responsibility of commanding soldiers under such conditions.'

Tweedman looked up and faced Stancombe:

'In our case we shall keep the numbers to the very

minimum. Ever heard of Admirante Miranda?'

'I am afraid not, sir.'

'Admirante Don Miguel de Oquendo, Count of Miranda, was a Spanish grandee who lost an arm at the Battle of Malaga, a leg at the Siege of Toulon and an eye at the Second Siege of Barcelona.'

'A most unfortunate gentleman,' said Stancombe, and waited.

'We're interested in him today, Stancombe, because he has given his name to a small submarine, similar to our B class. Built by Vickers in 1907 for the Spanish Navy, she was back in Barrow for a refit last summer. Although quite useless to us once hostilities began, being war material she was not allowed to leave. She is now more or less forgotten. I happened to see her last time I was up there.'

'Not on the Fleet Register, sir,' said Stancombe, raising his eyebrows.

'She requires a very small crew, is completely supernumerary to the Navy's requirements, unknown and unrecorded. It would be nice to keep her that way. Commission her secretly where she lies in Barrow, out of the way . . .' Then Tweedman stopped and shook his head.

It was left to Stancombe to put the impossibilities into words.

'There's the boat herself, sir – crew, stores, munitions, fuel. People are bound to know.'

Tweedman nodded. 'She'll have to come to Portsmouth,' he said sadly, then added crisply, 'As to crew, eight are enough to bring her down, and see that their postings don't coincide afterwards. Two men can gossip, it's harder for one.' Then he looked at his watch. Stancombe knew the signal. He had one hand on the doorknob when Tweedman said:

'I'm sorry, Stancombe, I forgot. Your boy John's joined up, hasn't he?'

'The East Surreys, sir,' said Stancombe proudly. 'Put his age up nearly two years.'

Tweedman smiled. 'That's the stuff!' But mark you, the Army'll spot his age all right. They'll know he's not eighteen. They won't send him to France, not for a long time.'

'Thank you, sir,' said Stancombe and withdrew.

Tweedman went to the wall chart. Although passenger traffic across the North Atlantic had fallen dramatically since the outbreak of war, it had been essential to maintain one fast sea-link with the United States. The *Lusitania* made the round voyage once a month, but to allow Cunard to operate the ship without loss or profit, her boiler power had been reduced by 25 per cent. The route was as it had always been, New York to Liverpool via St George's Channel and the Irish Sea. There was only one place for the attack, between the Fastnet Rock and Tuskar Rock, where the U-boats had now begun to operate. And to make things easier, the *Lusitania* now sailed under Admiralty instructions.

3

Early in his midshipman days, Tweedman had learnt that the higher the authorization, the fewer the questions. But there was another reason for him going to the top and seeking out no less a personage than the First Sea Lord. With the old Admiral's mental state the subject of considerable speculation, his decision-making process could, on one occasion, be quite swift and arbitrary; on another, vague or even confused. In this case, Tweedman hoped for the latter. Vagueness or confusion at the summit could only help matters.

In a dark suit, his large, portly frame hunched behind the desk, his left hand supporting his small, round head with its fine wisps of grey fringe, Lord Fisher looked every one of his seventy-four years. He stared up when Tweedman stumped in, pointed to a chair, then went back to gazing at the signal in front of him. Tweedman was surprised at the rapidity of the deterioration. The distress in eyes and face was getting more pronounced each day. The breakdown must be near.

'Well, Tweedman, what is it this time?' The voice was edgy and tired.

'I need your authority, sir, to commission a submarine and place it under NID control for a period of three months.'

The old head rose a little. The First Sea Lord was about to point out that the submarine service was fully stretched and that, as Tweedman must know perfectly well, the actual disposition of the boats was not his responsibility, when the Director of Naval Intelligence explained:

'I don't need to take one from operations, sir. There's one at Barrow, Vickers built, old B class, ex-Spanish

17

Navy. She'll do perfectly.'

'For what?'

Tweedman took a quick breath.

'Intelligence operations along the southern Irish coast, sir. Contact with Sinn Feiners . . . that sort of thing.'

'Submarines shouldn't be used for that!'

'We shall be simulating a U-boat, sir.'

'Dangerous,' said the First Sea Lord, shaking his head, 'damned dangerous! Never know where that sort of thing might lead. She might get sunk, then there would be no end of questions.' He stopped, looked at Tweedman, then added, 'You know, Tweedman, that I've always been one for innovations but this sort of operation − it's political double-dealing, could easily backfire, scupper the lot of us.'

'We believe the Sinn Feiners are helping the U-boats, sir,' said Tweedman strongly.

'Then leave it to MI5. It's their pigeon!'

'The sea element is ours, sir. It's a case of co-operation.'

Lord Fisher put his hand back to his forehead where it was aching again and looked down at the signal. He wished the young man would go away. He had enough on his plate with this damned Gallipoli business.

'If we've got a submarine and it works,' he said testily, 'and it can be spared from the Bight, then it ought to be out in the Dardanelles!'

Tweedman prayed. Not that the First Sea Lord should finally jump that narrow gap to complete madness, but for an inspiration. Then he remembered a note that had been lying on his desk for the last three weeks.

'If we could get hold of a trawler, sir,' he said with growing enthusiasm, 'I thought we might also try out that "trawler-submarine trap" idea. It's as good a place as any now that the U-boats have moved into St George's Channel.'

'The First Lord . . .' began Fisher, then shook his head.

'Mr Churchill's no problem, sir,' said Tweedman cheerfully. 'He's always pressing for U-boat counter measures.'

Lord Fisher glared up at the man in front of him, then dropped his head and stared gloomily ahead. He felt very old, very tired, and far beyond the point of argument. He knew there was a great deal more behind Tweedman's

18

request, but he seemed unable to continue the fight.

Tweedman struggled up from his chair. 'Have I your authority to commission her, sir?'

The call for a decision gave the old Admiral a moment of clarity.

'You wouldn't have come to me, Tweedman,' he said, staring straight up into the blue eyes, 'if you hadn't got something else up your sleeve?'

Tweedman saw the precipice, felt the cold and hoped he had not flinched.

'I know you too well, know your methods . . .'

'I have explained, sir,' said Tweedman lamely.

The old Admiral shook his head. There was silence. The wrong day and the wrong man, Tweedman decided, then heard a soft grating sound. The First Sea Lord was no longer staring at him, but down at the desk. He was slowly sliding the inkwell as if it were part of a battle squadron.

'Your authority to commission, sir?' Tweedman repeated.

The old Admiral put his hand through his hair.

'A full report in twelve weeks,' he mumbled, 'no more.'

'Yes, sir,' said Tweedman, and withdrew as quickly as his leg allowed. He reckoned the odds on Lord Fisher occupying that chair by the middle of May to be ten to one against.

Managing to obtain a minute from Churchill, just as he was about to go home, not only made Tweedman's blood flow faster, but considering his recent problem with Lord Fisher, almost laugh out loud. It also made him hurry down the corridor to an office near the stairs.

'Glad you're still here, Guy,' he said to the young lieutenant-commander who rose to his feet as Tweedman entered, 'I've got a job for you.' He held out the First Lord's minute. 'Don't bother about the preamble for the moment, just read the last paragraph.'

' "Pray let me have, as a matter of the greatest urgency, a note on the political effects should an ocean liner be sunk with American passengers on board . . ." ' Guy Carr stopped reading and looked up, 'That's a tall one, sir. It's so subjective. Washington might blow hot for a while, but these are hardly the days of Jenkins's Ear!'

Tweedman shook his head. 'Never underestimate national sentiment and prejudice, Guy. It only needs a tiny spark to set the whole of America ablaze. Remember the outcry over the *Amiral Ganteaume*? Do your best and make it convincing. You can see the way his mind is working.'

Lieutenant-Commander Guy Carr said a slightly doubtful, 'Yes, sir,' and Tweedman left the room.

Tweedman drove back home in a state of elation. It was raining, the street lamps were on, and in the light of his own electric headlamps the cobbles sparkled and the tramlines wound into the distance like wet snakes. He drove his 1913 thirty-horsepower Sheffield-Simplex as if pursued by a thousand jinn. The nerves of his amputated left leg throbbed, and the lost toes itched as they so often did when he was excited. This made changing gear difficult, and after each corner the car jerked away as if the driver was still a novice. Because of the rain, Tweedman had his goggles up, and in the yellow of the London evening the smile on his face seemed diabolical. It was good to have started, and it was good to have told Stancombe. Stancombe was a good fellow, he would soon come to see the need for it all. As for the First Lord's minute, Tweedman could hardly believe his luck.

Tweedman stumped into the drawing-room, the glow of weather and excitement still on his face. He scarcely took in the sight of his wife, Sarah, sitting on the couch, surrounded by balls of dark blue wool with a half-knitted balaclava on her lap; and only after taking the stopper out of the decanter and filling two glasses with whisky did he give her a cursory peck on the cheek.

If Gavin Tweedman was rough-cast earthenware, Sarah Tweedman was porcelain. Indeed, she had something of that look too, for although not a consumptive her skin was as clear and transparent as that of those unfortunate enough to suffer from the disease. However, for all her slenderness of limb and body, she was fit and exceedingly strong, as she needed to be to cope with her normally boisterous and exuberant husband. As so often happens, it was a case of a 14½-stone man married to an 8½-stone woman and thereby making her appear even slighter.

20

Sarah knew not to ask questions, but as tonight her husband's elation was something extraordinary, she could not resist a light-hearted comment. 'Don't tell me, Gavin dear, but you have trapped the German High Seas Fleet into another Dogger Bank and this time you are going to destroy them all?!'

Tweedman held up his glass. 'More than that, my dear, much more. I'm going to win the war almost on my own!'

Sarah was pleased. Not so much that Gavin was going to win the war, although it would be very good to get the wretched thing over and done with, but because her husband was so evidently happy. So often in the last three months since his younger brother had been killed, he had just settled morosely, hour after hour, with those endless Admiralty files. Perhaps tonight they could have a game of bezique together.

Henry Stancombe slept badly. At five, although it was still dark, he got up, went down to the kitchen, built up the fire and made tea. He left for the office an hour early, six-thirty instead of seven-thirty.

Sitting cramped in the train he went over the problem given him by his chief and saw no way out. In the office he moved his files about but nothing inspired him. He unlocked the safe and scanned through the Special Branch dossiers but there was nothing there either. By nine it was quite evident that although they even had information on Lord Fisher's correspondence with Admiral von Tirpitz, they had never bothered to collect information on their own submarine officers.

It was nine-fifteen when Stancombe looked at the signals before taking them into Tweedman's office. There were reports from agents in America and Turkey, decodes from Room 40, and the usual morning clutter. It wasn't until he was scanning through the Fleet Reports that his mind began to work. The submarine D-9, which he remembered had already been in trouble, was overdue and presumed lost. The submarine E-28, Lieutenant-Commander Esmond Bone DSC, had met, on her way home to Harwich, a British trawler and reported that she had torpedoed and sunk a

U-boat. The first time in the war that an underwater craft had sunk another. Stancombe had no idea why he did what he did, except that working with Tweedman had accustomed him to follow apparently quite unrelated paths. He asked Operations for the last known position of the D-9 and of the U-boat sunk by the E-28. They were almost coincident. When he saw the weather reports, the recurrence of south-westerly squalls, the bad visibility, he sat down and in his careful, neat handwriting, wrote a complete proposition.

Tweedman arrived late. Stancombe followed his chief into the office before he had had a chance to shut the door. Tweedman, who was not in the best of tempers, threw his cap on the mahogany hatstand and his attaché case on the desk and said, 'Bloody silly electric starters! Don't ever buy a car with an electric starter, Stancombe. And certainly not in the winter.'

'No, sir,' said Stancombe, knowing that he was never likely to buy a car of any sort on his Admiralty salary, and waited for the correct moment.

Tweedman saw the folder in Stancombe's hands. 'A homosexual who's had an affair with Crown Prince Frederick William himself?'

Stancombe's face showed a flicker of triumph.

'More a simple mistake, Captain, but one with great potential!'

'Ah,' said Tweedman, interested, 'let's have it.'

'Lieutenant-Commander Esmond Jasper Bone DSC. Thirty-one, only son of Rear-Admiral Henry Augustus Ewing Bone —'

'Henry Bone's boy!' shouted Tweedman. 'Have you gone mad, Stancombe? The boy's a hero!'

'Perhaps you would like to read this, Captain,' said Stancombe, laying the papers on Tweedman's desk. Tweedman sat down, pulling his left leg into a comfortable position, scowled and opened the file. When Stancombe saw his chief tap his pipe on his leg, he moved to the door.

'One thing, Stancombe,' said Tweedman without looking up, 'is this young man married?'

'No, sir.'
'Engaged?'
'There has been no announcement, sir, I have checked.'
Tweedman grunted. Stancombe left the room.

4

For Esmond Jasper Bone, life at the moment was difficult. Only four months ago, in November, he had been a hero. He had sailed into Harwich to discover that the E-28's exploits in torpedoing the German light cruiser *Antilope*, ten miles off Cuxhaven, was front-page news, vying with the official photos of the damage caused by German artillery to the doorway of Rheims Cathedral. The *Antilope*, a 2,600-ton cruiser of the *Gazelle* class, old and small, was of very little military significance, but the sinking came at a good moment. After the disaster off Coronel, the Admiralty badly needed a fillip. The sinking of the *Antilope* provided it.

Three patrols later and things were different. Here he was, in the depths of Hampshire, suddenly sent on what was turning out to be indefinite leave. True he had not succeeded in torpedoing that *Kaiser*-class dreadnought which had suddenly appeared from an early February squall; however, that had not been his fault, but the fault of the torpedoes. He had pressed home his attack, there was no question about that. The E-28 was only 800 yards away. He had seen the Bullivant net defences on the hull and even the barrels of the small twenty-four pounders below the bridge, but the torpedoes had 'dived under.' 'Diving under' had become quite a habit, and he had had to set the torpedoes to run deep to avoid the armour belt that encased the dreadnought's hull.

In a sense he had made up for it all the next day when he had surprised that U-boat on the surface. Again the weather had been bad, with sudden squalls coming up from the east and bringing visibility down to almost nothing. Like the

24

dreadnought, the U-boat had appeared out of one squall and was about to disappear into another. But this time the torpedo had run perfectly and his aim had been good. The shot had struck immediately forward of the conning tower and the U-boat had disintegrated. None of that seemed to call for this sudden rustication.

Esmond had intended to go shooting. It would have taken his mind off things, but all their shotguns had been loaned to the barracks for musketry instructions. So, instead of heading north on to the bare downs, Esmond had taken a stout walking-stick and set off south towards the valley. He had walked across the old chalk road, down the lane that led between the church and cottages, and across the river. The few cottagers about knew him. The men touched their caps, the women curtseyed. They saw him very much as their hero, along with the water-keeper's son who had done so well with the Horse Artillery at Mons. Indeed, the little village had much to be proud of. Two decorations for gallantry in the first seven months of the war.

Esmond stopped on the footbridge. For February the water was surprisingly clear, almost as clear as in the summer. With little mud in suspension, the chalk and gravel bottom contrasted with the long, dark, sinuous areas of weed. A 1½-pound brown trout lay in a patch of sunlight near the bank, flicking its tail to keep its position against the stream. In another few months Esmond would have been stalking it, selecting the right fly, but now it reminded him of only one thing, his own E-28. That is how they must look to an aeroplane or airship, just after diving. He was fascinated too by the trim of the trout. How perfectly it kept its position and depth. No Number One there, going the length of the vessel every morning and adjusting the ballast to compensate for changes in stores or torpedoes. Nor when it ate did its buoyancy suddenly seem to alter. He was startled from this reverie by a motor-car that descended to the bottom of the lane and then careered along the narrow footpath, scything the reeds on either side, until the damp ground at last made the driver decide it was folly to go further.

The apparition driving the car took all Esmond's attention. It was a man of forty to forty-five, tall, massively built,

25

with a shock of auburn hair that circled about his ears, and who, when he raised his driving goggles, stared through bright blue eyes. He then threw back the cape that encompassed his scarf, raised a gloved hand from the cockpit and cried, 'Bloody thing's gone to sleep! Come and get me out!'

Without questioning, Esmond did as he was bid. It was not until he had opened the car door and could see the lower half of the occupant that he gained an insight into the problem. The driver had a wooden leg, clearly visible where the trouser had been pulled right up. It was the other leg that had, with the tedium of the journey, gone to sleep. Esmond prised the man upwards as instructed, and watched him as he stood there massaging the offending limb. Then handing him his stick, he accompanied him the few paces to the bridge.

At the bridge, the man took off his gauntlet and held out a massive hand. 'Gavin Tweedman's the name. And I take it you are Esmond Jasper Bone DSC?'

Esmond, slightly confused by the addition of his decoration, which at the moment felt distinctly incongruous, had to admit that he was.

'Know your father,' said Tweedman, 'was on the old *Powerful* with him. Of course, I was just a cadet.'

'You're in the Navy too, sir?' inquired Esmond.

In answer, Tweedman dug deep into the pocket of his old tweed jacket, took out his pipe and tapped the bowl on his leg. 'Called in at the house,' he said. 'They said you'd gone for a walk down this way. Hoped I might catch you.'

Esmond decided that Tweedman, invalided out after losing his leg in one of the recent actions, found it embarrassing to be asked if he was in the Navy. He therefore put it another way.

'Was it Dogger Bank, sir? Were you with Admiral Beatty on the *Lion*?'

The *Lion* had been badly mauled.

'The *Lion*?' said Tweedman, puzzled.

'Your leg . . .?'

'Brooklands!' shouted Tweedman with a huge laugh. 'Damned tyre blew out on the Members' Banking!' Then he leant on the wooden handrail of the bridge and stared into the water. He spotted the trout but it failed to hold his interest. After a few remarks on the merits of camouflage, he took out his watch and said, 'I know of a nice place where we can talk,' and with that, led the way back to the car. Esmond, puzzled, hesitated. The big man beckoned, 'For God's sake, we haven't all day!'

'Who are you, sir?' cried Esmond, but Tweedman took no notice. As the engine sparked he shouted, 'Electric starting! Damned fine thing! Do you know, young man, that this is the first vehicle in this country with electric starting *and* electric headlights?'

Esmond did not know, but after a further moment of hesitation climbed in beside the driver.

They drove east, fast. The unmade chalk road was dry and they did not skid excessively. Nevertheless, Esmond was soon convinced that he would far rather be resting on the bottom of the Bight, listening to the ominous chug-chug of enemy ships passing overhead, than trying to survive on this mad switchback. He hung on grimly and waited. As they were dropping down into the Meon Valley, Tweedman shouted again above the roar of engine and wind. 'You're probably wondering what it's all about?'

Esmond *was* wondering, very much, but he was too frozen to do more than nod. Tweedman raised a gauntleted hand and pointed. 'It will all come clear when we get to "The Black Horse". An excellent inn. Good whisky and a good fire.'

'The Black Horse', black and white timbered, stood almost flush with the main road. The small private bar, a step above the public bar to accommodate the rise in the road, was to the right of the door. The single small round table had just sufficient circumference to allow a couch and armchair to be placed about it.

Tweedman was right. The landlord did have both a fine whisky and fine fire. Esmond thawed by the blazing logs; Tweedman rubbed his stump, then settled on the couch. He seemed to be well known, and was treated most respectfully. The small wooden table was carefully wiped and the drinks brought on a silver tray.

'An old haunt of yours, sir?' asked Esmond, at last warm

A.L. – B

27

enough to speak.

'They know me,' said Tweedman, filling and lighting his pipe. 'It's no distance from Portsmouth. Makes a pleasant change from the dockyard.'

Esmond sat and wondered and waited. They drank. Tweedman smoked, but neither spoke. At last, unable to contain himself any longer, Esmond leant forward and said, 'I really would like to know what all this is about, sir?'

'I've got a job for you,' came back the bland reply.

Esmond showed his surprise. He had been on leave longer than he had hoped, yet nevertheless he still assumed that his recall to command the E-28 again, or another submarine, was just a matter of time.

'I don't think I actually need a job, sir,' he replied carefully.

'You've been off for a while,' said Tweedman a little deprecatingly.

Esmond went on to the defensive. 'Who are you exactly?' he asked. 'All I know about you is that you call yourself Gavin Tweedman. You might be anyone. A newspaper reporter even. How do you know I've been ashore for some time?'

'Captain Gavin Tweedman RN. Director of Naval Intelligence.'

Esmond looked at the man sprawled across the couch.

'You're not in uniform, sir,' he said at last.

Tweedman laughed. 'Nor are you!'

'I'm on leave, long leave. And I was out for a walk.'

It was a challenge, but Tweedman did not respond. So Esmond switched to attack. 'How do I know you are the Director of Naval Intelligence . . . sir?'

'You could phone your father at Dover and ask,' said Tweedman quietly, 'or phone an Admiralty number I will give you.'

Esmond looked round the tiny room. 'Where am I going to find a phone here?'

'There is one,' said Tweedman. 'Mine host is very modern.'

There was a long pause, then Esmond suddenly sank back into the chair.

'All right, sir,' he said, 'why am I ashore? I'd like to know that first.'

'You're resting,' said Tweedman, 'like an actor.'

'But I want to get back!' cried Esmond. 'While I'm resting, the war could be over.'

Tweedman shook his head and laughed. 'It's got ages to go yet! Years! We're not half way through the first act.'

'Surely that's an exaggeration, sir?' said Esmond. 'It's run eight months already. The armies won't stand it.'

'They will, for another three years at the very least.'

'*Three years!*' Esmond thought of Elizabeth. He had intended putting the question when it was all over.

Tweedman was nodding. 'Could be four even, if the Eastern Front collapses.' Then he stared at the beam above his head. 'I've still got one or two things to arrange, but just as soon as they are settled I'll give you the details. In the meantime, I wanted to put your mind at rest and let you know that your next patrol will be for me.'

They did not speak again about Esmond's immediate future until they had roared into the entrance of Mortimore Place and down the gravel drive that ended in a circle in front of the colonnaded porch. As Tweedman turned the Sheffield-Simplex, gravel flew in a giant spray, falling on the flagstones, hitting the old brick wall and setting the dogs barking.

'Don't worry,' shouted Tweedman as he pushed his goggles up and proffered a gauntlet, 'you'll be on and under the sea again in next to no time. Oh, and one other thing. No need to tell anyone I've been, not even your father.'

Esmond did not go indoors at once, but walked in the garden. He heard the dogs barking and his mother at the door calling for him, but took no notice. He was pleased that his days of waiting would soon be over, but puzzled by Tweedman. He wished now that he had pressed for more information, and was surprised at the ease with which the big man had taken him over. In the end he settled for the fact that it must be an honour to work for NID, and slashed the heads off the molehills in his exuberance.

5

'I see there was an attack in Flanders yesterday, Stancombe,' said Tweedman, glancing up from his desk, 'a very small affair, just north of La Bassee. Battalion strength, simply to straighten the front. Reading between the lines, it seems that out of the 600 who took part, half were casualties within thirty minutes and the front was not straightened. I take it that as usual we had no hand-grenades, except those made from old bully-beef tins, no trench mortars and very little artillery support. Tell me honestly, Stancombe, am I any worse than the general who ordered that attack?'

'The Army has a different scale, sir,' said Stancombe carefully.

'300 dead and wounded for absolutely nothing?' cried Tweedman. 'Surely we wouldn't do that?'

Stancombe did not answer but continued sorting papers. Tweedman returned to the morning's reports.

'And another little statistic for you, Stancombe, and one that you won't find in the newspapers. Since 25 October last year there have been only ten dry days in Flanders, and then, more often than not, the temperature was below freezing.'

Tweedman suddenly pushed the reports away.

'How is it that when we lose 120 officers and ratings in some relatively minor mishap, a mine perhaps, the whole nation sheds a tear and questions are asked of the First Lord in the House? Yet when the Army lose a battalion, it's all quiet on the Western Front!?'

Stancombe knew the symptoms. Guilt. But he answered the question first.

'In so far as Mrs Stancombe is representative of the country, sir, she doesn't shed tears for the sailors but for the ship. With the Army there is no equivalent. But I take it that your real concern, sir, is for Lieutenant-Commander Bone?'

'Nice young man,' said Tweedman, sucking his pipe.

'And you are trying, are you not, sir, to equate the loss of him, his crew and the *Admirante Miranda* with that battalion north of La Bassee?'

'It helps,' said Tweedman, then his eyes suddenly brightened, he grabbed his trousers and tugged his wooden leg to the side. 'What about the boat?'

'She's on her way down from Barrow now, sir.'

'One day, Stancombe,' said Tweedman, pointing towards the window, 'there'll be a statue to you out there.'

Stancombe was flattered enough to blush. 'And may I ask, sir,' he said, 'whether Lieutenant-Commander Bone is likely to be suitable?'

'He'll do,' said Tweedman quietly, 'but, of course, we haven't come to the guts of the matter yet.'

'Should he demure, sir, the circumstantial evidence is very much against him.'

'That's what I'll tell him.' Tweedman suddenly hauled himself upright. 'But he'll do it all right. I feel it in my blood.'

'Should he still remain hesitant, sir,' said Stancombe quietly, 'you might say that the Germans have not announced the loss of any U-boat . . .'

Tweedman looked at Stancombe and wondered why he was still only a clerk.

With the submarine acquired, Tweedman moved fast. His first call was to an office in the basement of The Little Theatre in John Street, just off the Strand. It was in these humble and somewhat incongruous surroundings that MI5 operated. Tweedman had already laid the groundwork at lunch only a few days ago; now he proposed to do a little harvesting.

If Mark Beresford was surprised at another meeting so soon, he did not show it. Or perhaps it was that Tweedman never allowed him to show it. For Tweedman had hardly

31

tottered down the steps into the basement before he had launched into a tirade about U-boats off southern Ireland.

'One of von Henning's men from the U-18 gave the game away when we interrogated him the other day,' said Tweedman, with considerable enthusiasm. 'They not only spent their nights within a stone's throw of the coast recharging their damned batteries, they actually took bearings on individual houses! You must admit, Beresford, that that demands, at the very least, a pretty sympathetic population.'

Beresford had to admit that it did.

'Wouldn't put it beyond them to actually revictual the U-boats,' said Tweedman indignantly. 'But that's something I intend to find out. This new network the Huns are trying to set up. I take it that, as usual, they are aiming for the ports? In Ireland, Belfast . . . Dublin . . . Larne . . . Kingstown . . . Queenstown?'

'We know there's a new man in the south,' said Beresford. 'He's been right across to Rosyth. Very foolishly sent a telegram to Stockholm.'

At this point, Tweedman moved carefully. In all probability, Beresford would want to leave this particular agent alone for a while.

'I don't want to bust in on this,' he said, relighting his pipe. 'This agent is your affair and for reasons of your own you probably want to keep him where he is for a while. But the U-boat threat is getting damned urgent! The First Lord hammers away at it every day. The fact is, NID must have more on southern Ireland.'

Beresford understood, but as Tweedman had guessed, he did not want this particular man upset at the moment.

'Truth is,' said Tweedman, 'that I would dearly love to do a little *agent provocateur*-ing in that area and I don't want to tread on anyone's toes. Thought I might perhaps run a submarine in and see who they're signalling to. That sort of thing.'

Beresford was interested, provided his man did not take fright and run. Tweedman promised to be most circumspect.

As he climbed the steps to leave, Tweedman asked the name of the agent.

'Goes under the name of Frederick Childs,' said Beresford.

'His cover is that he's an American, interested in buying good livestock . . . horses for breeding.'

'My God!' cried Tweedman. 'A man interested in buying horses in Ireland goes all the way to Rosyth and sends telegrams to Stockhokm!'

Beresford laughed. 'That's just how short they are!'

Tweedman took Frederick Childs' address and left.

Stancombe entered as his chief's finger rose from the buzzer. A Norwegian tanker, the *Belridge*, had been torpedoed near the Varne Bank. She had not sunk and was now under tow to Dover. The papers on Tweedman's desk contained the first American reactions. Tweedman smiled.

'The Huns do half our work for us!' he said. 'A little more and NID could close for good.' Then he seemed to forget Stancombe's presence until his chief clerk reminded him.

'You rang, sir?'

'Stancombe,' said Tweedman, taking an unusually long time to knock out his pipe and refill it, 'I want you to find the most secret piece of information you can lay your hands on. Something that even you would happily secrete in your anus rather than let the enemy catch sight of it, and something that when passed to the dimmest agent will be instantly recognized as an absolute gem.'

Stancombe was unhappy. 'Real information, sir?'

Tweedman nodded. 'It's got to be so good, so red-hot, that when the agent gets his hands on it he won't want to slip it in a letter to Sweden or Holland, he'll want to take the first available ship and deliver it himself.'

'Are we not taking too much of a risk, sir?' inquired Stancombe anxiously.

'The whole damned thing's a risk!'

'We can never be sure of his reaction, sir. He might not take ship. He might just pass it on.'

'Then we'll have to see that he doesn't,' said Tweedman sharply and looked at his watch. He struggled up from behind his desk, took his cap and overcoat from the stand and held out his hand for Stancombe to give him his stick.

'Two other things while I'm away, Stancombe. I want that actor fellow we have in Dublin, Terence Ford, transferred to

Cork. There must be a theatre there.'

'He's very touchy about parts, sir,' said Stancombe quickly.

'I don't care if he has to give up Hamlet for a back row of the chorus in *The Belle of New York!* I want him in Cork by next week!'

'Yes, sir. And the second thing?'

'The moment you know he's in Cork, fix me a passage.'

'Yes, sir.'

Tweedman stumped into the corridor and into the lift.

Tweedman had a first-class corner seat reserved on the 2.50. He found it without difficulty, got the porter to put his portmanteau on the rack, laid *The Times* on his seat, then walked down the platform to inspect the locomotive. He had intended using his car, but the damp February weather had made the nerves in his leg jump and at the last moment he had got Stancombe to book him a seat on the train. Satisfied that he had not made a mistake, that his stump would be rested and that he could now work uninterrupted, he was walking back to his compartment when a tall man, wearing on his cap the braid of an admiral, appeared in front of him. Henry Augustus Ewing Bone MVO, RN stood, one foot on the step, the other on the platform, holding the carriage door open.

Tweedman swore to himself, wondered at his idiocy in catching this particular train and wondered too why Henry Bone was going to Portsmouth and not Dover where he belonged. Of all the men in His Majesty's Navy, this was the last one he wished to meet. It was going to be one hell of a journey; nevertheless, he smiled and saluted.

The Admiral threw off his greatcoat, helped the woman porter lift his baggage on to the rack and settled opposite Tweedman. He looked so evidently ill at ease that Tweedman began to sweat. They had scarcely passed Vauxhall, and No. 721 was still picking up speed, when Henry Bone announced in a voice of doom that he had been up to the Admiralty. It was perfectly natural that the Rear-Admiral commanding Patrol Area XI should go to the Admiralty. Nevertheless, Tweedman felt so uncomfortable and had

34

such grave misgivings that he had difficulty inquiring just who Bone had visited.

'The First Sea Lord,' said Henry Bone non-committally.

Tweedman managed a nod. After all, Fisher knew very little, and certainly none of the details.

'In a bad way, Lord Fisher,' he said, as casually as he could. 'Quite disturbing seeing him these days. Can't believe he'll be staying with us long. But tell me, sir, why are you going back to Portsmouth?'

'The *Attentive* is in the dockyard,' said the Admiral. 'Going back on her tonight.'

Again it was perfectly natural that the flagship of the Commander of Area XI should put into Portsmouth Dockyard, yet Henry Bone's very evident preoccupation could not be easily dismissed. That sad, brooding look he gave the countryside was very definitely not that of a senior officer in the prime of life and on full pay.

Tweedman, unsure which line to take and not wishing to broaden the conversation, suddenly blurted out, 'At least you're lucky, Henry, you've got an operational command. You actually see the water. You're not stuck behind a desk all day.'

'Too old, Gavin,' said Henry Bone sadly. 'That's the trouble. This is going to be a young man's war.'

They both thought of the same young man at the same moment. The only difference was that Tweedman kept quiet.

'Chaps like Esmond,' said Henry Bone, 'they're the ones we need. Young brawn and young brain, used to this mechanized age.'

Tweedman took out his pipe and tapped it so violently on his leg that the Admiral, indicating Tweedman's left trouser, asked whether it hurt. Tweedman, delighted to have changed the subject, muttered something about nerves and lost limbs. Henry Bone might have followed that with a 'You remind me of Long John Silver' or 'Still driving your fast cars, Gavin?' but he didn't. He said, 'Something else is worrying me, Gavin. You're at the Admiralty, you have your ear to the grapevine. What's wrong with Esmond? Why is he at home so damned long?'

'He's earned his leave,' said Tweedman carefully. 'Great strain, you know, submarine patrols, particularly where he's been going, right inside the Bight.'

'Saw him the other day,' said the Admiral. 'No life in him. Looked like a ghost.'

'Losses are high in submarines,' said Tweedman. 'It's a nasty, dangerous life. Not easy for old hands like you and me to understand. It affects them all.'

The Admiral raised an eyebrow. 'Are you suggesting that my boy might be going off his head?'

Tweedman laughed. 'Good God, no! Just overstrained, that's all. After all, how many patrols has he done? Five . . . six? That sort of concentration under those conditions affects the chap's psyche.'

'I hope he's back on the bridge again soon,' said the Admiral. 'It'll destroy him if he's not.' then he leaned forward and touched Tweedman just where his stump went into the leather socket. 'You're in the swim, Gavin, you've got influence up there. Do what you can to see that he gets another command soon.'

Tweedman nodded and took refuge behind the newspaper.

At Portsmouth Town Station they got up and put on their greatcoats. As Tweedman was struggling into his, the Admiral suddenly asked, 'Still all mixed up with spies and codes and things?'

'Doing my best on the Home Front,' said Tweedman.

The Admiral looked at him quizzically, then said, 'Don't think that we're all fools, will you, Gavin?'

Tweedman, who had just been congratulating himself on getting this far intact, felt his good leg weaken.

'Fools?' he said, smiling nervously.

'I see in the latest Fleet Lists that you are still putting the *Audacious* with the Second Battle Squadron, whereas every Jack knows that she's lying up there mined off Tory Island! Sometimes I wonder just whose eyes you fellows think you are pulling the wool over?'

'The enemy's,' said Tweedman blandly.

The Admiral opened the carriage door, then turned and asked, 'Anyway, what brings you to Pompey? Some pretty young blonde tucked behind the C-in-C's cot taking notes for you?'

There was a distinct touch of nastiness in the remark and it made Tweedman react.

'As a matter of fact, I'm taking a close look at a submarine.'

'Good God!' said the Admiral, 'you're not actually thinking of going in one?'

'No, but I hope to use one soon.'

'Esmond!' said the Admiral, inspired, 'the very man for you!'

Tweedman gave the same nervous smile but said nothing. The Admiral squeezed his arm, helped him down on to the Harbour Station platform and inquired whether he was being met. Tweedman said he was, and was thankful when they parted.

The *Admirante Miranda* was one of six old submarines moored alongside the aged mother ship *Dolphin*. She was the furthest one out, distinguished by having no large white pendant numbers on her conning tower, and like all the rest looked small and dirty. An engineer-lieutenant helped Tweedman on to the deck of the equally forlorn A-6 and on to the gangway that linked the boats. Tweedman stood on the steel deck of the Spanish submarine and tapped the rusty casing with the ferrule of his stick. The boat rang with a hollow clang. He looked from stem to stern and was not impressed. He walked over the torpedo-loading hatch to the bow and looked into the murky water of the harbour. More of the boat went on under the surface, perhaps fifteen feet, and down there, somewhere beneath the flotsam, were the torpedo-tube doors.

'Is she serviceable?' he asked in amazement.

'Well, sir,' said the engineer-lieutenant hesitantly, 'the Spaniards haven't exactly done her any good, but then you wouldn't have expected them to, would you? The batteries are a bit old, we'll charge them as best we can . . . and there's quite a lot of corrosion.' He stopped, thought for a moment, then added more cheerfully, 'But there's still life in her if she's properly treated. After all —' and he indicated the next three boats, ' — she is a B class, and here the Bs are stand-bys for the Second Flotilla.'

Tweedman turned his attention to the inside of the boat, and went up the steel ladder to the small conning tower. The entry hatch was open and he peered down. He tried to remember how long it was since he had been inside a submarine, and decided that they had got smaller with his own advancing years. In contrast with the outside, everything he could see in the control room seemed to be clean and reasonably efficient-looking. He lowered himself down the ladder and marvelled at the lack of space. With a beam of no more than thirteen-and-a-half feet, it seemed impossible that more than a dozen men could even survive. Uninhabited for several months, the boat smelt of oil, sea-water and chlorine. Head bent, he went forward past the battery tanks to the mess table where the spare torpedoes would be stored. He stood there for a while deep in thought, then went aft to the engine. It was a Wolseley sixteen-cylinder, horizontally-opposed petrol motor of 600 brake horsepower. He liked the look of it, but without hearing it fire, could not be sure.

'Petrol,' he said, as if surprised.

The engineer-lieutenant nodded.

'Not everyone's favourite, not these days. But they're handy little boats,' he added cheerfully, 'lively enough.'

When he was once more in the daylight, Tweedman turned, stared at the engineer-lieutenant and said, 'Lieutenant-Commander Esmond Bone will be commissioning her.'

'Bone?' said the engineer-lieutenant, instantly alerted. 'Not the chap who sunk the *Antilope*?!'

'The same.'

The engineer-lieutenant would have whistled, but thought better of it. After a moment he said, 'He's going to find a second-hand dago submarine a bit of a comedown after the E-28, sir.'

Tweedman looked up at the clouds.

'Then let's make the second-hand dago submarine as good as we can for him, shall we, because he's a bloody good commander?'

'Of course, sir,' said the engineer-lieutenant, and slowly followed Tweedman back up the ladder of the *Dolphin*. On

38

deck, he asked where the boat was to operate.

'Operate?' said Tweedman, taken off guard.

'North Sea . . . Channel . . . Med . . .?'

'Does it matter?' asked Tweedman.

'Well, if it's the Med, sir, she might want something special . . .'

'North Sea,' said Tweedman sharply.

'Remember, sir,' said the engineer-lieutenant, 'she's not got all that much range.'

'How far?'

'A thousand miles, maybe twelve hundred, not much more.'

Tweedman hoped he hadn't made a mistake.

'And one other thing, sir,' said the engineer-lieutenant, 'she needs a class number and pendant. As to all intents and purposes she is a B class, I suggest, sir, that she be the B-12 with a pendant 04.'

Tweedman did not want the boat to have any numbers. If it had to be called anything, he would have preferred *Miranda*, but with all His Majesty's submarines neatly lettered and numbered, it would have stood out as too much of an oddity.

'B-12, 04,' he said, looking the engineer-lieutenant straight in the eye, 'but remember, this is a very short-term commission. She'll be back with the makers in twelve weeks.'

'And the Fleet Register, sir?'

'I'll look after that.'

'Yes, sir,' said the engineer-lieutenant, and saluted.

6

'The job, sir?' asked Esmond eagerly.

There was a long silence. They were alone together in the private room of 'The Black Horse'. Tweedman got up and walked to the window. Outside, the pale morning sun made long shadows on the wet road. Winter leaves still lay by the flint wall, and a seagull, driven inland by the weather, flew languidly over the bare elms.

'Novelists call it cloak-and-dagger,' said Tweedman. 'So far as I'm concerned it's an operation of war that calls for a cool-headed commander who presses his attack right home.'

'You mean off the German coast?' asked Esmond, his excitement rising.

'Irish,' came back the reply. 'It's a hot-bed these days, and with the U-boats extending their activities from St George's Channel to Fastnet Rock, likely to be a damned important one.' Tweedman turned, faced Esmond and added with great intensity, 'It could be that this war will be won not on the Western Front as the generals seem to think, but *on the western ocean*.'

This was a completely new concept to Esmond. Like most Englishmen he thought that although the Navy was the country's shield, shields by themselves did not actually win wars.

'Starved out by U-boats?' he asked incredulously.

Tweedman nodded. 'The lifeline between us and the Americans cut. Oh, it's all perfectly possible,' he said, seeing Esmond's face. 'You're a submarine commander, wouldn't you make hay against nothing but slow, wallowing tramp-steamers? Fisher foresaw it years ago, but their lordships laughed him out at the time. Mind you, they have second thoughts now!'

'And this operation?' asked Esmond.

Tweedman did not answer directly, but said, 'Pick the best of your old crew but remember, you'll need less than half of them. It's a much smaller boat.'

'Smaller boat?' said Esmond puzzled.

Tweedman nodded. 'Ever run a B class?'

'Trained on one, sir.'

'Fine!' said Tweedman. 'The B-12's at Portsmouth waiting for you.'

'The B-12?!' said Esmond in disbelief, 'There isn't a B-12. The B-11 was the last, before Vickers went over to the Cs.'

'For the next three months there is a B-12,' said Tweedman urbanely. 'We've borrowed the *Admirante Miranda* from the Dons. She was at Barrow having a refit. She's a B class in all but name.'

'But the Bs are obsolete, sir!' gasped Esmond. 'A thousand miles' range, petrol driven, and devils with the wind ahead or astern!'

'They're small and this one can be spared,' said Tweedman quietly. 'There's no E boat available, and if one was available it would be quite unsuitable.'

'The operation, sir?' said Esmond for the third time.

Tweedman called for two more drinks then settled on the couch.

'A highly secret, two-pronged anti-U-boat patrol. One part will involve close inshore work, for which a small boat is ideal. It is aimed at finding out who amongst the local Irish are helping the U-boats, revictualling them, passing information on ship movements, that sort of thing.'

'And the second?' asked Esmond cautiously.

'Heard of the "trawler-submarine trap"?'

'Just a whisper, sir.'

'We hang you down behind a trawler with a tow rope and a length of telephone line. When a U-boat surfaces and starts shelling the trawler with her deck gun, the skipper picks up the phone and gives you range and bearing. You then slip the tow and work yourself into a nice position for a torpedo shot. You should have a sitting target.'

'Sounds interesting, sir,' said Esmond hesitantly. 'But a B boat! That really is the very bottom. Couldn't we have a C?'

'Good agile little craft!' said Tweedman cheerfully. 'And you've got a damned famous sister to live up to! You've seen the details of Holbrook's patrol?'

Esmond nodded. 'Nine hours submerged, five more than the design time, periscope fogged up, defective compass, flat battery, exhausted crew −'

'But she made history!' cried Tweedman. 'The first submarine to sink a battleship.'

All that was true. In December, the B-11 had navigated the Narrows from Cape Helles to Chanak and torpedoed the old Turkish battleship *Messoudieh*. But as a submariner, Esmond knew the sharpness of the knife-edge on which they had operated.

'Saw the B-12 yesterday,' went on Tweedman, his enthusiasm for the old craft seeming to grow. 'She's in fine shape.'

Esmond could only shake his head. Forty feet shorter than the E class, with a beam of almost half − as far as he could remember thirteen-and-a-half against the E's twenty-three − a range of a third and a speed of two-thirds, no submarine captain in his right mind would wish to give up one of the new Es for a nine-year-old B.

'God,' he said with a groan, 'back to white mice.'

Tweedman was puzzled.

'All the petrol-driven boats carry white mice, sir,' explained Esmond. 'They're the best early warning for carbon monoxide.'

'This patrol won't be hazardous,' said Tweedman cheerfully. 'Enemy activity won't be the sort you're used to. Except for U-boats, the vessels around you will be ours. You'll be in home waters.'

'A B class,' said Esmond flatly, then after a while added, 'What are facilities like at Queenstown, sir?'

Tweedman shook his head. 'You won't see Queenstown.'

'I'm thinking of our limited range, sir,' said Esmond puzzled.

Tweedman laughed: 'You just work that boat up with the pick of your old crew. Get her diving fast . . . trimmed right . . . all the things you submariners do. Then I'll tell you about your contact. Oh yes,' he said with a chuckle, 'just like steamship companies and corn merchants, we have local agents.'

Tweedman struggled upright and held out his hand for his stick. They sat together in the back of the old naval Wolseley and only one more thing was said of the B-12.

'You'll work up from *Dolphin* at Portsmouth,' said Tweedman thoughtfully, 'but your crew will keep their old cap tallies. Ratings will continue to wear FORTH.'

Nothing surprised Esmond any more.

A hundred yards from the gates of Mortimore, Tweedman told the driver to stop, and by leaning across Esmond and opening the car door on Esmond's side, indicated that this was where he got out.

'Everything should be plain sailing,' said Tweedman. 'I can't see any snags, nothing but smooth water ahead. The boat's waiting for you, your first lieutenant will be there tomorrow, the crew only want a call and the C-in-C Portsmouth knows you're to be given every assistance.'

'And if I need to contact you, sir?' asked Esmond.

Tweedman looked up at the sky.

'Keep clear of the Admiralty and don't telephone. If it's really urgent, contact mine host at "The Black Horse".' Then he pushed the driver in the back with his stick and the Wolseley picked up speed in a cloud of chalk-dust. Esmond now realised why that obscure, remote inn had a telephone.

Twenty-four hours after leaving his office at the Admiralty, Tweedman was back. Everything seemed to be in order, but his meeting with Esmond's father had shaken him. He rang for Stancombe and while waiting, scanned the signals. Nothing eventful seemed to have happened in his absence and for that he was thankful.

Tweedman let Stancombe have first go. As expected, their man, Terence Ford, was most unhappy to leave Dublin.

There was no comparable theatre in Cork. The Palace in King Street had no part for him, and he had no wish to play there if they had.

'Why can't the blasted man just rest?' asked Tweedman. 'That's what most actors do.'

'Mr Ford takes his profession most seriously, sir,' said Stancombe.

Tweedman rubbed his large chin with his hand.

'He hasn't got much of a part now, has he?'

Stancombe shook his head.

'Well, then,' began Tweedman and stopped.

'He also writes.' Stancombe proffered that piece of information like a prompt. Tweedman took it up instantly.

'Does he, by God! Then he can get down to Cork and damn well write!' He paused, then a further thought struck him. 'We can even commission a play. There's nothing in Admiralty Instructions to say that we can't, is there?'

Stancombe thought not. Certainly nothing explicit.

Satisfied that for the moment Terence Ford was dealt with, Tweedman moved on.

'And what's wrong with Admiral Bone, for God's sake? I saw him on the train yesterday and he was like a dog with a sore nose. He talked a lot of rubbish about being too old, but, and this is what worried me, Stancombe, *he'd been up here nosing about!*'

Stancombe had nothing to say.

'You find nothing strange in that?' asked Tweedman, angered at the impassivity in front of him. 'You find nothing strange in the fact that the father of our man comes up here and then glares at me in the train as if I was wearing horns?'

'Rear-Admiral Bone is the Commander of Area XI, sir,' said Stancombe. 'The First Sea Lord would naturally expect to see him from time to time.'

Tweedman shook his head. 'You've got chums amongst the First Sea Lord's clerks, see what you can find out.'

Stancombe gave one of his rare smiles. 'As for the Admiral's visit to the First Sea Lord, sir, I may be able to shed a little more light on that. I understand that the First

44

Sea Lord is none too happy about Admiral Bone's performance at Dover. The meeting was in the nature of a reprimand.'

Tweedman beamed. 'Stancombe,' he said, 'I'll put up that bloody statue myself!'

7

They stood on the bridge, hands grasped round the rails, looking forward. The immediate view was of the surface engine vent, the periscope and the new steel-bladed net-cutter, with its supporting planks bolted on either side, that ran right down to the bow of the casing. The distant view was of grey hulls and the equally grey waters of Portsmouth Harbour. Their thoughts at that moment ran along identical lines. How to turn this rusty, obsolete old craft into something alive and responsive.

Hugh Paynter had been Esmond's first lieutenant on the E-28. Now he searched the deck to find something nice to say.

'Well, I suppose we can be thankful for one thing, Skipper,' he said at last, pointing at the forward hydroplanes. 'They have at least moved them. From the look of her, they might have been still admidships.'

Esmond said nothing. The move from E-28 to B-12 was certainly not upwards, no matter what the operation. None of the crew could be expected to be happy at the change.

'Petrol driven too!' added Paynter with a grimace. 'We'll have to be damned careful.'

'But good agile little craft,' said Esmond with a smile, echoing Tweedman's remarks.

Paynter grunted, turned and gently spun the wheel. The master compass lay in front of them.

'Primitive, antediluvian,' he said, stopped, then stared at Esmond. 'I don't understand. You've done damned well in the E-28.' He indicated the small blue-white-blue ribbon

46

near the lapel of Esmond's jacket. 'You've sunk the *Antilope* and that U-boat, and now they bring you down to a second-hand Spanish junk!'

'I've told you,' said Esmond, 'It's a very special job.'

Paynter shook his head and glanced once more round the casing. 'Four days in summer, three in winter, that's about all you can do in one of these and keep the crew on their toes.'

Esmond led the way below. In the tiny, cramped control room, Paynter pushed back his cap, showed his deeply furrowed forehead and leant against the bulkhead door. His eyes settled first on the bilingual Spanish/English instructions, passed on to the depth-gauge in metres and ended up on the periscope.

'They'll have a lot to learn,' he said, 'and as for winching that thing up every bloody time — my God, who does that now?'

'I grant you it's not motorized,' said Esmond philosophically, 'but when the *Admirante Miranda* came back into Barrow last July, that periscope was fixed, and the whole boat had to be taken up and down.'

'Another thing, Skipper,' said Paynter, 'you do realize, don't you, that this tub uses the old Mark V GS torpedo?'

Esmond nodded.

'Eighteen inch!' said Paynter. 'And you know what trouble we had with the new Mark VIIIs! What's it going to be like trying to hit anything with a Mark V?'

'One seems to have hit the *Messoudieh* all right,' said Esmond.

'A petrol engine, a hand-winched scope, no wireless, internal ballast tanks, and Mark V torpedoes!'

It was a procession of despair. Yet the very mention of the mechanics of the boat made Esmond concentrate. He needed no reminder that the B-12 would call for very different handling.

'Remember, Hugh,' said Esmond, 'the Bs are still fully operational in the Med as I have already been forcefully reminded.'

'The Med's not the North Sea.'

'We're not going to the North Sea.'

Paynter's eyebrows rose.

'Not going to the North Sea, Skipper?' He savoured the thought with surprise. 'But that's what the engineer chappie said. He got it right from the horse's mouth, your horse.'

'Hugh,' said Esmond quietly, 'I've told you all I can, and I don't know much more myself. Our job at the moment is to get this boat worked up. Get it looking and feeling like one of His Majesty's submarines.'

They squatted round the mess-room table and Paynter brought out the old crew list of the E-28.

'Another thing, Skipper,' said Paynter, 'B boats are a lieutenant's command, with a-sub as his second.'

'Not this one!' said Esmond firmly.

Paynter spread the list across the table:

'I've done this much, Skipper. Coxswain, CPO Phillips. Engine tiffy and electrical tiffy, ERAs Fletcher and Warren. Sick-bay PO, Mills. Leading stoker, Lampton. Scott, Prentice and Bennett, leading seamen, and that gives us a good signaller and torpedoman. Hancock and Milton, two of the ordinary seamen, and we're still three ordinary seamen and a stoker short.'

'And we need a cook,' said Esmond.

They ran through a dozen names, ratings that did not automatically pick themselves. Men who were all equally reliable. They filled two more of the ordinary seamen and the stoker. The B-12 was still short by one.

'It's between Grant and Campbell,' said Paynter. 'Campbell's good on porridge, but Grant's range is a bit wider. He'd be my choice if it wasn't for his knack of getting waylaid by every passing skirt. You said we were working for NID, all hush-hush. Does that mean we're not going into port anywhere?'

'We're going to have to be refuelled,' said Esmond, 'but maybe that will be done at sea.' He took a penny from his pocket, 'Heads, Grant; tails, Campbell.'

He tossed the coin. It ricocheted from an overhead pipe and clattered on to the deck.

'Does that count?' asked Esmond.

Paynter nodded, bent down and picked up the coin.

'Heads,' he announced, then went back to the mess table

and in his sprawling handwriting added the name of PJ 10273 P. Grant at the very bottom of the list.

'We'll get the telegrams out today,' he said, 'and don't worry, Skipper, in ten days you won't recognize the old wreck!'

Esmond was going back to the bridge when a sudden impulse made him turn and say, 'We're having a dance at home tonight. Would you like to come?'

Paynter was surprised. As captain and first lieutenant they were close, but Esmond had never asked Paynter to his home before.

'I'm afraid it's nothing much,' said Esmond apologetically. 'It's just that my mother loves arranging these things even in wartime.'

Paynter happily accepted both invitation and lift.

They drove back at five in the morning under a dome of stars and each with his own thoughts. For Paynter it had been a moment of brightness and a glimpse of how some others still lived. For Esmond much more. It had been one of his rare chances to see Elizabeth. They had drifted into the gun-room more by chance than design. It was cold but at least semi-private. Almost her first words had upset him. She was joining the FANY.

'Soldiers!' he had said deprecatingly. 'You'll be dealing with soldiers!'

She had held the lapels of his jacket, her head slightly on one side, smiling.

'Dear Esmond, you know I would love to clean your guns and torpedoes and make mine-nets and things like that, but the Navy won't have women.'

He had told her that she was far too intelligent for a nurse, that anyone could tie a bandage, and pleaded with her to find something else. She had teased him with her blue eyes, threatening to become a ticket collector on the Midland Railway, a woman policeman or even a munitionette. When he had dismissed all three possibilities, she had kissed him lightly on the lips and laughed, saying, 'A Fanny it must be! Now, stop being jealous and tell me about you?'

He had told her that he was back at sea, and although she

had said that she was pleased for his sake, her eyes had clouded and she had frowned. He had told her too that the war might last three more years, but by that time he should have made commander. She had known exactly what he had meant, and it had seemed an awfully long time. When he had run his fingers through her hair, he had whispered about his next patrol. It was in home waters. If she went to France, he would be safer than her. She had laughed although she had wanted to cry.

They crossed Portsdown Hill with the dawn. Portsea Island was slowly unfolding from the grey-blue of night. The ancient walls of Porchester Castle were light, although not yet sunlit, and on the harbour waters the first ferry boats of the day had begun their passage. Paynter pointed just to the east of the great dockyard cranes.

'Funny, Skipper, to think that Nelson must have seen much this same view when his carriage came over the top on his way to the *Victory*.'

'For God's sake, Hugh,' cried Esmond, 'haven't you any soul!'

Paynter laughed.

8

Tweedman crossed from Pembroke Dock in an old destroyer, the black hull of which was marked more by the streaks of rust than by the large white letters of her pendant numbers. The sea, as so often in those approaches, had a heavy swell, and after several hours struggling to keep his feet Tweedman gave in to a troubled sleep. Thus, in spite of his profession, he was not the least disappointed to enter the relative calm of Cork Harbour, see the hills of Great Island through a dawn squall, and eventually step ashore beneath the tall, grey stones of St Colman's Cathedral. At Queenstown he carefully avoided the Naval facilities and hired the only car he could find. A two-year-old green Morris Oxford, the tiny 1018 cc engine of which was now to face the sternest test of its life.

Tweedman's first stop was only a few hundred yards away in the square by the Rob Roy Bar. He got out and walked slowly up the hill. The address led him to a terraced house close by the cathedral. He did not knock on the door, for this was merely a reconnaissance. For five minutes he stood at the end of the street, then he walked back to the near-by grocer and newsagent. He inquired whether the American gentleman, Mr Childs, had picked up his paper yet and was shown the last four copies of *The Cork Examiner*. He returned to the car and drove the thirty-three miles to Kinsale.

Terence Ford, deeply hurt at having to exchange the relative sophistication of Dublin for this back of beyond, had no intention of adding to his ills by being uncomfortable. He had therefore rented an eighteenth-century house, not large

51

but of pleasing elegance, on the slopes of Compass Hill. From its small bay window on the second floor, he could see the whole harbour of Kinsale and beyond. It was at this window that he was standing, disclaiming that bit of Lear's speech to Cordelia – 'Be your tears wet? Yes, 'faith. I pray, weep not: if you have poison for me, I will drink it' – ending with a flourish and draining his glass, when he saw the tiny bull-nosed Morris grind up the steep lane directly beneath him, and the immense form of Tweedman struggle out from beneath the canvas hood.

With the presence of a star about to make his first entry of the evening, Ford walked slowly down the stairs, unhurried by the continual clamour of the bell, and with considerable solemnity swung open the door. With nothing more than a theatrical bow, he led the way back upstairs. When Tweedman too reached the top, some moments later, Ford proffered the decanter. Tweedman declined and settled for a coffee, the order being passed in a loud voice as if intended for the back of the gallery, but in fact destined for Bella, invisible beneath the banisters.

To Tweedman's testy inquiry as to Ford's health, the reply was cold.

'I think you will agree, Captain,' said Ford, going to the bay window and indicating harbour, hills and the distant sea, 'pleasant enough even at this time of the year, but not really the place for one of my capabilities.'

No two men could have been more strikingly incongruous. Ford, tall, thin, with an Edwardian demeanour, dressed in a green smoking-jacket and crowned by a tasselled cap of rich peacock blue, although it was not yet ten-thirty in the morning; Tweedman, a huge bundle in knickerbockers and cape with a workmanlike magnificence. It was as if a clipper ship had met an ironclad.

Tweedman let himself down into the widest chair, pushed out his legs and balanced his stick against the left one.

'Whether this is the place for your capabilities or not, my dear Ford, remains to be seen.' He looked at the furniture, the curtains and the carpets. They were of considerable quality. Ford watched him, reading his thoughts.

'I had to give up an excellent part, Captain,' he said in

52

his clear, measured voice.

'£300 has been put in your bank in Cork.'

Ford bowed, refilled his glass and settled in the other chair, his face to the window.

'Now that that important matter has been settled, Captain, you might as well tell me the worst.'

'You're writing a play.'

Ford's aquiline nose twitched. 'Really, Captain, how very, very interesting.'

Tweedman nodded. 'You're writing a play set in the south of Ireland, and in the course of it you are likely to travel about getting your quota of local colour.'

Ford was distinctly pleased.

'And the subject of this play?'

'The sacrifice of the few for the many. A very traditional theme, goes well back before Christ and constantly comes up in mythology . . .'

The coffee arrived, brought in by an Irish girl with long auburn hair that almost matched Tweedman's in colour. The moment she had gone, Ford leaned across and looked at Tweedman over the rim of his glass.

'And while I'm writing this play?'

Tweedman lowered his voice. 'How well do you know this coast?'

Ford shrugged. 'Like anyone who lives in Dublin.'

'I want somewhere to hide a submarine,' said Tweedman.

'My dear fellow,' said Ford, 'what a funny request! Whatever's wrong with Queenstown or Haulbowline Island?'

Tweedman shook his head. 'West of here and secret.'

Ford lit a Fribourg and Treyer, Tweedman lit his pipe. At last Ford said, 'You're not telling me very much, are you?'

Tweedman mentioned the increase in U-boat activity off the Irish coast, the great concern in Whitehall, his hopes of trying out the 'trawler-sub trap', and his intention of finding out who on land were giving succour to the King's enemies.

'Ah,' Ford clasped his hands and smiled, 'the wicked Sinn Feiners again!'

Tweedman nodded. 'I want one of our smaller boats to operate off this coast impersonating a U-boat, and I want you to find an isolated anchorage — secure, not overlooked in any

53

way — where it can be refuelled and revictualled.'

'Have you anywhere in mind?' asked Ford without a touch of facetiousness.

Tweedman produced a crumpled map and laid it across his knees.

'There are several inlets here,' he said, indicating, 'but from the map it's not easy to see exactly how hidden they are, how protected from the weather and how accessible for a lorry.'

Ford looked at the map.

'It so happens, Captain, that I do know that area. Not intimately, mind you, but three years ago I borrowed a friend's gig and drove all along there. Forbidding, inhospitable and lonely,' he shivered, 'especially in the driving rain.'

Tweedman smiled. 'Exactly what we want.'

'And when is all this to happen?'

'The submarine will be here early in May.'

Ford's eyebrows rose. 'Then I shall have to get on with that play, won't I, Captain?'

Tweedman got up and leant on his stick.

'Do you know much about horses?'

'You can't live in this country and remain in complete ignorance for long.'

'I want you to meet a Frederick Childs,' said Tweedman. 'Lives in County Kildare but also takes lodgings in Queenstown. Ostensibly he's here on business, buying bloodstock for shipment to America. Not that he seems to have bought much lately. Put an advert in *The Cork Examiner*. Something to catch the eye. Do you know anyone with a stud?'

Ford smiled. 'Several.'

'Then take him to one, show him around, get his confidence. You know the sort of thing.'

'May I know the purpose, Captain?' inquired Ford politely.

'I'm not sure we shall want Mr Childs in the district. It may well be a case of enticing our friends in the Special Branch to pick him up.'

Ford nodded. He had not worked for Tweedman here and in America for the last seven years without learning something of his ways.

At the door they shook hands.

'One thing I forgot to ask,' said Ford. 'These bays and creeks are tidal. A moored ship can quite easily find itself high and dry for hours. I take it you would not want that to happen to your submarine? How much water does she need?'

'Twelve feet. And she's 142 feet long.'

Ford stood at the door while Tweedman squeezed back into the car, then he went back upstairs and refilled his glass. None of it would be too arduous. He knew of an inlet that would probably do. It had an island on which stood the remains of an abbey. There was a wall of sheer rock to the sea, not too high but deep enough, he thought, to shelter the submarine. He would hire a car and have another look. As for the German agent, the prospect of taking him round a stud and perhaps even to the races cheered Ford immensely.

Tweedman had no wish to stay in Ireland a moment longer than necessary. By eight that night he was safely aboard a destroyer and watching the long, low outline of the ramparts on Spike Island as they disappeared into the darkness.

9

Kapitän-Leutnant Walter Schwieger could be forgiven for a little daydreaming. By this time tomorrow they should be south of the 54th Parallel and approaching the Frisian Islands. Germany was little more than twenty-four hours away, leave at home in Berlin perhaps three days. From the bridge of the U-20, the North Sea was empty. All around, the waters had that cold, grey merciless look they always had whenever the sky was clouded and the wind laden with the chills of the Arctic. There was nothing to look at and only the cold to fight.

Although his boat, the U-20, was a veteran – in Schwieger's predecessor's hands, Kapitän-Leutnant Droescher, it had sniffed out the defences of the Firth of Forth within a month of the outbreak of war – this was Schwieger's first patrol as captain, and he was far from contented. He had obeyed his orders, penetrated the Bristol Channel and Liverpool Bay, but for seas supposed to be swarming with ships his sinkings had been few. A collier and a single small steamer were not going to impress his colleagues in Emden. An old British cruiser would make a fine last picking, but at the moment none was to be seen.

Surrounded by nothing more inspiring than a wilderness of windswept sea, Schwieger warmed himself with recollection and anticipation. The war had already begun to affect Berlin, he had noticed that on his last leave. It wasn't just that uniforms and bicycles were plentiful, private cars and taxis few, it was the already quite apparent air of seediness and shortage that seemed to have arrived with bread rationing.

On the other hand, the cafés were still doing good business, as were the hotels; and although luncheon at the Adlon had deteriorated, there was still that excellent restaurant in the Leipzigerstrasse where the platter of roasts would make a welcome change from the everlasting soup and cabbage of his U-boat. No doubt there would still be theatres to go to, and it would be nice to buy the London *Times* again and brush up his English.

Through his binoculars, Schwieger scanned the horizon. It was still empty. On his last leave the hate campaign against England had been in full swing, and was beginning to include America. Everywhere, postcards and cartoons lampooned the English and extolled German martial prowess, the Zeppelin being a particularly emotive weapon. In Schwieger's opinion, except for those in *Simplicissimus*, many of the cartoons were over-heavy and lacking in finesse. Not that Schwieger really enjoyed the hate campaign. Like most of his colleagues and the officers he met from the front, he found it unreal. His regard for the British, and in particular the British Navy, went deep. After all, it had been the model for their own Imperial Navy. Nevertheless, the many patriotic articles on sale in the shops, from cups decorated with Iron Crosses to girls' garters sporting motifs of German valour, all amused him. Indeed, some of them had found their way into his boat. Schwieger had been surprised and not a little disappointed that more was not being said of the U-boats. Already they had transformed naval warfare, and it always gave him a feeling of pride to see a U-boatman in his all black leather uniform, with the two long neck ribbons flowing from the back of his broad-crowned cap, striding down a Berlin street.

Yes, it would be good to see the Unter den Linden again, the girls, go dancing, eat fine food and drink fine wines, and for a few precious days feel his old gaiety return and forget the smells and squalors of his command.

'Smoke, bearing green, one-seven-zero!'

One look through the glasses, the scream of the klaxon, the order for both motors to go full ahead, the race down from the bridge, the clipping shut of hatches, and the U-20 dived. As the smoke gave way, first to a single funnel, then to a funnel and superstructure and finally to a complete ship, Schwieger knew that here, almost certainly, was his last chance on this patrol to add a few thousand tons to his score. He took an all-round look through the periscope, found that with the exception of this one small steamer the North Sea was quite empty, and decided it was not worth a torpedo.

'Stand by to surface! Shut main vents! Surface!'

Compressed air, racing into the ballast tanks, hissed like a thousand snakes. The depth-gauge needle swung back, and Schwieger waited on the steel-runged ladder, his hand on the hatch lever. As the conning tower burst into daylight, Schwieger swung open the hatch and raced up on to the bridge. The gun crew followed, sliding on the wet, slippery plating.

At 500 metres Schwieger ordered a warning shot to be fired over the steamer's bows. To his surprise the vessel did not heave to, but turned hard to port and, with black smoke streaming from its single funnel, made straight for the U-boat. Three more shots in rapid succession failed to stop her. Schwieger pressed the klaxon button.

'Dive! Dive! Dive! Full ahead together!'

For the second time in an hour, gun crew, watch officer and captain raced down the hatch. The cover was slammed down, the vents opened and the hydroplanes set to dive. But the U-boat took a long time to submerge. She hung on the surface as if held by an invisible hand, while Rudolf Zentner at the depth-gauge willed the needle upwards. With terrifying slowness it moved. 'Seven metres . . . ten . . . twelve . . .' As Zentner called 'Fifteen metres', a noise, like a gigantic rumble of thunder, pounded overhead. Instinctively, every man enclosed in that steel hull clapped his hands to his ears, the boat rocked, shook as if hit by a giant maul, and without anyone touching it the periscope swivelled in its casing. The sounds of the ship, reciprocating engine, propeller and turbulence died slowly away and they were left with their own quickened hearts and the dripping of water as the North Sea found its way in through the wrecked periscope housing.

'A close one, Herr Kapitän,' said Zentner, mopping his brow. 'Two seconds more and we would have been cut in two.'

Schwieger nodded. 'That, Zentner, is the danger of trying to do as some people in the world would have us do. Fire a warning shot.'

'We should rely more on our ability to fight from under the sea, Herr Kapitän! This is what we were designed for.'

Schwieger laughed. 'You should tell that to the President of the United States, Zentner, then we shall all live to take our grandchildren hunting butterflies in the Tiergarten!'

The meticulous Tweedman, the one seldom seen, went through every detail. Stancombe had brought the file right up to date. The Admiralty had, of course, had a hand in the design of the ship from the first. Indeed, both the *Lusitania* and her sister ship the *Mauritania* had, with a loan to the Cunard Company of £2,600,000, been built to Admiralty specifications, which had included the ability to cross the North Atlantic with 2,000 passengers and 900 crew at an average speed of twenty-four knots, or maintain the same speed and range with twelve six-inch guns.

Two years ago, in May 1913, war with Germany considered near, the *Lusitania* had gone into dry dock in Liverpool to have her gun-mountings positioned. She had returned to operations in July, and four days after the outbreak of hostilities she had been moved back into dry dock for full conversion to her armed merchant cruiser role. The lower deck, 'F', had been gutted and a large part of the shelter deck, 'C', had been strengthened and enclosed. Beneath 'C' deck, all forward passenger accommodation was now sealed off and in Admiralty control. This included the second-class smoke-room and the third-class dining-room on 'D' deck. Thus equipped, the *Lusitania* had entered the Fleet Register as an AMC.

The next page Tweedman skipped. He knew it by heart. They had decided not to use the steamer in the AMC role and the Cunard Company had been told to operate the ship on a once-a-month high-speed round trip to New York, the Admiralty trade division having control of the cargo space, the Government having priority for all passenger bookings. In addition, the liner's course on each crossing was to be an Admiralty matter and no contact was to be made with her at sea, even by the owners, except through the Admiralty.

Her first outward voyage from Liverpool after her release had been on 24 October last year. Then followed a note on Cunard's decision in November to reduce the crew to lower costs. This had meant manning only three of the four boiler-rooms and reducing the cruising speed from twenty-four to eighteen knots and the maximum speed from twenty-six to twenty-one knots. In his careful handwriting, Stancombe had added the words: 'It also saves Cunard 1,600 tons of coal per trip.'

Tweedman scanned the sailing dates. On 20 February the *Lusitania* had left Liverpool under the command of Captain Dow. Now, at the end of March, she was in New York, this time under the command of Captain W.T. Turner. There was another handwritten note by Stancombe to the effect that Captain Dow had been considerably disturbed at having to transport fuel-oil as cargo in a ship carrying passengers through waters becoming infested with U-boats, and that this, with the subsequent drop in his morale, had no doubt led to his replacement by Captain Turner. A further note, added later in amplification, mentioned the torpedoing of the steamer *Bengrove* by the U-20 on the *Lusitania*'s homeward course. It was anticipated that the *Lusitania*'s next docking in Liverpool would be on 11 April. The tentative date for her westward voyage was 17 April and that would place her arrival in New York around 23 April.

Tweedman counted on his fingers. Allowing six or seven days in New York would mean a sailing date of 30 April or 1 May. His estimate to Terence Ford to expect the B-12 in the first few days of May had not been far out.

It was 8 pm and Tweedman had just locked his desk when one of the First Lord's personal staff put his head round the door and said the Chief would like to see him.

'At this time of the night?' asked Tweedman testily. 'And the subject?'

'The *Falaba*,' said the aide, 'what else?'

Tweedman grunted, got to his feet and searched for the correct file. The 5,000-ton Elder Dempster steamer *Falaba* had been torpedoed in the approaches to St George's

Channel. Amongst the 101 lives lost was an American.

'I should warn you,' said the aide, 'his mood's none too good. He still hasn't got over the eighteenth. Of course, it's not the loss of the old *Ocean* and *Irresistible* that's upsetting him, it's this damned awful grinding to a halt.'

'With the Dardanelles his baby,' said Tweedman, 'it's a wonder he hasn't gone out there himself!'

'Just thought you'd like to know,' said the aide, 'until things start up again, it's all U-boats.'

'Thanks,' said Tweedman, and headed for the open door.

Churchill's first request was for an up-to-the-moment situation report. Tweedman ran through the statistics. Twenty-five merchant vessels totalling 80,000 tons had been sunk since the German declaration of a war zone last month.

'And four to six thousand ships enter and leave our ports every month,' said Churchill thoughtfully, 'with only twenty-five lost . . .'

Tweedman nodded.

'At the moment, not a matter of great significance,' said Churchill. 'Now tell me about the U-boats themselves.'

'Sixteen sailed,' said Tweedman, 'we know that for certain. They test their radios when they're about fifty miles out as a matter of routine. However, we don't believe that more than six were on station at any one time.'

Churchill looked at the signal.

'What I am really interested in, Captain,' he said, 'is neutrals. Neutral ships and neutral passengers.'

Tweedman was getting to know the First Lord, but this was the first time he was quite certain that their lines of thought were running parallel.

'American neutrals, sir?' asked Tweedman.

Churchill grunted and waved the signal.

'Now we have an American citizen as a casualty, have you seen any *private* reaction to this barbarous attack on the *Falaba*?'

Tweedman remembered the signal passed by his agent in the United States Embassy cipher room. 'The Americans have asked their consul in Plymouth to get all the details, particularly of the U-boat commander's behaviour.'

61

'Ah, the U-boat commander's behaviour,' said Churchill with rising anger, 'another sea pirate!'

'No, not really, sir,' said Tweedman, 'from all I have heard it looks as if this U-boat captain stuck pretty close to the Cruiser Rules, fired across the ship's bow first, gave passengers and crew five minutes to take to the boats and then only torpedoed her when one of our armed trawlers came up.'

'Then why did she blow up and not just sink?'

'She was carrying high-explosives,' said Tweedman blandly.

Churchill made a grating noise deep in his throat, closed the file and handed it back to Tweedman. 'In which case, Captain, I trust you will be circumspect enough to keep her manifest secret?'

'Naturally, sir.'

'And you've seen this morning's telegrams on the reactions of the American newspapers?'

'I have, sir,' said Tweedman, with unconcealed enthusiasm, 'and they make very good reading.'

'This consul in Plymouth interviewing survivors,' mused the First Lord, 'I don't like it.'

'His report will take time, sir,' said Tweedman soothingly. 'Meanwhile our official communiqué and this outcry will have set the mood, and we have many friends in the United States.'

Churchill got up and went to the large map that stood propped on the leather couch behind his desk. He drew his hand expressively across all the blue waters that made up the south-western approaches to the British Isles.

'Historic seas, Captain, where the great trade routes from the Americas converge. They must be teeming with vessels of every sort. Fishing smacks . . . colliers . . . coasters . . . packet-boats . . . torpedo-boat destroyers . . . cruisers . . . steamers . . . even great liners!'

Tweedman nodded.

'. . . And now, all the way from Fastnet Rock to Liverpool Bay, and southwards past the Scillies to the Straits of Dover the sea wolves are on the prowl.' Then he turned to Tweedman and added, 'At the summit, where I am, Captain, true politics and strategy are one. The manoeuvre that brings an ally into the field is as serviceable as that which wins a great battle. Remember that, Captain.'

Tweedman's pulse raced. He was about to blurt something out when he stopped. 'I will, sir,' he said, 'I certainly will.' He turned to leave. He had reached the grandfather clock by the door when Churchill called him back. The First Lord was holding out a folder of papers.

'I take it you have seen this, Captain?'

Tweedman went back and took the folder. It was the paper written for the First Lord by Guy Carr. Tweedman nodded. 'Yes, sir, I helped to draft it.'

'I greatly enjoyed reading it,' said Churchill. 'It is lucid, precise, and I would agree with the conclusions. If an ocean liner were to be sunk with Americans on board, the balance of power would be greatly changed . . . in our favour.'

Tweedman left the First Lord's room in a state of euphoria. As a serving officer, whose conditioning had entailed the receipt and carrying out of orders, the First Lord's words were like the lifting of an immense weight. No longer did it seem that the preparations he was making were the result of a self-generated, almost deceitful idea that had had to be hatched behind closed doors, but the results of quite specific orders from above. But for his wooden leg, Tweedman would have skipped down that august corridor. As it was, he held himself in check and called in upon Guy Carr.

'Good show, Guy,' he said, 'that paper of yours really pleased the First Lord!'

'I'm glad it was all right, sir,' said Carr, 'but I don't mind admitting that it worried me once I got going on it. It's a dangerous area. I didn't want to go giving people ideas.'

Tweedman said nothing more, but patted Carr on the shoulder and left the room.

10

Esmond reached 'The Black Horse' in a Daimler ambulance. He hoped that wasn't an omen, for it had been the only vehicle leaving the dockyard and going in the right direction. The landlord ushered him into the private room where the fire was already burning. There was no sign of Tweedman and to Esmond's inquiry as to how long Tweedman might be, the landlord thought not long or he would have telephoned. Esmond ordered a brandy and soda and made himself comfortable by the fire.

It was neither the electric lights nor the electric starter of his Sheffield-Simplex that was making Tweedman late. For once, both were working perfectly. Tweedman was late because, having decided to drive down, he had been able to stay at the Admiralty longer, and that had allowed two events to occur that he had not foreseen. Stancombe had produced that most secret piece of information requested some days ago, and Terence Ford had sent a second communication.

Stancombe's arrival with a brown manila envelope containing a copy of the minutes and drawings of the projected armoured land vehicle with the endless track, called 'Tank', and one of the pet ideas being promoted by the First Lord, had sent a chill down Tweedman's good leg. The thought of accidentally losing it, or of it actually passing into enemy hands, was more than he dared contemplate. For the moment the envelope and its contents were securely locked in his safe.

Ford had not only found what he thought a suitably safe and secret haven and sent more details of it, but repeated inserts in *The Cork Examiner* having failed, he had taken the bull by the horns and visited Frederick Childs personally. However, it wasn't Ford's letter about his meeting with Childs that had kept Tweedman in London, it was Childs' reaction to his meeting with Ford. Childs had promptly written to an address in Putney assessing Ford as a 'dangerous theatrical charlatan' and asking urgently for further information on him. Fortunately, Tweedman's own private mail interception service, quite separate from and unknown to MI5, had done its job. Now, by the relatively simple process of prolonging his impending visit to Parkhurst, Tweedman could put an entirely different, but well-forged, letter from Childs into the same envelope, where it would no doubt in due course be reopened by MI5 before onward transmission. But it had been a close shave.

As Tweedman remarked to Stancombe when writing his cautionary letter to Ford, the only thing that Childs had not complained about was Ford's knowledge of horses, but maybe that was because as Childs' own knowledge was so evidently meagre, it had been beyond him to spot it.

Tweedman was thus two hours late at 'The Black Horse', but as he was now in a much better position to brief Esmond, he considered the delay justified. Esmond, however, was fretting. The thought of working with Naval Intelligence had begun to worry him. Should anything go wrong with the operation, about which he still knew so little, the Admiralty would doubtless disclaim all knowledge and responsibility, as they had in 1910 when two marine officers, Trench and Brandon, had been caught charting the German sea-coast defences on the Frisian Islands. The prospect of being left stranded or made a scapegoat did not please him. The late arrival of Tweedman therefore had one quite distinct effect. Esmond had drunk more brandies and sodas than he had intended, and when Tweedman's car roared into the yard he was feeling distinctly truculent.

Tweedman threw two rolled charts and his goggles on to the couch and held out a hand in greeting. Esmond got up but glanced quite openly at his watch, pointing out that he had cut short the B-12's second trial immediately upon receipt of Tweedman's signal.

'Terribly sorry,' said Tweedman, 'but it's all in an excellent cause.' Then, calling the landlord to serve the duck and bottle of Pomerol he had ordered that morning on the telephone, he settled in the big chair.

'And how's she going?' asked Tweedman, ignoring Esmond's ill humour. 'Now you've got used to her, a much better boat than you expected, eh?'

Esmond found it hard to equal Tweedman's enthusiasm. 'I've got a damned good first-lieutenant and crew, sir, that's about it!'

'Dived yet?'

Esmond shook his head. 'Tomorrow, if all goes well.'

'You've got plenty of time,' said Tweedman, 'three weeks at the least, so you should be able to get her into pretty good shape.'

Esmond felt reassured. For wartime and with his experienced crew, that wasn't bad. It all depended on the faults they found when they started working up properly. So far they had only made two mild excursions out of the dockyard into Stokes Bay.

'And make sure you carry at least a dozen rifles,' said Tweedman, 'and that someone can shoot straight.'

'Charts, sir?' said Esmond, looking at the rolls Tweedman had brought and, for the first time, warming a little to the operations.

'From Portsmouth to the entrance of St George's Channel, then the Irish coast to Valentia Island.' Tweedman unwound a chart on the floor, using one hand and his good leg, 'Do you know this coast?'

'Only Queenstown and Cork Harbour as a midshipman on the old *Leviathan*,' said Esmond.

Tweedman spoke quickly, indicating all the time. 'There's an inlet between Cape Clear and Galley Head. It goes under the name of Carridleagh. To the west is Fhininskagh, White Sheep Island straight ahead and, to the east, Anliem Point. It's apparently a God-forsaken area, completely uninhabited. On the north of White Sheep Island there is the remains of an abbey. Around the abbey it is well wooded and there is this

66

sheer rock cliff to the east. You should be able to tie up there quite nicely.'

Esmond picked up the chart. The east channel, 'The Ferries', leading to his rocky quay was marked five to nine fathoms. Deep enough, but there seemed to be no lights or other aids to navigation anywhere in the vicinity. Finding it in the day was going to be difficult enough, finding it at night the very devil. Tweedman read his thoughts.

'When you're there, the moon should be three-quarters full and rising early. And we could arrange with your contact to provide a light for short periods on the promontory at Anliem Point.'

The way Tweedman was putting it, it was all far too simple. Esmond shook his head. 'That channel's not much more than fifty yards wide and with the tides there must be one hell of a current there. I'd like to see it in daylight first.'

Tweedman sipped his claret and thought.

'How close could you take her submerged?'

Esmond made a guess, pointing at the chart. 'A few hundred yards off there, but that depends on the weather. I'm assuming a clear day and very little sea.'

'You couldn't take her all the way in submerged?' asked Tweedman.

'It might be possible just on the turn. The trouble is that even if we had the room, on a short spurt, I don't think we're going to get much more than five-and-a-half knots out of her submerged and that's not going to give us much leeway if the tide is running.'

Tweedman refilled their glasses, then tapped his unlit pipe on his leg. 'We'll arrange it so that your movements are at the turn. I would much prefer that you had a go at it submerged.'

Tweedman rolled up the chart. After a while Esmond asked about his contact.

'His name is Terence Ford,' said Tweedman. 'He is an actor by profession, but no Henry Irving. His mother was Irish, his father English. He is a Protestant, fond of the bottle and has quite expensive tastes. As his profession seems to bring him little financial reward, money is always welcomed. That is not to say that he is not loyal, for he is – completely loyal. As a person, he is almost always theatrical and at times over-garrulous.'

'Interesting . . .' said Esmond, not at all sure.

'Amazingly reliable, though, for one of his profession and character,' added Tweedman, and Esmond was pleased. The thought of a drunken actor placing a light on Anliem Point in a Force Ten gale was not a very reassuring one.

'And now,' said Tweedman, 'you're worried about fuel, right?'

Esmond nodded. 'I haven't had a chance to check it, sir, but from here to your inlet, Carridleagh, looks about 450 miles. It depends, of course, on what you want us to do, but with charging batteries and the like, by the time we get there we won't have that much range.'

'Your fuel capacity is thirteen tons,' said Tweedman. 'You'll leave here with full tanks, and another six tons will be provided at Carridleagh. That should see you home again. Also, as a bonus, expect a few choice victuals — Irish butter, eggs, bacon, prime beef and mutton.'

Esmond was impressed. Tweedman had not only been doing his homework, he was also being very considerate. The whole enterprise was beginning to look far more hopeful. Indeed, under the aura of roast duck and claret, Esmond was once again enjoying life. He saw the distinct possibility of several interesting, unusual, and he hoped exciting days off the south coast of Ireland playing cops and robbers with Sinn Feiners and sinking U-boats.

'And the trawler, sir?' he asked.

'Trawler?' said Tweedman vaguely.

'For the "trawler-sub trap"?'

'Ah,' said Tweedman, 'in hand. Depends entirely what Queenstown can come up with.'

When Tweedman dropped him off at the naval barracks, Esmond had only one regret. He liked to know about his enemies. He knew a lot about the Germans, their ships and harbours. The Sinn Feiners he knew nothing about except that along with the Irish Volunteers they were classed as rebels.

In the morning, Tweedman had his car slung aboard a naval

lighter and crossed to the Isle of Wight. From Cowes he drove the few miles to Parkhurst Prison and there, as was his custom, was allowed as long as he liked in the private company of Charles Stoddart, who until three years ago had been a trusted member of one of the nation's foremost merchant banks. In a very short time, Tweedman had in his case not only an innocent letter from Childs to the 'post box' in Putney but an order to the Commanding Officer of HM Submarine B-12, signed by the First Sea Lord, instructing him to 'carry out a controlled attack upon the steamer *Lusitania*'. As for Charles Stoddart, he was warmed by the knowledge that when at last his term of imprisonment came to an end the nest egg awaiting him would have grown considerably and that, in the meantime, his wife's weekly postal order remained completely secure.

When Stoddart had been returned to his cell, Tweedman did not rush away as usual from the grim surroundings of the prison, but saw one more inmate. Petren was a professional anarchist, reputedly a friend of Peter the Painter, and known in the underworld as one of the finest practitioners in the developing art of explosive sabotage. Although Tweedman had never consulted Petren before, he had attended part of his trial and had earmarked him as a potentially useful contact.

When Petren was brought into the simple whitewashed room with its single high, barred window, Tweedman wasted little time. When a man was serving life there was not much to be gained in discussing the weather. Tweedman came straight to the point, laying before Petren a metal object that could best be described as a mushroom with a propeller on top, in all about eighteen inches long and varying in diameter from six inches to one.

Although Petren had not seen this particular mechanism before, the shape, shine, texture, accurate turning and threading all combined to stir him.

'Know what it is?' asked Tweedman.

'Part of an aerial bomb?' queried Petren, evidently interested.

'Not far out. The piston of a standard Mark V GS torpedo. That is to say, the detonator and primer.' Tweedman picked up the device to illustrate his words. 'The mechanism is safe when the torpedo is fired. The passage of the weapon through the water turns the propeller and arms the detonator. The whole affair slides into the warhead, which contains 265 pounds of amatol.'

Petren nodded, impressed.

'. . . I want a delayed-action device hidden in there so that it will explode at some predetermined time.'

'The torpedo is not to be fired?' Petren asked in surprise.

Tweedman shook his head.

Petren raised his dark, bushy eyebrows, smoothed down his equally dark but drooping moustache, and looked up from the mechanism. 'A torpedo that is not to be fired . . . a big man who comes into a prison, does not want to give his name, yet who wants to blow people up!'

'No questions,' said Tweedman testily, 'and I pay damned well.'

Petren spat the word, 'Money!', then laughed when he saw Tweedman's face. 'That is exactly what I would expect from you!' he cried. 'Money! Make all the wheels you want to turn go round with money! Just put the gold sovereign on the palm of your hand and the world will bow down before you!'

Tweedman was surprised by the outburst, but had no wish to get entangled in a philosophical debate, and certainly not with this man.

'All I want is a mechanism for this,' he said, tapping the pistol angrily, 'and I know you can do it!'

'I do not even know your name,' said Petren.

'Robertson.'

Petren nodded. 'Tell me, Mr Robertson,' he said, laying his hand upon the pistol, 'who is to die because of this torpedo?'

Tweedman slowly shook his head.

Petren looked up at the small, barred window, the tiny patch of sky, and shrugged.

'You have a wife in Belgrade,' said Tweedman, watching the anarchist. 'In spite of the war, we can still see that she is well looked after.'

'You must be a man of great power,' said Petren. 'You

come into a prison, bring that with you −' he indicated the pistol, '− you have me brought here, you say you can send money to Belgrade . . .'

'I cannot get you released, if that is what you mean. I can only help your dependants.'

Petren laughed.

'Doesn't that mean anything to you?!' asked a shocked Tweedman.

Petren shook his head. 'Very, very little.'

Tweedman tapped his artificial leg, glared and considered his next move:

' "Life" can be very long sometimes,' he said at last. 'There is just the possibility of a little remission.'

Petren picked up the pistol and examined it. 'Some men are to die so I have a little remission . . .'

'Good God, Petren,' cried Tweedman, 'you're behaving like an outraged girl! You made bombs, blew things up! That's why you're here!'

'*Things*, maybe, Mr Robertson, *not people*!'

'The Bosnian assassination,' said Tweedman coldly, '. . . Zvornik . . . 14 May 1912. You made the bombs!'

Petren slowly shook his head.

'We have a copy of the police dossier . . .'

'False! You know that!'

Tweedman shrugged. 'The charge anywhere within the Austrian Empire is murder.'

'But you are at war with Austria! They are your enemies!'

'They would be pleased to have you back. It could be arranged.'

Petren put down the pistol and stared straight ahead. His tongue moved slowly across his lips. Tweedman shifted uncomfortably upon the hard floor. His stump hurt and he wondered how much longer he could contain himself.

'One other thing,' he said at last, 'this operation could shorten the war by a year and save a million lives.'

'Lies!' cried Petren suddenly. 'Everything you say is lies. However good the explosion, it will not shorten the war by one day. This war has to run the course decreed by the land-owners, the generals, the profiteers. You cannot alter it, no one can!'

Two thoughts ran concurrently through Tweedman's mind. Put in motion the returning of the anarchist to Austria and see if that changed the man's mind, or take the damned pistol away and try someone else. But who? It would be too dangerous to involve the dockyard or any of the manufacturers. There was the Russian, Alexei Toupitsin, who the French had arrested last summer. His techniques were reputed to be impressive, but there were considerable difficulties in trying to employ him. Time was short and it would mean going through the Deuxième Bureau. Tweedman's relations with French Intelligence were not particularly good.

'I wish to go back to my cell,' said Petren moving towards the door. 'The air is cleaner there.'

Petren would know none of the difficulties with Toupitsin. A threat and a challenge were all that Tweedman had left.

'I am sorry I cannot interest you,' he said, stretching out his hand towards the pistol, 'for I am sure the Austrian Police won't be anything like as understanding as we have been. Fortunately, I have another string to my bow. Your old chum, Toupitsin . . .'

'Toupitsin!' spat the anarchist.

'An expert,' said Tweedman, 'a detonator specialist.'

'Toupitsin cannot do it!' cried Petren. 'He is not a master-craftsman!'

'The French were most impressed with his work.'

There was silence. Petren looked down at the pistol. Tweedman's hand stayed where it was.

'How long is this delay that you need?'

In his excitement, Tweedman lifted his hand and offered it in friendship. Petren ignored it. 'I said, how long is this delay that you need?'

'Eight to ten days.'

'Toupitsin could not do that. No one can. It is too long. A lot can go wrong in that time.' The anarchist picked up the pistol. 'Toupitsin will say he can do it. He will say he can do anything, for the man is a Russian and has no morals. But he cannot guarantee it, and I have a feeling that you will want this mechanism to be guaranteed, otherwise *you would*

72

not have come to me!'

Tweedman nodded. 'It is absolutely essential that it works perfectly. There is no room for error.'

'If it were to fail,' said Petren questioningly, 'there would be some other, maybe diplomatic catastrophe that you would not wish to face?'

Tweedman said nothing.

'. . . With Toupitsin you would be in that trouble.'

'In which case,' said Tweedman, with well-judged graciousness, 'I am completely in your hands.'

Petren stared at the pistol. 'If I do this, Mr Robertson, it will not be for *you*, nor to shorten *your* war, nor even to save me from the Austrian Secret Police. It will be because Toupitsin is a fraud.'

'I understand perfectly,' said Tweedman.

'Good. Now, the first thing you have to do is reduce the time. For the sort of reliability you demand, I will have to duplicate the mechanism. Even so, I cannot guarantee anything beyond seventy-two hours.'

While Tweedman was digesting that, Petren explained.

'There are three ways I can do this, by clockwork, acid or electricity. I assume that in this case, as the pistol will be within a movable torpedo, it cannot be connected to anything electrically?'

Tweedman nodded.

'. . . In that case it must be either acid or clockwork. Clockwork will be the bulkier but more exact.'

Tweedman thought rapidly. He would now have to arrange for the doctored pistol to be inserted into the spare torpedo not in the dockyard, as he had intended, but in the temporary anchorage at Carridleagh. It was not what he would have wished but there seemed no alternative.

'It will make it more difficult,' he said, 'but if that's the limit of your reliability I will have to accept it. But it must not show!' He added quickly, 'The whole mechanism must look perfectly normal. And it must be silent.'

'It will be as silent as the quietest Genevan watch,' said Petren soothingly. 'Now, how long have I got?'

'Ten days.'

'Ten days!' cried Petren in horror. 'This is the work of a month!'

'Ten days,' said Tweedman, 'not one day more.'

Petren stared gloomily at the pistol.

'Everything you need can be here tonight,' said Tweedman coaxingly.

'Two duplicate mechanisms ... tools ... materials ... lathe?'

'Everything.'

Tweedman provided the paper. Petren sat at the table and wrote. When at last he had finished, Tweedman scanned the list.

'The Governor won't exactly welcome this!'

'Surely, Mr Robertson,' said Petren sarcastically, 'it is all in an excellent cause?'

Tweedman did not answer. At the door he turned and said, 'I think you understand, Petren, this entails absolute secrecy?'

'No blackmail on my side, no Austrian police on your side, is that what you mean?'

Tweedman stood for a moment staring at the man. 'I repeat, if this mechanism works, I might be able to get you a little remission.'

Petren smiled and fondled the pistol.

'I am a master-craftsman, Mr Robertson, all my mechanisms work!'

Tweedman drove back to the jetty at Cowes satisfied that his work in England was almost done.

Euston had an air of somnolent industrial beauty. It was that brief afternoon moment when the platforms were uncrowded and porters and ticket collectors could settle with the first editions of the evening papers. Ten minutes ago, a troop train had left for Liverpool, its khaki-clad occupants en route to Egypt. In less than sixty minutes, the rush hour would engulf the station a second time. Stancombe, unhurried, dark-suited, with bowler and umbrella, fitted into the background perfectly. Too old to go to war, he gave the impression of helping to keep the home fires burning in a thoughtful rather than an active way.

Stancombe had dealt with Peder Mortensen on three previous occasions, and had no difficulty spotting the giant Norwegian stoker as he entered the forecourt just as the hands of the station clock reached three-thirty. Over a cup of tea in the buffet, he placed the envelope in Mortensen's massive hands.

'The man is called Frederick Childs. Tall, six foot two, fifty-five, and talks with an American accent. You are to meet him in the main post office in Cork at noon on Friday. He will bring with him proof of identification.'

'Cork post office, noon Friday . . . Frederick Childs . . .' repeated Mortensen.

Stancombe nodded. 'Give him the package and tell him you got it from the baker at Putney. Remember that, the baker at Putney.'

'The baker at Putney . . .' repeated Mortensen, staring at Stancombe over the top of his teacup, his large melancholy eyes unblinking.

'And here's the first £20,' said Stancombe, sliding a second, smaller envelope across the table.

Mortensen grunted and put the money into his inside pocket.

In view of Childs' reaction to Ford, they could no longer risk using that channel and the only other available, within the limited time at NID's disposal, was this merchant seaman whose ship, outward bound from Liverpool, had Cork as its first port of call. Now, in a moment of doubt, with a glance at the precious envelope that contained the plans of 'Tank', Stancombe hoped they had chosen the right man. Feeding any information to an agent was tricky; feeding real, live, hot information, frightening.

Stancombe glanced at his watch, paid the bill, bought a platform ticket and escorted Mortensen to his seat. He watched the large brown envelope go in the stoker's suitcase, and the train leave. He prayed that, for all their sakes, this crazy idea of his chief worked.

11

Schwieger was short of sleep. He had had a quiet enough evening, but nevertheless it had been later than he had intended when he had said goodbye to a few of his fellow officers and gone back to his boat. It was not his habit to turn the night before sailing into an orgy, but before any patrol there were always things to talk about. In this case, Admiral von Tirpitz's first submarine offensive against merchant ships using the waters around the British Isles was now in full swing, and for every U-boat crew, and particularly their commander, it was a busy and testing time.

They had, of course, swopped stories of their new heroes. Of Kapitän-Leutnant Hersing, who had sunk the British cruiser *Pathfinder* and who was now on his way in the U-21 to the newer hunting grounds of the Mediterranean. Of Weddigen, perhaps their greatest hero, who had in September sunk the three cruisers *Hogue, Aboukir* and *Cressy* off the Dutch coast and who was now reported lost in the U-29; and, with another touch of sorrow, of the recent disappearance of Stoss in the U-8, Kratzch in the U-12 and Wilcke in the U-37. Indeed, it was the loss of the latter boat that had caused the naval authorities to decree that from henceforth no U-boats were to force the Dover Straits, but all heading for the south-western approaches to the British Isles should use the long sea passage around the north of Scotland. Hence the heavy loading of the U-20. Every available inch had been crammed with provisions. The most perishable had been placed in the cool of the bow near the torpedoes, but even under Schwieger's own bunk, sacks, boxes and cartons were packed like sardines, and from an overhead pipe in the control room two huge smoked hams swung gently with the tide.

Two other boats of the Emden half-flotilla had already sailed, the U-30 and U-27, but the U-20 had had to await the repair of her periscope. With the packing of the glands completed, her departure had been fixed for the early morning of Friday, 30 April.

The collar of his old leather jacket turned up against the chill night air, Schwieger leant over the bridge rails.

'Let go forward, let go aft! Midships! Slow astern together!'

212 feet of steel, built in the Danzig dockyard only two years ago and looking like a cold, grey shark, the U-20 was the home of thirty-five dedicated men, all proud to wear the insignia of the 'Deutsche Unterseeboots Flotille'. She was armed with two 3.4-inch guns and four tubes of the deadly twenty-inch torpedo, and was once again ready to sail against England. So was her ambitious commander.

The waters were dark and murky as Schwieger slipped the U-boat stern first from its berth. The only lights were those of the buoys marking the Ems River, and in the far distance, on the port side, the lights of the Dutch coast.

'Slow ahead together! Steer two-seven-zero!'

At that hour, the only other craft to be moving was a fishing-boat, but it veered off and away from the naval anchorage so that Schwieger was left to pass alone beneath the towering masts and funnels of cruisers of the High Seas Fleet. The *Prinz Adalbert*, motionless at her moorings, was the last to signal, 'Good hunting!'

By dawn, the U-20 had left the friendly shores of Lower Saxony, lost the lights of neutral Holland and was heading into the choppier waters of the West Ems Channel. The Island of Borkum, marking the last landfall before the waters of the North Sea proper, passed slowly to starboard. They signalled to the crew of the Borkum lightship, and with the 650-ton boat making a steady ten knots, a blue haze trailing behind her from the exhaust of her throbbing diesels, the cook preparing veal stew and cabbage, and the yelping of the ship's dachshunds rising through the open hatches, Schwieger went below. In his tiny cubicle he took another look at his orders. Like orders the world over they were not particularly precise, but the destination was clear: the Irish Sea, Liverpool and the Bristol Channel, and the quarries he was to await seemed to be large English troop transports coming out of the south- and west-coast ports.

Helmsman Lang joined his captain for coffee. A reservist from the Merchant Navy, Lang was an acknowledged authority on British ships. Now his eye caught the boat's copy of *Jane's Fighting Ships* on the tiny bookshelf above the captain's bunk. It was the latest edition, 1914. Balancing the mug of coffee on the edge of the flap that acted as a table, he took the book, opened it and turned the pages methodically until he came to page thirty-one. Pages thirty-one and thirty-two contained the silhouettes of British liners of eighteen knots and over. They started with the one-funnelled *Orantes* and ended with the four-funnelled, *Mauritania*.

'Brushing up your identification, Lang?' asked Schwieger with a grin.

Lang, always a little serious, nodded. 'You said we were to expect large troop transports, Herr Kapitän.' He ran his finger across the shining page. 'The question is, which one is it to be?'

Schwieger had to peer at the book upside down.

'I fancy the *Olympic* myself,' he said, 'she is the fattest goose!'

Lang looked at the lower, left-hand silhouette. 'The fastest, Herr Kapitän. That is what I fancy. The greyhound that took the blue riband away from our own *Deutschland*. The *Lusitania*.'

Schwieger laughed. 'My dear Lang! Ever the optimist! Somehow I don't think she will be our luck any more than the *Olympic*. We shall probably have to make do with an old Mersey river steamer that has lost its way!'

At that moment, with the U-20 forty miles out on her west and northward passage, the wireless operator calibrated his radio frequencies with the Borkum station. The signals were picked up in England, passed to Room 40 at the Admiralty and were in Stancombe's hands an hour later.

Stancombe placed two sets of papers in front of Tweedman. The first, a single sheet, reported the departure of the U-20 from Emden and reminded Tweedman of her destination. The second set contained the latest reports on the torpedoing of the American tanker *Gulflight*.

Tweedman looked at the single sheet first.

'Operations,' he said sharply, 'and remind them that that's the third U-boat heading for the west coast this week.'

Stancombe had noticed that with each passing day, Tweedman was getting more touchy. No doubt, like everyone at the Admiralty, he needed a few days' leave, and no doubt he would take it when things calmed down. But there was more to it than that. Stancombe knew Tweedman well enough to know when he was under strain, and what with the mess in the Dardanelles he was under strain now. But the big one, of course, the one that was really sapping him, was the *Lusitania* project.

Just as the moment, however, it was all *Gulflight*. An unknown American tanker had suddenly become an international star. Better known even than Mabel Normand, Mack Sennett or Charlie Chaplin. The U-30 had been playing havoc with shipping off the west coast for the last three days. From an intercept of her orders she was supposed to be heading for Dartmouth, but it was doubtful if she would have any torpedoes left even if she got there. Three days ago she had sunk a 2,000-ton collier; two days ago, four more ships; and yesterday she had made her third victim of the day this obscure American tanker. That, of course, had brought a flood of minutes from the First Lord and the most intense activity from the political branch of NID.

Tweedman scanned the papers with an ill-concealed temper.

'Are you telling me that this tanker was actually being *escorted* to St Mary's in the Scillies when attacked?' he asked incredulously.

'Yes, sir. The hired Hull trawlers *Filey* and *Iago* were on

79

their way to a reported sighting of the U-30 when they intercepted the *Gulflight*. The skipper of the *Filey* seems to have been suspicious of the *Gulflight*'s activities and ordered her to accompany him to St Mary's. The U-30 then surfaced and ordered the convoy to stop. The *Filey* tried to ram the U-boat, which dived and torpedoed the *Gulflight*. The rest you know, Captain. Two of the American crew were drowned and the captain died of a heart attack.'

'And had the *Gulflight* not been escorted?'

'That morning the U-30 stopped a Dutchman, then allowed her to go.'

'So the U-30's attack on the *Gulflight* was, in the circumstances of her being escorted by British warships, reasonable?'

'It would appear so, sir.'

Tweedman sighed. 'The First Lord doesn't think so. He's already called it "a murderous and unprovoked attack". And your version, Stancombe, will do us no good whatsoever. If all the details of this come out, the Royal Navy stopping a neutral American, forcing it into one of our own harbours, turning it into a sitting duck by reducing its speed, making it a target by our presence, we shall lose a lot of friends across the Atlantic. On the other hand,' said Tweedman more cheerfully, after a lengthy pause, 'properly handled it could be damned useful. After all, a U-boat *has* torpedoed an American ship and three of her nationals *are* dead. Uncle Sam isn't going to like bald facts like that! So a murderous and unprovoked attack it is, Stancombe.'

'Yes, sir,' said Stancombe, and collected the papers.

'You know,' said Tweedman, looking up at Stancombe, 'I don't like the way this war is developing. I like to know that somewhere you can still find the truth when you need it. It's not only a foundation for our daily lives, it's reassuring, and we all need reassuring sometimes.' He struggled up from the desk and walked to the window, 'I forgot to ask, how is your boy liking the Army?'

'He's had two nights' embarkation leave, sir,' said Stancombe, 'Mrs Stancombe baked him a fruit cake, and he sails tonight.'

'Don't worry, Stancombe, there are no U-boats in the Channel and the Army'll spot his age all right. He'll get an L of C job. Shouldn't be a bit surprised if he doesn't end up in the RTO's office in Calais.'

'That's exactly what I told Mrs Stancombe,' said Stancombe smiling.

Tweedman came back from the window and looked at his watch. 'It seems to be a day of events. Thank God it's Friday the thirtieth and not the thirteenth!'

At two-fifteen in the morning, with a new quarter moon high in the sky, Esmond had nosed the B-12 out of Portsmouth Harbour. As Tweedman had hoped, their stealthy departure had gone virtually unnoticed.

The working up had not been all that traumatic. The boat was old but serviceable, and the dockyard had done their best. Esmond would have liked new batteries but none were available in the time. There had been several leaks to attend to, the most serious where the capstan drive shaft entered the hull and in one of the pipes to the main ballast tanks. The engine-cooling circulating pump had had to be replaced and a good many glands repacked. 'Tiffy' Fletcher had stripped the Wolseley down to its casing and pronounced it worn, but with an even chance of lasting 2,000 miles if they did not push it too hard. The aft hydroplane had jammed on their third test-dive and scared everyone, but with the tanks blown the boat had come back to the surface, leaping from the water like a porpoise. In the three weeks, Paynter had whipped the crew into their new mould and already the grumbles at leaving the E-28 were receding into the past.

The anti-cyclone that had begun to build over the British Isles, and was to stay for the whole of the following week, had thrown a haze over Spithead. The water, ruffled by the faintest of east winds, had sparkled like roughly pressed gold beneath the crescent moon. Behind them the colourless light had caught the cranes of the dockyard and the long, low forts on Portsdown Hill, turning the red bricks a pale magenta. In the harbour itself, the mirror of water had been so still that but for the grey of the cruisers and the black hulls of the

81

ubiquitous destroyers they might have been leaving a tropical lagoon.

They had followed the Southsea shore and could just make out the Trafalgar monument and castle to port. Once past Horse Sand Fort, Esmond had brought the B-12 to her economical eight-and-a-half knots cruising speed and headed south-east towards the swept channel between Bembridge Point and the Nab Light. At the entrance to the channel he had turned south and through it. The sixteen-cylinder Wolseley settled to a steady 360 revs, and as the bow wave rose over the guide cables the submarine sat in two distinct troughs of sea, the second crest immediately below the conning tower. They had passed three armed trawlers of Patrol Area XII, and as they had turned south-east for the southern tip of the Isle of Wight they had almost collided with elements of the Fifth Battle Squadron returning to harbour. The old battleship *Venerable* and her escorting cruiser *Topaz*, together with four destroyers, had run for two miles on an exactly opposite course. At seven in the morning they had seen their last of St Catherine's Point, and at five in the afternoon they passed the most southerly tip of Devon with the Eddystone Light ahead.

On the same day that the U-20 was heading north for its apogee around Fair Isle and the B-12 westwards down the Channel, at Pier 54 on Manhattan's waterside the *Lusitania* was experiencing all the problems and frustrations that beset any great liner in the hours immediately before sailing. For one thing there were to be more passengers on this voyage than on previous wartime voyages, and with most of the stewards now very temporary, Staff Captain Anderson, acting as Captain Turner's aide during these difficult crossings, had problems.

The cargo too was larger than usual, and although the *Lusitania* had not been a cargo ship since the gutting by the Admiralty, almost the whole area forward of the No. 1 boiler-room had been turned into a hold. However, with the decks still in place, accessibility was exceedingly difficult, resulting in much manhandling, cursing and frayed tempers. Another worrying problem for Anderson was which items of cargo to put on the 'open' manifest to be handed to the customs for clearance and which to put on the 'closed' second manifest to be handed in later when the ship had sailed.

As far as Anderson could see, a great proportion of this particular cargo was contraband. There were nearly 5,000 cases of small arms ammunition, weighing in all about 170 tons, and over 1,200 cases of shrapnel shells weighing just over fifty tons, as well as numerous other packages, cases and barrels, the exact contents of which Anderson had grave doubts. These ranged from several hundred bales of furs to several thousand boxes of cheese. Indeed, Anderson was in the hold while some of the latter were being taken out of the slings. When he remarked about the great quantity of cheese going aboard, a stevedore unloading the sling laughed.

'Cheese,' he said, 'they're no more cheeses than I am, Captain. I know a guy who packed some of these. It's an explosive used in guncotton. Fancy name, can't remember it, but if sea-water gets on that!' He whistled most expressively, 'I'll tell you, man, I wouldn't like to be on this ship. It only wants a few drops . . .'

The stevedore sent the sling up. Anderson looked at the cases, tons of them, and grew angry. The sling brought down another consignment.

'Are you certain about the explosives?' he asked the stevedore.

The stevedore nodded. 'Dead certain, Captain. I wouldn't fool you on a matter like this. Still, it shouldn't worry you, not with the speed of this boat. Besides,' he added with a grin, 'I don't suppose they'd dare have a go.'

Anderson climbed the ladder to the deck. The fresh air felt good and the bustle all around did something to allay his worries. He thought of finding Turner or the Cunard agent but knew it was pointless. There was a war on and the *Lusitania* was under Admiralty orders. Nevertheless, like the *Lusitania*'s previous skipper, Captain Dow, now resting in England, he did not like mixing munitions with passengers, and certainly not with U-boats about.

Around nine in the evening, loading was completed and the last coal lighters left the ship's side. By that hour too the final touches had been applied to both the cabins and staterooms. The inlaid mahogany had received its final polish and the fabrics of every sort, from curtains to carpets, their final cleaning. But for her passengers and the last minute orders to her captain, the *Lusitania* was ready to sail.

12

Frederick Childs stood before the mirror clipping his neat, grey moustache. A tidy man, his left hand was cupped directly below his chin, collecting the trimmings which he then tipped into the wastepaper basket that stood ready at his feet. Tonight he was dining out, and amongst the guests would be naval officers. He would like to have worn his own mess uniform, that of a Korvetten-Kapitän in the Imperial German Navy, but even had it been with him in Queenstown instead of lying in mothballs in a tin trunk in his sister's house near Kiel, it would not, of course, have been possible. Nevertheless, within the limitations imposed by mufti, he was determined that his own appearance should be as correct as that of the British.

Childs was looking forward to an evening he knew he would enjoy. To dine with British naval officers, not an onerous task in itself, was also, of course, most useful in his present position. A surprising amount was still to be gathered at the Queenstown dinner tables in spite of wartime security. In addition, some of the officers would have their wives, and it made a pleasant change for him, a widower, to sit between the ladies.

Childs finished his moustache, stood back from the mirror and gave himself a very critical appraisal. Satisfied, he tied his black tie and brushed the collar of his jacket. A knock on his bedroom door and his landlady announced that the visitor he had been expecting had arrived. Without any apparent hurry, Childs completed his dressing, unlocked the drawer of the table by his bed, took out a long, crumpled brown envelope, placed it within a new white one, collected his cape from the hook on the door and went downstairs. Willem Stöver, second mate on the tramp steamer *Irene*, had his broad back to the door as Childs entered. He turned at once, and gave a toothless smile. 'You wished to see me, Mr Childs?'

Childs politely offered the Dutchman a drink, then directed him to the better chair, taking the other himself.

'I have an envelope I would like delivered to my friend in Rotterdam.'

Stöver nodded. Childs took the envelope from the inner pocket of his jacket and laid it on his lap.

'Important is it, Mr Childs?' asked the Dutchman, looking at the envelope and considering his likely payment.

'That is just what I'm worried about,' said Childs. 'If it really was important, then I suppose I should take it myself. On the other hand . . .' and he shrugged.

'Falls sort of midway?' said the Dutchman, draining his glass.

'Maybe I am a little old fashioned,' said Childs, 'and, of course, I have been a naval rather than a military man, but the idea of a vehicle, loaded down with armour and fitted with an endless track, that is supposed to cross trenches and silence machine-guns would seem to me to be somewhat ludicrous.'

Stöver, still assessing his fee, nodded.

'I would have thought', said Childs, 'that if it didn't bury itself in the mud or fall headlong into the first shell-hole, it would certainly be a sitting target for our excellent field artillery.'

'Don't you worry yourself, Mr Childs,' said the Dutchman getting to his feet, 'I'll see that it's in your friend's hands, safe and sound, within the week.'

Childs handed Stöver the envelope and a bundle of notes. The Dutchman counted the notes, shook hands and left.

As he had anticipated, Childs enjoyed the dinner party. It had a fine blend of Irish, Anglo-Irish and English, and although he picked up little of military or naval importance he did have a very pleasant conversation with the wife of a

Commander whose husband was on the old cruiser *Sutlej*, one of the three vessels whose funnels could be seen from the dining-room window while they ate.

For Mrs Cynthia Maitland too the dinner party was enjoyable. Not only was the food excellent and even to her gourmet palate something of an experience, but she enjoyed sitting next to the tall, distinguished American whose gentle voice, manners and wide cultural interests made such a pleasant change from the unsophistication of her husband's fellow officers.

Together the couple ranged from ballet to literature, and at first neither could find a weak spot in the other. Childs had seen Diaghilev's production of Mussorgsky's *Boris Godunov* at the Metropolitan Opera House in New York, Cynthia had seen the same production at Drury Lane four months later. Both had heard Chaliapin, watched Isadora Duncan and read Henry James. Over crème brulée, Cynthia mentioned Thomas Hardy. To her surprise and joy, Childs had only a passing knowledge. She at once promised to lend him her own first edition of *The Woodlanders*. As she so sweetly put it, 'Now that Mr Hardy is pledged to devote all his writing to the Allied cause, we must take even more notice of him.'

Childs tilted his head and smiled graciously. Cynthia Maitland's matronly heart beat a knot or two faster.

After the cold, wet winter, the extraordinary warm spring that enfolded northern Europe in the last days of April brought a more than usual sense of regeneration. Nowhere was this feeling stronger than in Tweedman. Sitting at his desk at the Admiralty after a morning of seemingly endless, niggling worries, he suddenly realized what had been missing from his life. Whereas some men would have taken themselves off to the Turkish baths or for a stroll around Kew Gardens, he left the office early and drove down to Brooklands.

The race track was officially closed, although not to Tweedman. He borrowed one of the few cars still there, the big V12 Sunbeam and took it round twice before opening it up. The track had deteriorated since his last visit; RFC Leyland and Thorneycroft lorries had cracked the surface in many places. Holding the great car steady took all his strength and will. He was in the railway straight, with the famous sewage farm between him and the Vickers works, when he suddenly realized how frighteningly narrow was the margin between life and death, success and failure. Instead of sitting quietly 400 miles away in Ireland, by now Frederick Childs should have booked a passage to Holland and been picked up on the gang plank by the stalwarts of the Special Branch. And, more important, those precious drawings of that weird creation called 'Tank' should by now be back in the safe. A Vickers gun bus took off, turning Tweedman's relaxation into a race, and they lapped together at 90 mph. He suddenly found himself screaming above the roar of the wind, 'If that's the way the stupid Hun wants to play it, I'll go over and get him myself!'

Then he put his foot down to the floorboards and, to the cheers of a dozen RFC mechanics, beat the gun bus into the finishing straight by twenty yards.

13

NID got their first information of the German warning before it had appeared on the streets of New York. A compositor at the offiecs of the *New York Tribune* passed it to the British Consulate. It was on Tweedman's desk by ten. He was out all morning, but Stancombe had made the signal so evident that he was reading it before he had hung up his cap.

NOTICE! Travellers intending to embark on the Atlantic voyage are reminded that a state of war exists between Germany and her allies and Great Britain and her allies; that the zone of war includes the waters adjacent to the British Isles; that, in accordance with formal notice given by the Imperial German Government, vessels flying the flag of Great Britain, or of any of her allies, are liable to destruction in those waters, and that travellers sailing in the war zone on ships of Great Britain or her allies do so at their own risk.

IMPERIAL GERMAN EMBASSY, Washington DC,
22 April 1915

Stancombe came in with two more signals and, without a word, laid them alongside the first one. Tweedman glanced at his watch. 'Eight-thirty, New York time. She sails in less than two hours.'

'It's in all their morning papers, sir,' said Stancombe, 'and in at least one it appears next to Cunard's own advertisement.'

Tweedman got up and walked to the map. 'Two U-boats in the Irish Sea, one heading there, and now this quite blatant notice, published on the morning she sails. My God, Stancombe, they mean to sink her themselves!'

'It would certainly appear so, sir.'

Tweedman shook his head. 'They're mad! Crazy! Two days ago it was the *Gulflight*. The trouble with the Huns is that they have no finesse. They're so heavy handed about everything. Here they are, doing their very best to help *us* get the Yankees into the war!'

'Lieutenant-Commander Bone and the B-12?' inquired Stancombe.

Tweedman stood looking at the map.

'The sea is a large, lonely place, even if it doesn't look so there,' he said, pointing to the narrowing of the waters as they approached St George's Channel. 'A submarine's horizon is very limited. The Germans might just miss her. No! This is too good an opportunity to call our side off yet. The sea teeming with U-boats, this warning in the paper . . . when something does happen, it won't be all that unexpected.'

Stancombe indicated the second signal. 'Several passengers were sent warning telegrams, sir. They appear to have been intercepted by Cunard's staff and not distributed.'

Tweedman read quickly.

'It gets better and better!' he cried, looking up and smiling. 'The Huns really must have a death wish.'

At the door, Stancombe turned. 'Forgive me, sir, for even thinking this, but did you by any chance have that warning put in the paper, or those telegrams sent?'

Tweedman dissolved into floods of laughter.

Half an hour later, Tweedman had an unexpected visitor. Rear-Admiral Henry Bone put his head round the door.

'Just want to thank you, Gavin,' he said gruffly. 'Was passing by and didn't want you to think I was churlish!'

Teedman struggled to his feet, puzzled and alarmed.

'Damned kind of you getting Esmond that submarine,' said the Admiral. 'Know you Intelligence fellows don't like letting your left hand know what your right's doing, but it's damned nice of you. He was a different chap, I can tell you, when he knew he had a command.'

Tweedman's hands were wet, but he managed to mutter a few words about it being an old craft yet the best he could do.

'Understand it's a job for you?' queried the Admiral.

Tweedman nodded, Rear-Admiral Bone grunted; then, to Tweedman's dismay, instead of a cheery wave and goodbye, the Admiral dropped into the leather chair, laid his arms along the arm rests, his legs straight out, and looked as if he might stay all afternoon. Tweedman was quite sure that the next sentence from Bone would be, 'Now tell me, Gavin, just between the two of us, what exactly is young Esmond up to?' It wasn't. It was even more shattering. The Admiral stared at Tweedman for several seconds, a far away look in his eyes, then said, 'I suppose you've heard the news?'

Tweedman, who prided himself on normally being first with the news in Whitehall, shook his head.

'I'm off to Queenstown,' said the Admiral flatly.

That cold, prickly feeling went down both of Tweedman's legs. In his brain, his amputated foot itched abominably.

'*Queenstown?*' he said, '*Ireland?!*'

'For God's sake man, there's only one Queenstown, surely?'

'You mean you're taking over Patrol Area XXI?' asked Tweedman in disbelief.

The Admiral shook his head. 'The Eleventh Cruiser Squadron.'

The Eleventh Cruiser Squadron was based at Queenstown and came under the command of Patrol Area XXI. It consisted of four old cruisers and four armed boarding steamers. It was a demotion, but it wasn't that that was upsetting Tweedman. It was the endless vista of complications and the awful implications. This wasn't the moment, nor was this the enterprise, for father and son to be closeted in the same Patrol Area.

'When, sir?' asked Tweedman anxiously.

'I'm off tomorrow night,' said the Admiral. 'They've got a destroyer for me at Milford Haven.'

'So by this time on Sunday,' said Tweedman, riding the shock, 'you'll be flying your flag in the *Juno*.'

'Never liked Ireland,' said the Admiral, 'always thought it a dirty, wet, ugly place. Now, Dover . . .' he said with great nostalgia, 'handy to Town, easy enough to slip home for a night . . .' Suddenly the Admiral sat upright in the chair, 'Gavin, these damned U-boats. The First Lord swears that they are still all coming through Dover, but we're quite sure they're not. It's all pretty well netted with Bircham indicators and stiff with armed trawlers, and it's not a month ago we dug the U-8 out.'

Tweedman now knew why Rear-Admiral Bone had been demoted and why operation 'Deliberate Diplomatic Miracle' was taking on the aspect of a Greek tragedy.

'The First Lord should know,' said Tweedman. 'We've told him often enough.' He got up, walked to the map that detailed the waters around the Britsih Isles, and stabbing his finger angrily on the chart, indicated. 'At this moment the U-20 is probably somewhere between Fair Isle and the Little Minch heading south, and the U-30 is somewhere in the area of St George's Channel, having come round Scotland on much the same course. The U-27 was heading that way but seems to have turned back. So far as we know, not one U-boat has used the Straits in the last month.'

The Admiral got to his feet. 'I'm grateful for that, Gavin. It's cleared the air.' Then he laughed and added, 'But it doesn't look as if I'm going to get away from submarines wherever I go, does it?'

Tweedman's throat was too tight to answer. First he hoped that the U-30 would be lying off Milford Haven tomorrow night, then suppressed the thought as being too ignoble. But the moment the Admiral left the room, he poured himself an enormous Scotch.

They were just over a hundred miles north-west of Land's End. The sea had that same glassiness that it had had all day, with a long, low swell rolling in from the Atlantic, and the sun was a red ball ten degrees above the horizon, when Esmond sprung his first surprise on the crew. He told Paynter that he wanted a roll of canvas run round aft of the

92

conning tower and fixed to the stanchions that supported the bridge, and the large white numbers '04', on the conning tower and bow, obliterated. Paynter made no comment but sent a party on deck. The canvas completely altered the silhouette. Gone was that well-known characteristic of the B boats, a small conning tower with a 'veranda' astern. From anywhere but the closest range, the boat riding on the sparkling sea might have been one of the U-17 class.

With the canvas in place, Ordinary Seaman Milton set about the painting with a bucket of one part black to twenty parts white by weight. It was not a difficult job and the result did not have to pass the scrutiny of the selection committee of the Royal Academy. Milton had it finished at the beginning of sunset.

'We're now nobody, is that right, Skipper?' asked Paynter, as he joined his captain and peered ahead into that area where, under conditions like this, it can sometimes be difficult to tell sea from sky. 'No lights, no ensign, no recognizable shape, and now no pendant number.'

Esmond saw the pained look on his first lieutenant's face.

'Thanks for being patient, Hugh. I know it hasn't been easy keeping morale up when everyone's in the dark. I'll tell you what I know, then I'll brief the whole crew.'

On the B-12, the captain's cubicle was even smaller than on the U-20, so Esmond took Tweedman's charts and unrolled them on the small table in the control room.

'Ireland!' said Paynter in anguish. 'I knew it must be from the course you set, but it still doesn't make sense.'

'Ever heard of Carridleagh?' Esmond asked, laying his finger on the long, thin inlet. Paynter shook his head.

'Supposed to be like the Sahara, completely uninhabited. Fhininskagh to the west, White Sheep Island in the middle, Anliem Point to the east.'

'We're not going in there, Skipper, are we?' asked Paynter in consternation.

'That's the idea.'

'Whatever for?'

'To the locals we're a U-boat.'

Paynter winced. 'I hope we're not to the Navy.'

Esmond laughed. 'It's a game . . .'

'Thank God for that!'

Esmond pointed out Carridleagh Abbey, the sheer wall of rock, the wooded surround. 'We tie up against the granite and a gentleman from the theatre looks after us.'

'You're pulling my leg, Skipper,' said Paynter.

Esmond shook his head. 'It sounds like a music-hall joke, I know, but it's not. We're going there for a very specific reason. To find the Sinn Feiners who are refuelling the U-boats.'

Paynter whistled.

'. . . And after that, we're going in for a little destruction ourselves. If Queenstown can provide the trawler, we're going to be the other half of a "trawler-sub trap" double act.'

Paynter grinned.

14

Little at the start of the voyage had been auspicious. It had been drizzling and the clouds across New York had been low and unbroken when the *Lusitania* had left Pier 54. There had been the reporters and cameramen the moment the morning papers had appeared with the German warning, and the telegrams. Just as they had left the quay, there had been the discovery of the three stowaways with the camera who had turned out to be Germans, presumably trying to photograph any guns on board, and who were now safely locked in the ship's cells. Indeed, nothing that Saturday morning had been particularly reassuring unless it was Captain Turner's statement that no submarine could ever catch the *Lusitania* and that anyway, when they neared the Irish coast, the British Navy would take care of them. Nevertheless, the men selling photos of the ship and crying out, 'Last Voyage of the *Lusitania*!' had taken some stomaching.

The sailing itself had been a little late. The liner had not left the quay until twelve-thirty when, with her ensign, house flag, pilot's flag, the Stars and Stripes and flags of identification for the blockading British warships all hanging damp and limp, the tugs had pushed her gently out into the Hudson River. With her band playing 'Tipperary', the sun took its cue and broke through, sparkling first on her white superstructure, then all across her wet hull. Just beyond the three miles limit she had met two cruisers and one of her own kind, the 20,000-ton *Caronia*, now an AMC and sporting her eight 4.7-inch guns. After collecting homeward mails, the *Lusitania* had increased speed to twenty knots and steamed north-westwards towards the distant coast of Ireland, nearly a week away.

If the start had been inauspicious, at least the weather was good. Early-morning fog seemed their only enemy. On Sunday morning Captain Turner had conducted matins in the first-class lounge and, as was the custom, had offered prayers for His Majesty King George V and all upon the High Seas. By noon they had covered 501 miles and were south of Nova Scotia. Before lunch Turner went over his numerous War Notices. He had a new one dated 15 April:

> German submarines appear to be operating chiefly off prominent headlands and landfalls. Ships should give prominent headlands a wide berth.

Another dated 10 February warned him that

> . . . so far as is consistent with particular trades and states of tides, vessels should make their ports at dawn.

While Turner sat in his cabin brooding over these sometimes contradictory memoranda, planning his timing and proximity to the Fastnet Rock and the southern Irish coast, Anderson knocked on his door.

As captain of the *Lusitania*, Turner had no real wish to discuss the weighty matters he was now considering with anyone. He believed ardently in the loneliness of responsibility, and although Cunard had seen fit to supply this extra captain, Turner was very loath to share either his worries or his privileges. Nevertheless, when Anderson came in and saw the bulky form of Turner bowed over the mass of papers, he quite naturally expressed the wish to help. He knew that Turner had received no new course-instructions for this particular crossing, that he was following much the same course as for their previous voyage, and that amongst the passengers there was considerable concern about the possibilities of a submarine attack, but that was all he did know. He therefore started the conversation by inquiring whether they were likely to have any naval escort.

'I am told, Captain Anderson,' said Turner in his precise way, 'that elements of the Eleventh Cruiser Squadron out of Queenstown will rendezvous with us forty miles west and ten miles south of Fastnet. Probably the *Juno*.'

Anderson shook his head, remembering all he knew about the old *Eclipse*-class cruisers now over twenty years old.

'The *Juno* may have the guns, Captain, but what about speed? I doubt if she can sustain much more than fifteen knots. That would leave a clear five knots between us.'

The first intervention of his aide had done nothing to allay Turner's anxieties.

'I dare say, Captain,' he said, 'that with this Dardanelles business there has been quite a call on the Navy's vessels. And, as you say, the *Juno* does have the guns. No doubt properly placed in escort, even if we have to reduce speed, she should be able to stop any U-boat from showing its periscope and thereby denying them the possibility to see.'

With that he grunted, got up and intimated that as it was Sunday he would take lunch in the dining saloon and not on the bridge as was his usual custom. His last act before leaving the cabin was to check the safe. In there lay the lead-weighted canvas bag containing despatches from the Embassy in Washington to the Foreign Office in London and which, in the event of a German attack, he had orders to throw overboard immediately.

293 other diners ate with Captain Turner in that saloon, of which Alfred Vanderbilt was without doubt the wealthiest and Charles Frohman, the Broadway producer, one of the best known. Elsewhere in the ship another 1,669 souls were eating in relays. Some 900 of them, second- or third-class passengers, were having to make do with a single dining-room at the stern, now that the Admiralty had closed the third-class dining-room in the bow. The rest, the remaining 700 odd, were the crew, plus of course the three Germans in the cells.

Within two hours of his arrival at Queenstown, and before his kit had been properly stowed aboard his aged flagship, Rear-Admiral Henry Bone had thoroughly shocked the officers and men of the Eleventh Cruiser Squadron. He ordered steam up for an immediate exercise. The fact that it was Sunday morning, that many of the crew were ashore and that those that were not were getting ready for church parade, had no effect. Rear-Admiral Bone, still smarting over his demotion from Dover, was going to ensure that his new command was as efficient and effective as his tired-out fleet allowed. So the cruisers *Juno*, *Sutlej*, *Isis* and *Venus* were to be made ready for sea with all possible speed.

Rear-Admiral Bone, however, had yet to be made aware of Admiralty standing orders for the Irish ports. In the first place he was not supposed to take the whole squadron to sea without the prior authority of the Admiralty; in the second place, since the triple disaster to the *Hogue*, *Aboukir* and *Cressy*, their Lordships were not at all keen that one of the few remaining sister ships, the *Sutlej*, now almost worn out and with her engines only capable of very short spurts, should ever go outside Cork Harbour again, and certainly not with U-boats about. Of the three remaining ships of his squadron, the *Isis* was still coaling, her boilers like those of the *Venus* being cold; only the boilers of the *Juno* were warm. And so in the end it was only the flagship, the *Juno*, that cast off. Slowly she thread her way down the uterine West Passage, through the narrows between Haulbowline Island and the strand of Queenstown, then southwards past the forts of Camden and Carlisle.

Once upon the Atlantic, with her twenty-four furnaces blazing, Rear-Admiral Bone brought the old warship up to her full speed and for more than two hours steered a westerly zig-zag course at over nineteen knots. The exhilaration of the vessel slicing her way through the calm, clear waters; the shaking of her hull under the hammering of her engines; the dense black smoke that poured from her two stacks to smudge her clean, white wake; together with the rapid traversing and occasional firing of her six-inch and twelve-pounder guns, did something to compensate the crew for the sudden interruption of their Sunday.

By five in the afternoon, feeling that he had now made his mark upon his new command, the Rear-Admiral's heart softened and he thought again of Queenstown. In the interests of both the structure of the ship and economy, he first ordered speed to be reduced to fifteen knots, then consulted the charts in the company of the *Juno's* commanding officer, Captain Towers. Without bothering to read the

name of the long, thin inlet due north-west of their present
position, Henry Bone ordered that the *Juno* be turned about
when the inlet was due north. Towers peered at the writing
and eventually uttered, in a careful and very anglicized way,
the single word, 'Carridleagh'.

Henry Bone walked out on to the bridge and stared at the
flat, shining water. If any U-boat dared to show its periscope
it would be seen immediately. He noticed that the double
look-outs he had posted before leaving Queenstown were still
at their posts and he felt satisfied.

For the crew of the B-12, lunch was a memory; already they
were looking forward to a mug of tea. It was the first Sunday
afternoon in May. The air was hot and the sea warm, and the
crew were as contented as sailors could be away from home.
It was the sort of day when men and women like to walk as
couples, to parade their new summer best, a day for blazers
and boaters, flower-patterned dresses, sunshades, canoes on
the lake, punts on the river, walks along the esplanade. The
war seemed an era away. Flanders, the Heligoland Bight and
the Dardanelles might have been on another planet. For the
sixteen souls on that submarine, there had been only one
small reminder of the holocaust that now gripped most of
Europe. Four hours ago they had passed through the scattered flotsam of a torpedoed merchantman. Yet already the
sodden planks were being bleached by sun and sea. In
another few days they would be washed ashore to become the
walls of pigsties or kindling for the bothies, the disaster that
brought them to sand and shingle forgotten.

The boat lay on the surface fifteen miles from the Irish
coast, drifting gently eastwards. The hatches were open and
the sun poured in, making vivid, contrasting areas of light
and shade where eyes ached trying to match the sudden
changes. From the forward hatch came the sound of a gramophone playing, for the third time that afternoon, 'Alexander's
Ragtime Band'. The record was already scratched, and in its
unacoustic surroundings needed a devotee to listen.

After reducing speed in the night, they had arrived at their
present position soon after noon. They had seen the distant
coast of Ireland, pale and indistinct through the midday

haze, and its presence brought the excitement that stirs every sailor on sight of land, even though in this case their journey had been of little more than two days' duration. Esmond did not want to approach Carridleagh until evening high water, and had therefore let the boat drift back, away from the sea lanes.

They had already dived twice that day to avoid being seen, and Esmond was now watching the smudge on the horizon, deciding at what moment to sound the alarm and disturb the peace of his crew. It was odd taking evasive action at the sight of friendly merchant ships, and Esmond wondered whether the skippers had any idea that a submarine was so near. He now realized the ease with which the U-boats could operate, and how different their patrols must be from his in the Bight.

'She's changed course, sir,' called the coxswain, and Esmond pressed the alarm button. The spine-chilling *ooogh-aagh* filled the boat and the still afternoon air. Esmond and the coxswain raced down the steel ladder into the control room. With hatches shut and clipped, the Wolseley stopped, its air inlet closed as it made its last revolution, and the electric motors running, the B-12 dived. After their briefing the previous evening, the crew knew that any passing ship might send them beneath the sea, so instead of the usual suppressed excitement there was nothing but a workmanlike determination that the vessel, old as she was, should at least behave like a modern submarine.

Esmond went up to periscope depth. 'Steer zero-six-five!'

The ship's new course, away from land, would bring her across the B-12's bows. It was an ideal opportunity for a simulated attack. The ship, too fast for a merchantman, was still too head-on to identify with any certainty. When she was about 3,000 yards away, she turned several points to starboard, unfolding her silhouette. She was a two-funnelled cruiser of either the *Pelorus* or *Eclipse* class, making about sixteen knots.

'Steer zero-four-seven!'

CPO Phillips brought the boat round to its new course.

'Flush deck,' said Esmond to Paynter, as he turned the periscope. 'Four sponsons amidships mounting what look like six-inch guns.'

'*Eclipse* class,' said Paynter.

'Two white rings on forward funnel . . .'

'*Juno*.'

'Flagship of the Eleventh Cruiser Squadron,' said Esmond. 'She must have just come out of Queenstown.'

Paynter nodded. Esmond gave a new course, turning the B-12 slightly to port. If both vessels continued on their present paths, the *Juno* should pass, a perfect target, just 600 yards away. Although no torpedo was to be fired, for the first time since leaving Portsmouth, Esmond felt the excitement of the chase.

The *Juno* did not change course, nor did she see the short-lived appearance of the periscope on her port side. Thanks to Paynter's efforts, the trim of the B-12 was perfect and she responded sweetly to the hydroplanes. Even though it was an old, hand-winched affair that had so disgusted his first-lieutenant, Esmond was able to bring the periscope up for the briefest of exposures and then correct his course. When he took his final look, the cruiser was exactly where he had calculated. He held her in his sights for no more than ten seconds, during which time he gave the order 'Fire' to tubes that had not been made ready. He called 'Down periscope!' then turned to Paynter and said, with unconcealed excitement, 'Right between the bridge and forward funnel! She'd have broken in two. We'll send them a note when all this is over. We should get a free dinner or at least a bottle of Scotch.'

Paynter grinned.

The engines of the *Juno* grew fainter as Esmond's father's flagship turned through 180 degrees and headed back to Queenstown.

They surfaced again and waited, dispelling the foul smells of the boat and filling the hull with delicious fresh air. After half an hour they moved in towards the coast, diving as they went. Anliem Point was the most evident of their landmarks. It was hardly a point in the true sense of the word for it stood no further into the ocean than did the southern end of White Sheep Island, but it was higher and from seawards much the most dramatic. Its top was crowned not by the usual stunted, windswept trees, but by a slab of dun-coloured rock, the west side of which now reflected the dying sun.

Even submerged and with condensation clouding the periscope, Esmond had no difficulty in steering for the inlet. Two miles out they stopped and waited for a curragh to pass and had to watch the time carefully. They they moved again towards the dark shadow that marked their harbour. The same deep yet silent excitement that had gripped them six months ago when they had stalked the *Antilope* gripped them now. The crew knew that they had to navigate a narrow entrance submerged, with little room for manoeuvre and no room should things go wrong. They were blind. Only their captain could see, and he carried their trust.

Esmond, eyes to the periscope, chanted small alterations to the course and dropped speed to two knots. The tide was just on the turn. Yard by yard the B-12 crept between the towering overhang of the Point and the rocky flanks of White Sheep Island. Suddenly they were in. Esmond swung the periscope. The view, even from his low vantage-point, was breathtaking. They were in a narrow defile, bounded by rock and dark, sinuous trees. Now that the sun was down, the water was a sombre purple. The colour gave it a sense of immense age and depth, as if the limpid surface was the lid of a primeval world with the long, thin neck of a brontosaurus a far more likely object to be leaving a delicate, feathery wake than the periscope of a submarine.

Esmond handed the periscope to Paynter and mopped the sweat from his face.

'Bloody fantastic, Skipper!' said Paynter, taking an all-round look. He handed the periscope back.

Esmond brought the boat slowly down the middle of 'The Ferries', the channel widening as they went. Suddenly, on his left, he saw the wall of rock that marked the north-east corner of White Sheep Island, and looking upwards waited for a parting in the trees. From the chart, the abbey stood back from the cliff, and Esmond wondered how much, if any, of it would be visible. It turned out to be a gable with a huge perpendicular window, in the ruined tracery of which the mullions still hung like stalactites. With the dark stones silhouetted against a still bright-green sky, the effect was dramatic indeed.

Esmond brought the B-12 to the surface, then ran up to the

dripping bridge. He shaded his eyes and looked into the gloom of trees, grass and stones above him. A man stood waving his hat. As Esmond's eyes became accustomed to the light, he saw two other figures, a petty officer and a rating, both ready with lines. Still running on electric motors, Esmond brought the B-12 gently towards the rocky face. A decaying wooden landing-stage that might not have been used for the last twenty years jutted six feet into the water. Moored at the end were a skiff and a wherry. When they were still twenty feet away, Esmond saw that the landing-stage had been recently repaired. Large tree-trunks now reinforced the rotten buffers, and a derrick and a ladder that led down from the cliff-top to the landing-stage were new.

'Lieutenant-Commander Esmond Bone, Royal Navy?' shouted the figure waving the hat.

'Mr Terence Ford?' called Esmond into the gathering darkness.

'Welcome to the Emerald Isle, welcome to Carridleagh!' shouted Ford.

Esmond handed over to Paynter, climbed down to the casing and jumped on to the landing-stage. Petty Officer Blackmore and Leading Seaman Wright were waiting.

'We're your harbour party, sir,' said Blackmore, saluting. 'Sorry there isn't much in the way of facilities, but we understand that it's all pretty temporary.'

Esmond acknowledged their salutes, and assuming they were from Queenstown announced with considerable glee that they had just made a successful attack on the unsuspecting *Juno*.

'We're not from Queenstown, sir,' said Blackmore. 'I'm from Devonport, Wright's from Sheerness. We were given the Crossley tender at Kingstown and told to drive her.'

If Esmond was surprised he did not show it. He glanced at the badge on Wright's arm.

'Torpedo and gunner's mate, higher standard!'

'That's right, sir,' said Wright.

'We're here to look after the torpedoes in particular and everything else in general,' said Blackmore.

Esmond nodded and climbed up the rope ladder.

15

The moment you climbed out of Carridleagh on to the ridge behind Anliem Point and looked back, you realized why the stretch of land beneath you was called White Sheep Island. A fat, woolly ewe might have fallen into the waters and drowned. Her humped back was to the south-west, clothed in tightly-packed, windswept trees; her head to the north-east, where oaks, elms and thorns, unbent and in luxurious profusion, were broken only by the rich, green grass on which stood the remains of Carridleagh Abbey. The wild Atlantic could hurl itself against the rocks a mile away, the wind could screech across the ridges of Fhininskagh and Anliem, but on that small head where the old, grey stones stood draped in ivy, there was silence. Like Cistercians everywhere, the builders had sought shelter and found beauty and peace.

In the corner of the great cloisters, sheltered by the west wall of the monks' dorter and the remains of the warming house, Blackmore and Wright had pitched their bell tent. Old, cracked flagstones which had known nothing but the sandalled tread of white monks or the bare feet of summer fishermen now resounded to British hobnails that scuffed the surface and kicked the moss balls on to the cropped turf. To this, as the evening wore on, was added the heavy clop of submariners' boots as those off watch climbed the ladder from the landing-stage.

For sailors used either to the cramped conditions of a submarine or the rough amenities of a naval port, Carridleagh was extraordinary and bewildering. The crew had been ordered not to leave the area of the ruins, and after a cursory exploration most of them were back, clustered round the tent asking questions. Neither Blackmore nor Wright had much to offer. For them too, a billet in a ruined abbey in southern Ireland was an entirely new experience. They had one or two spares and bits of equipment in the Crossley over on the Anliem side and rations for ten days, and that was all. So, like most of their compatriots, whether they were in Scapa Flow or Flanders, it was a case of more tea and cigarettes while they waited.

Esmond's main concern at that moment was the safety of his ship. Tied up alongside the landing-stage, the B-12 was a sitting target for anyone of ill disposition who might find their way into the inlet. As soon as CPO Phillips had brought half of their dozen rifles ashore, and stacked them under cover of the subcroft, Esmond tackled Ford. Ford was amazingly sanguine. He could see no possible danger anywhere. The two tongues of land either side of Carridleagh, Anliem and Fhininskagh had been sealed off by the Army. A barbed-wire fence had been built right across the narrowest part of Anliem, and on Fhininskagh a fence had been built from the waterside to the Great Quarry, and no one even went through the Great Quarry. Remembering the curragh that had crossed the entrance only a few hours ago, Esmond asked about fishermen. As the military now had posts on both Anliem Point and Fhininskagh, and there was no cottage on the whole of Carridleagh, Ford saw very little chance of interference.

'All right,' said Esmond, 'then when do we start?'

Ford threw back his head, laughed, and put an arm round Esmond's shoulders.

'I see you stand like greyhounds in the slips,' he cried, addressing not only Esmond but those shadowy forms across the cloister visible only by the glow of their cigarettes or the thin rays of the single hurricane lamp, 'Straining upon the start. The game's afoot: Follow your spirit; and, upon this charge cry "God for Harry! England and Saint George!" '

It was well delivered and greeted first with silence, then with a round of scattered, self-conscious applause, and finally with a few muttered obscenities.

'Thank you, kind fellows!' said Ford, then turned and took Esmond away into the darkness of the trees. 'Tomorrow night. You leave at sunset and work your way westwards along the coast towards Cape Clear. You will signal with a lamp at prearranged points I will point out later, and take bearings on any lights seen in return. Stay surfaced for fishing vessels but dive for merchantmen and warships. And do remember, dear fellow, you are playing the part of a U-boat, so do try and think like one.'

'Are there in fact any about at the moment?' asked Esmond, remembering the flotsam he had seen on the way in.

'Always one about,' said Ford cheerfully. 'Present chappie's been playing the very devil. Sinking ships all the way to Liverpool!'

'And our trawler?' asked Esmond.

'Not my province, old man,' said Ford. 'She's RN at Queenstown. Understand they're having a spot of bother over the submarine telephone cable. Still,' he added, reverting to his theatrical voice, 'no doubt the good captain will sort it all out.'

Esmond asked when Tweedman was coming.

'Towards the end of next week,' said Ford. 'By then, of course, we shall be able to tell him just where those Sinn Feiners are, and all he'll have to do is send the military to round them up.'

'These Sinn Feiners,' asked Esmond, 'who are they?'

Ford smiled. 'Fishermen ... farm labourers ... carriers ... schoolteachers ... even doctors and priests. They have this mad idea that Ireland should not be part of England! Of course, they couldn't last like that for a moment.'

'No ... no, I suppose they couldn't,' said Esmond, 'and they actually *help* the U-boats?'

'The worst ones are so deluded as to be actually pro-German.'

With that Ford shook his head, walked back to the circle by the light, took a watch from the fob pocket of a heavily embroidered waistcoat and said that he must be going back for his supper. He offered to take Esmond or his first lieutenant, but Esmond declined for both. He must stay with his boat and he needed Paynter.

They walked together to the rope ladder and climbed down to the landing-stage. Ford got into the skiff.

'You're very welcome to come,' he said. 'Mrs Sullivan cooks a fine cottage pie, I could always do with a bit of civilized company and I did have the foresight to bring a dozen of my own clarets with me.'

Esmond thanked Ford and declined a second time.

The actor maneouvred the skiff with considerable skill, and Esmond watched until he could no longer make him out in the darkness. He saw a lantern lit on the opposite shore and a light wound slowly away and upwards. Somewhere on the track, behind the rocks, Ford had a car. No doubt it was down that same track that their supplies would arrive.

Monday's patrol was abortive. They kept close to the coast as ordered, reduced speed at three points, and lying still on the surface signalled the code they had been given. There was no response from the shore. Such lights as they did see, faint and flickering, were those of ordinary homes, the occupants of which seemed supremely indifferent to the present of a U-boat. The return to Carridleagh was something of an anti-climax.

Tuesday, after the mist had risen, was another lovely warm day. The abbey ruins, only thirty-six hours ago the object of such wonder, had already become a sailor's rest home and recreation centre. The gramophome was up there, the off-duty watch lay stripped on the grass, underclothes and towels were drying on the stones; besides their tent, Blackmore and Wright cleaned and checked their smaller stores as they tanned under the sun, and the damp conditions of the submarine were almost forgotten. The world seemed altogether too peaceful.

Esmond went to the cliff-top by the derrick, looked across the conning tower of his own submarine to the narrow stretch of 'The Ferries', and felt ashamed. This should be the Narrows of the Dardanelles. There was going to be much work for submarines in the Sea of Marmara, and while his colleagues risked their lives through the Turkish minefields he was idling his days away here. Even Elizabeth was probably in France by now. All he could hope for was that the Sinn Feiners came out soon, and he prayed that it might be tonight.

Paynter came across in the skiff. When he had tied up and climbed to the top of the ladder, he pushed his cap back and looked worried.

'Something very rum's going on, Skipper. I've just had a look in the Crossley and amongst all their other clutter they've got two warhead Mark V GS.'

'Spares?' said Esmond.

'Spares for what?' said Paynter.

Esmond shrugged. 'Have you asked Blackmore?'

'He doesn't know any more than we do.'

'I'll ask Ford,' said Esmond, 'just as soon as he gets here.'

Ford arrived late in the afternoon and called for the skiff to fetch him. As soon as he reached the cliff-top, Esmond asked him about the two warheads.

'My dear fellow,' said Ford, 'I don't know about things like that! I'm an actor, not a mechanic. But I will tell you something. Your little excursion last night has certainly put the cat amongst the pigeons. The coastguards saw you, if no one else did, and they've reported it not only to the police and military at Skibbereen but the Navy at Queenstown.'

Esmond failed to see the joke.

'Don't you see,' cried Ford, ' once the peelers know, the military know and the Navy know, the Sinn Feiners are *bound* to hear of it.'

Esmond looked surprised but said nothing.

'And another thing, dear boy,' said Ford, his eyes shining with excitement, 'I've made doubly sure. I've fed it into the hands of a Mr Frederick Childs, a buyer of good horse bloodstock!'

Esmond decided that the man had really gone off his head. He stared in amazement. Ford laughed. 'Mr Frederick Childs also happens to be a German agent.'

Esmond had an extraordinary feeling, a numbness he could not remember before. As a submarine captain, as a sportsman, he knew of the thrill of the chase, but this was a

108

colder excitement. He had never seen an enemy spy, and doubted whether any of his crew had ever seen one. Photos of enemy soldiers and sailors were commonplace in the papers, one knew what they looked like, but spies were different. They were few, wore mufti and were never photographed. Special people. Indeed, deceitful people, for they lived as friends amongst their enemies. Spies were both exciting and repellant and, of course, when they were caught they were shot.

'This spy,' said Esmond, 'do you actually know him?'

'Met him once,' said Ford, 'charming old gentleman. Lives in Kildare but has lodgings at Queenstown. Handy place, you see, to keep an eye on chaps like you. Dines with the Navy whenever he can, picks up no end of tit-bits.'

'And we don't arrest him?!'

Ford laughed at such naïvety. 'He's wonderfully useful at the moment.'

'Useful?!'

'Leading MI5 hither and thither. Oh, we agents are quite used to being played with,' said Ford, seeing the disgust on Esmond's face, 'it's part of the cross we must learn to bear. Ours isn't the clean Christian war that you young fellows fight!'

Esmond stared down at the grass. 'Was it wise to tell him? Might he not be suspicious and ruin it all?'

'I didn't actually *tell* him,' cried Ford, with a dramatic wave of the hand, 'I just leaked the information into a reliable channel! And one other thing,' said Ford, pointing upwards, 'do stop your cook throwing potato peelings over the side. We share Carridleagh with the gulls, you know, and we don't want to draw more attention to you than we need.'

On the evening of the same Tuesday that Esmond waited to take the B-12 out of Carridleagh, on a sea equally calm and devoid of whitecaps, and beneath an almost cloudless sky, the *Lusitania* was approaching the half-way mark of her journey. In slightly choppier conditions, Kapitän-Leutnant Schwieger, one torpedo down after making an abortive attack on a Danish vessel, sighted the north-west coast of Ireland.

Keeping a steady surface ten knots, he set course for the Fastnet Rock.

At the same time that Schwieger was heading south, the boat he was to relieve, the U-30, was heading north, having completed its not inconsiderable depredations. The two U-boats were to pass one another off that wild, west coast, just beyond the 54th Parallel.

The next fifty-six hours were going to call for all Tweedman's stamina and resourcefulness. He was due to travel to Ireland overnight to tie up the loose ends, some of which were now beginning to worry him a great deal. The briefing of Esmond was the key to the whole operation. Tweedman believed that he had a persuasive case, but could not be certain until he had actually presented it. Before leaving, however, he had one more engagement to keep at the Admiralty. The First Lord wanted to see him at four-thirty.

Tweedman had seen the First Lord earlier that day in the great map room. Standing beneath a giant fathomless chart, all of ten yards long and covering the whole of one wall, they had already considered the disposition of all ships, both Allied and enemy, that were at that moment going about the oceans of the world. In particular they had noted the squares that denoted the locations of U-boats and the many coloured discs that indicated the positions of British ships that might be in their paths. The biggest disc of all, way out in the Atlantic but closing towards southern Ireland at twenty knots, had not been missed by any present, even though it had drawn very little comment. It was as if there was a conspiracy to silence. As if no one in the Admiralty, from the First Lord downwards, wanted to breathe the name *Lusitania*.

'I have just seen Lord Fisher, Captain,' said the First Lord. 'He is not in good health and beset by a multitude of anxieties. One of his worries is your activities off Ireland.'

'I am going over there tonight, sir,' said Tweedman quietly.

The First Lord nodded, stared at the ceiling, then got up

110

from his desk. 'The steamer *Lusitania* will be passing there on Friday.'

'Yes, sir.'

'I thought of going over to Flanders tomorrow, to see Sir John French.'

'A good idea, sir.'

'You think so, Captain?'

Tweedman nodded.

'That is settled then,' said the First Lord. 'I will telegraph the Field-Marshal and make it a definite engagement, and I will not be back until after the weekend.'

Tweedman took a deep breath and said nothing.

'I am seeing the King this evening,' said the First Lord. 'He is sure to ask after your various enterprises?'

It was a question and Tweedman was not quite sure how to reply. The First Lord prompted him. 'Last time you talked of a "Deliberate Diplomatic Miracle". His Majesty is rather taken by the expression.'

'You may tell him, sir,' said Tweedman, 'that it is still very much in mind, particularly at the moment.'

Churchill nodded and Tweedman left the room, his heart pounding so hard he could no longer hear the squeaking of his left leg.

Sarah Tweedman folded the shirt for her husband to pack in his portmanteau. Tweedman was quiet and detached, with none of the *joie de vivre* he had shown two months ago.

'I think I know how poor Cradock must have felt when he turned the *Good Hope* four points to port to meet von Spee,' he said, placing the hairbrush carefully in the open bag, 'although, of course, he was going with them, that would have made it easier . . .'

'Going with them?' asked Sarah, puzzled.

'With Spee superior in every quarter, Cradock must have known that he had just signed a thousand death warrants. On the other hand, he had also signed his own.'

'Freddy Sturdee soon made up for all that at the Falklands,' said Sarah staunchly.

Tweedman smiled. 'The loneliness of command, my dear,

the responsibility of sending men into battle. It helps to be with them.'

Sarah kissed her husband on the cheek. 'I am quite sure that whatever you have to do, Gavin, is for the best. For England's best!'

'Thank you, my dear.'

When she had left the room, Tweedman opened the gladstone bag he had placed beneath his bed and checked the pistol of the Mark V torpedo he had collected from Parkhurst the previous day.

16

Now that the sea was so calm and his rheumatism better, Pádrig O'Callaghan had a mind to go collecting gulls' eggs and was up well before the sparrows' chirp. The night was clear and star-lit, but there were pockets of mist on the water. He took his curragh out of Dinish Bay and pulled west along the coast. Through a gap in the mist he saw Claghan Strand and knew he was half-way to Anliem Point. He knew this piece of the ocean so well he needed no more landmarks, but brought his curragh on to the shingle in the shelter of a great rock. He scrambled out, dragged the boat up to the bleached-white tree-stump that had laid here ever since a gale had tossed in on to the ledge years before, then climbed the steep side to the top. The ridge was clear, and he could look into the basin of mist that filled Carridleagh. The ruins of the abbey seemed to be rising from the flood. Pádrig crossed himself and went about his work.

On the rocky face of Anliem Point, where it looks south-west towards the Fastnet Rock and the wide ocean to the Americas, seabirds of every sort had made their nests since the waters first covered the Earth. Puffins, guillemots, kitti-wakes, herring gulls, razor-bills, black-faced gulls and petrels fought for space and vied with rabbits to scratch homes in the scant earth.

Pádrig was an expert not only at collecting eggs but at wringing the necks of roosting puffins and pulling rabbits from their shallow burrows. By the time the sun was up and the thinnest of the mists dispelled, his shirt was filled with warm eggs, and from a rope round his waist hung more than

113

a dozen rabbits. He had been working down from the top on the open face towards the sea. When he knew he could carry no more, he turned to retrace his steps back to the curragh. He would lay all he had found in the boat and make one more journey. He was standing, warming his back in the first of the sun's rays, when a strange sight caught his eyes. Carridleagh was still in dark shadow, and the mist was grey and not white as it was further to east and west where the sun had already caught it. But even in the shadows the mist had dispersed a little, and it was in the midst of a clearing that Pádrig saw a dark grey monster rise slowly from the loch, shake itself free of water and move gently towards the abbey. He watched the apparition for perhaps two minutes, then crossing himself again, and with a cry of 'God of Virtues, t'is a thing from the deep!' fled down the path back to his currag and the sea.

None of the military saw him arrive and none saw him leave.

The same mist that had helped Pádrig O'Callaghan, very nearly aborted the B-12's second expedition along the coast. Several times they had been completely engulfed, navigation had become impossible, signalling pointless. As it was, Esmond had brought the boat much nearer the shore than he had intended, and once had had to dive suddenly to avoid a patrol boat. While still submerged they had passed too close to a river mouth, and the efflux of fresh water had upset their buoyancy. They had bumped the rocky bottom stern-first and could well have damaged rudder and aft hydroplanes. But the boat had slowly levelled itself and the manoeuvrability seemed to be unimpaired.

Esmond was about to turn back for Carridleagh when the mist suddenly lifted and two cottages appeared on the distant hillside. Without any expectations, he had ordered Leading Seaman Scott to try once more with the lamp. To their surprise, the letter 'M' was flashed five times in reply from a spot just uphill and behind the higher cottage.

With the location firmly marked on their charts, they turned for home. Even the mist that covered the entrance to Carridleagh no longer seemed a hazard.

When Pádrig had put sufficient distance between himself

and Anliem Point, he rested on his oars. He realized now that it was a submarine and not a sea monster and laughed at himself for thinking as he had. Nevertheless, even a submarine running into Carridleagh was a matter of concern and excitement, for although along with many of the fisherfolk, he had, in the last few weeks, seen submarines on the surface and heard of them coming inshore, he had never before seen one actually do so. The war was bringing strange things to their doors, but this was the strangest so far.

While Pádrig lay resting in the early sunshine he even thought of going back to Anliem, climbing the ridge again and having another look. He was no longer afraid. He had much to thank the submarine for. The people of the shore had never lived so well in all their lives. The cargoes being washed up after each torpedoing had brought riches beyond their wildest dreams. There was not a cottage now that did not have its full quota of wood for the winter, a shirt and spare breeches for every man, a Sunday dress for every girl, cheese for the next year, oranges for midsummer and even binoculars and watches. In his own case, even the oil for his lamps had come from the sea in a barrel.

But Pádrig did not go back to Carridleagh. He returned to Dinish Bay, left his curragh on the shingle and sought out Shaun Mehigan. Shaun was in the Volunteers and would know exactly what to do.

Shaun was the schoolmaster at Béal na Liam. He was teaching when Pádrig arrived, but he gave his pupils a poem to learn by heart and came outside to see him.

'Faith, Shaun,' cried Pádrig, the moment he had his breath back, 'you'll never believe what is happening now in Carridleagh! A submarine has gone there to rest itself!'

'In the name of God, man,' said Shaun, 'a submarine has gone into Carridleagh!?'

'It rose like a porpoise from the water, shaking and draining itself as it did so.'

'A German submarine?' asked Mehigan

'Are not all submarines German?' asked Pádrig.

'They may be,' said Mehigan, 'for it is true that I have never heard of one that is not. But there, the English too may have submarines.'

'God have mercy upon us,' said Pádrig, 'what would the English want with a submarine off the coast of Ireland?'

Mehigan thought for a moment, then said, 'You are right, Pádrig. It must be a German submarine. Your soul to the devil if they are not bringing us revolvers and rifles!'

With that he grasped the man, and to the surprise of those of his pupils looking from the schoolroom window, hugged him to his chest.

'Tell no one, Pádrig,' he shouted as Pádrig walked away, 'tell no one of the submarine!'

Mehigan dismissed his class early and set out to see for himself. When he reached the narrow neck of land that led towards Anliem Point, he was surprised to find the track closed, two sentries on guard and a barbed-wire fence running east and west as far as the eye could see. His innocent request to continue his cycle ride was turned down and he was waved away.

Mehigan was not a member of the newly-formed Irish Volunteers for nothing. If Pádrig was right and there was a German submarine there, then it was his duty to have a look at it. He rode back down the track for half a mile, then hiding his bicycle behind a hedge set off across the fields. He reached the fence and followed it towards the sea. When it went into a shallow dip by an old stone wall, he decided to crawl through. He was more than half-way, lying flat on his back lifting the last of the low strands of wire up over his chest, when a voice from above and behind him, called upon him to halt.

Mehigan turned his head. A man of great build and with a shock of auburn hair stood at the top of the slope looking down at him. Two soldiers pointed their rifles at Mehigan's chest. The man limped down the slope. Looking backwards, his neck twisted and the wire tight across his chest, Mehigan felt like a rabbit awaiting a stoat.

'Did you not know that this is now a military area?' asked the man.

Mehigan tried to shake his head.

'Where do you live?'

'Béal na Liam.'

Tweedman turned to one of the soldiers and asked where

116

that might be. The soldier pointed away to the north.

'Then what are you doing here?' asked Tweedman.

'I am a schoolmaster,' said Mehigan defiantly. 'I am teaching my class of Finn MacCoul, who swum around this point when he led the Fenians against the Clann Morna.'

'See that he goes back to this Béal na Liam place,' said Tweedman to the soldiers, then turned to Mehigan, still lying penned beneath the wire. 'Consider yourself a very lucky man. If you are caught here again, not even Cuchulain, your hero of heroes, will be able to save you.'

The two soldiers dragged Mehigan out from under the wire and marched him back to the track. They were about to put him in a lorry when he told them of his bicycle. They let him go and laughed.

For a picnic they ate and drank well. This was the first time any of the crew, other than their captain, had ever seen the Director of Naval Intelligence. Not that any of them knew him as that. Nevertheless, they were all quite conscious that the impressive-looking visitor in their midst, who exuded as much mystery as importance, was not just a salmon fisherman, even if he dressed like one.

Only three people — Esmond, Paynter and Tweedman himself — actually constituted the luncheon party under the canvas awning in the cloisters, but it was watched with considerable interest by the rest of the crew as they queued at the cookhouse and collected their bottle of India Pale Ale, brought by Tweedman as the ratings' equivalent of the Dom Pérignon that he and the two officers of the B-12 were now enjoying.

It was a jolly, light-hearted affair with succulent, Irish sirloin for all, extras such as fresh bread, butter and vegetables, and Ordinary Seaman Grant, dressed in a white mess overall, doing his best to give the impression of one of the bigger wardrooms in the Grand Fleet. The officers of the B-12 might have been forgiven for thinking that they had reached a submariner's paradise, but that would have been to discount the boredom. A minute of signalling in the night did not really make up for their departure from the war.

Tweedman was politely interested in the night's events,

and carefully noted the location of the cottage that had responded to the signals, but did not seem greatly stirred. Esmond decided that if you spent your life amongst spies, no doubt you grew blasé about them.

'Now we've flushed out a Sinn Feiner or two, sir,' said Esmond cheerfully, 'how about the trawler? Ford said there was some problem with the telephone cable?'

'That'll sort itself out soon enough,' said Tweedman affably, then lit his pipe, picked up his gladstone bag and expressed the wish that Esmond would take a walk with him.

They went towards the north-west corner of the island, by the abbot's hall. For the first time since leaving Portsmouth, Esmond had the feeling that there was more to their visit to southern Ireland than setting traps for either Sinn Feiners or U-boats. Nevertheless, he was still taken by surprise when Tweedman lowered himself on to a stone wall and suddenly said, 'Damned bad show about that submarine.'

'Submarine?' said Esmond, puzzled. 'What submarine, sir?'

'Turning out to be the D-9.'

'The D-9?' Esmond asked stupidly, dragging his mind back to the war.

Tweedman nodded. 'Look,' he spoke quietly, sympathetically, 'I've been an operational sailor. I know what it's like to have to make snap decisions under filthy conditions in foul weather. And in your case, not even on a bridge in God's own fresh air but through a damned periscope, all covered with oil and condensation . . .'

The horror of Tweedman's implications made Esmond gasp. 'Are you saying *I sank the D-9*!?'

Tweedman was nodding. 'The light poor, one snow squall following another, the surface broken, whitecaps all around, and that low silhouette suddenly coming into your sights . . .'

Stunned by the accusation and the matter-of-fact way the man was putting it, Esmond cried, 'My God, I know damned well it was a U-boat! *I saw it*!'

Tweedman held up a calming hand. 'An error of judgement, and under the circumstances, one anyone could have made.'

118

'It was a U-boat,' said Esmond quietly, fighting to contain his anger, 'U-9 class!'

'No one else in your crew saw it. You are the only witness.'

'That's not unusual. Not in submarines!'

'No identification signals.'

'We were submerged! We stayed submerged!'

Tweedman patted the stones beside him. 'Sit down.'

Esmond resolutely remained standing.

'It's a preposterous suggestion!' he blurted out. 'Unbelievable!'

Tweedman opened his gladstone and took out a file of papers.

'Documents relating to the court-martial of Lieutenant-Commander Esmond Jasper Bone DSC . . .' he read slowly.

Esmond felt a sudden iciness. A sense of unreality engulfed him. The stones, the grass, the sky, the inlet, and most of all Tweedman, were all ingredients in a nightmare. To survive he had to fight, reassure himself, dispel every doubt, remember every detail of that attack. The mechanical sounds, the electrical sounds, the stale sickening smells, the everlasting condensation, the drops of icy North Sea falling on his neck as he had put his eye to the glass and swung it. And there, the dark grey shape only 500 yards away. Suddenly he knew why he had had no doubts that the boat in his sights had been German and he had ordered that single torpedo to be fired.

'It was on the surface, sir,' he cried excitedly, 'and it was still daylight! No British submarine would be on the surface so near the enemy coast in daylight!'

'The D-9 reported that she had been crippled,' came back the impassive answer, 'and could no longer dive. She had spent a bad night and was doing her best to get away on the surface.'

'Crippled,' repeated Esmond over the pounding of his own heart, 'crippled . . .'

'And now, of course, she's missing, believed lost,' said Tweedman, shifting his wooden leg into a better position. 'Did you know Prescott?' he asked after a while. 'Nice fellow. Nice young wife too . . .'

Esmond said nothing. He felt violently sick.

'But there, that's war,' said Tweedman, breaking a long silence, 'a nasty business, and this is one of the oldest of military problems, an error in identification. That, of course, is why the Army trooped the colours. Tell 'em which side they were on.'

'I saw the ensign,' said Esmond.

'Awfully alike,' said Tweedman, sucking his pipe, 'both a cross with something in the top left-hand corner. I knew that one day that would lead to confusion. Pity we aren't fighting the French. There'd be no mistake then. And when you have a grey sky, snow squalls, a rough sea . . .' He stopped and shrugged.

'Why are you telling me all this?' asked Esmond. 'Why isn't it the Officer Commanding Submarines?'

'This is a very delicate matter, an Admiralty matter.'

Esmond stared down at the grass, but all he saw was that dark grey silhouette alone on the stormy sea. Would a British submarine on the surface so close to the enemy coast be flying an ensign? Unless, of course, unable to dive they had decided to fight it out. Yet the shape, the conning tower, the flat line of the casing, everything pointed to it being a U-9 class.

'I'm quite certain, sir,' he said slowly, 'that it was a U-boat. I can still see it, and in spite of the weather, I am quite certain!'

'My dear fellow,' said Tweedman cheerfully, 'so you might be. You might be as certain that it was a U-boat as you are that you can't get a fifteen-inch shell into a 13.5-inch breech.' He paused, relit his pipe, then said, 'And supposing, and I'm just saying supposing, you were right. It wasn't the D-9 but the U something or other after all. You'd have a hell of a job persuading anyone. Same place, same time, you're what our friends at the Yard call a victim of circumstances.'

' "Sit back and shut up," ' said Esmond bitterly, 'that's what you're saying, isn't it?'

'Sorry, old chap, but there it is.'

'The court martial,' said Esmond eagerly, 'the truth would come out then!'

Tweedman shook his head. 'You wouldn't stand a chance. Everything would be tilted against you. It's wartime. Errors like that can't be forgiven in wartime, it's bad for morale.'

'There was no error!' said Esmond firmly.

Tweedman shrugged. 'No one on the court would understand you, let alone believe you. None of them would have ever seen the inside of a submarine. They'd be superannuated, pompous old shore dogs who'd think the control room of the E-28 like the admiral's cabin on the *Iron Duke*!'

For a while neither spoke, Esmond too sick at heart, Tweedman waiting. Then Tweedman remembered Stancombe's words.

'Besides, had you sunk a U-boat, we would have known by now. Either through prisoners, wireless signals, agents, or the Germans themselves. *And there hasn't been a word!*'

There was a long silence. A squirrel stood up on the grass, looked at them, then bounded back into the trees.

'The Admiralty communiqué gave the D-9 as lost through enemy action,' said Esmond defiantly.

'A British submarine torpedoes another!' cried Tweedman. 'We'd be the laughing stock of the whole world!'

Esmond stared into the water of the inlet.

'My father . . .?' he asked, after a while.

Tweedman fingered the file. 'He knows nothing yet.'

'You didn't bring us here to flush out Irish rebels or U-boats did you, sir?' asked Esmond.

Tweedman got up and stood beside Esmond, looking down the length of Carridleagh.

'There are many ways of helping your country, just as there are many ways of winning a war. I told you the other day, it doesn't have to be won on the Western Front. Nor will it be decided by any one weapon, although unless we find counter-measures the U-boat might come close to succeeding. In the end, the side that wins will be the side with the greatest all-round resources in munitions and men. And with Russia on the decline we need a new companion, but I can do no better than quote some words of the First Lord: "The manoeuvre that brings an ally into the field is as serviceable as that which wins great battles." '

Esmond thought about the words as well as his numbed brain allowed, but he was still quite unprepared for what was to come.

'In this case,' said Tweedman, 'the ally is the United States and the manoeuvre is to attack the *Lusitania*.'

Esmond turned and stared at Tweedman. He could remember no previous time in his whole life during which he had felt so far from reality.

'Attack the *Lusitania*?' he repeated like a puppet.

Tweedman nodded. 'She is due past here in less than forty-eight hours, and amongst her passengers are 159 Americans. But that is not all. As you know perfectly well, the name *Lusitania* has a particular potency on *both* sides of the Atlantic. An attack on her is almost an attack on the White House!'

'Sink it?!' said Esmond in total disbelief.

Tweedman shook his head.

'Who said anything about sinking anything? I said attack it, that's all we want.'

'We?'

Tweedman pulled an envelope from his gladstone:

'These orders are from the First Sea Lord. They are extremely simple. You are to memorize them, then I will destroy them.'

'Let me understand you, sir. You are asking me to take the B-12 out and torpedo the *Lusitania* in exchange for the dropping of my court martial?'

'There are two torpedo warheads in the Crossley,' said Tweedman. 'Each contains only one half the normal explosive. 130 pounds of amatol instead of the usual 265. On a liner as big as the *Lusitania*, with her multitude of watertight doors, the effect will be no more than that of a pea-shooter on a crocodile. The most you will do is give her a five-degree list and send her limping into Queenstown. But that will be enough! With sentiment as it is, the whole world will rise as one man and condemn Germany for an act of the utmost barbarity, *and the United States will declare war*.'

Esmond gave a laugh of amazement and release.

'I didn't even know that we had a department like this, sir! I don't think any of us operational sailors know!'

'If we are to survive this war,' said Tweedman coldly, 'we need America in and on our side. An attack on the *Lusitania* by a U-boat, and that is what you are now, will do it.' He looked round the ruin, then lowered his voice. 'You have the perfect cover. One U-boat has just left the area, at least one more is due in today. And as the *Lusitania* is under Admiralty orders, she will be diverted towards Queenstown to narrow your search area.'

'And if I prefer the court martial . . . sir?'

Tweedman fingered the envelope. 'It is too late. These are your orders.'

Esmond stared at the envelope. Tweedman opened it. The instructions were clear and concise. Esmond saw the Admiralty crest and the signature. He had never seen the First Sea Lord's signature before and had no reason to doubt its authenticity.

'There is no need for you to examine your conscience,' said Tweedman, watching Esmond's face. 'As I have explained, the operation is a strategic necessity and the chance that anyone will be killed, a thousand to one.'

Esmond said nothing but continued to stare at the sheet of paper, at the words ADMIRALTY WHITEHALL around the anchor. Tweedman prepared his *coup de grâce*.

'You mentioned your father just now,' he said quietly, 'a most distinguished naval officer. For his son to be court martialled for sinking one of His Majesty's ships, or for disobeying orders, would not help him at the moment.'

'At the moment?' said Esmond, surprised.

'The First Sea Lord is already less than satisfied with your father's performance at Dover.'

'That is blackmail, sir!'

Tweedman looked at the sky. 'I also have my duty to do.'

They lapsed into silence. Tweedman took the orders and thrust them back into his gladstone. 'You have no choice,' he said, snapping the bag shut, 'nor is it as onerous a task as you seem to think. In the end it could well save a million Allied lives.'

'I have a crew, sir,' said Esmond doggedly, 'I am responsible for them.'

'Good God, Bone!' cried Tweedman, near the end of his patience. 'So far as your crew are concerned, these are orders! They will obey orders just like you and I obey orders.'

'But attacking one of our own ships . . .' began Esmond,

123

when Tweedman interrupted.

'Your crew will know nothing. Only you and your first lieutenant will know. You said yourself that only you saw the submarine in the Bight. In this case you will submerge on reaching your intercept position and use only one or other of the two torpedoes already in the tubes. You will aim aft of midships, for the rear boiler-room, No. 4, which will be empty. Remember that, aft of midships, beneath the fourth funnel. You will then clear the area staying submerged to the limit of your endurance. While your warheads are altered, all the crew will vacate the boat. Take them for a row on the loch, or a run round the shore. Exercise will do them the world of good!'

'Everything's been thought out, hasn't. it, sir?' said Esmond bitterly.

'We aim to be efficient in NID.'

'And what do we say we've torpedoed?' asked Esmond. 'Fourteen men in a boat like ours are going to ask questions.'

Tweedman laughed.

'Why, a U-boat, of course!'

Kapitän-Leutnant Walter Schwieger pointed to the lighthouse away on their port side. 'An old friend, Lang?'

'Indeed yes, Herr Kapitän. The Fastnet. I have passed it many times.'

'One week to travel here,' said Schwieger, 'one week to hunt, and then one week to get home. We must hope that the one week in three is a fruitful one.'

'It will be, Herr Kapitän,' said Lang cheerfully, 'I can feel it in the marrow of my bones.'

They both laughed. Lang thought how young his captain looked. Tall, broad shouldered, with blue eyes and blond hair, he had the true stature of an officer in the Imperial German Navy. Yet, with his round face, which was small for his body, and the slight turn-down at the corners of his lips, the features of a child.

They swung hard to port and set a course south-east.

17

Ford was at home when Bella ran down the lane crying out that something fearful was happening off the Old Head. Ford opened the bay window and shouted at the girl to be quiet. The girl took no notice but pointed back the way she had come.

'Faith, Mr Ford,' she cried, 'there's a German submarine off the Old Head and he's after sinking my father's ship!'

Ford asked no more. He collected his binoculars, pushed the girl into the car and drove like a banshee to the narrow neck of the long peninsula that made up the Old Head of Kinsale, and where for centuries the land fortifications of that ancient settlement had begun and the ruins of the De Courcy's castle still bar the way.

The ocean was visible to east and west but all the craft seemed to be going about their daily business unmolested. The hump of land to his immediate south which obscured the lighthouse also obscured the whole southern arc of sea. Whatever was happening must be happening there. Ford had no choice but to drive down the grass track to the lighthouse and pass the military post by the old gun emplacement.

As it happened, no soldiers were to be seen. Like everyone else they were standing in the late afternoon sunshine by the cliff-edge walk that projected from the lighthouse, looking just west of south. There on the flat ocean were half a dozen vessels, but it was just three that caught the eye. A broad-beamed schooner, her dirty brown sails now enfolding the still sea, lay on her side like a child's toy blown over in the wind. Yet there was no wind. On the land side, her crew sat glumly in the ship's boat, watching their recent home disappearing for ever. On the seaward side, a dark grey U-boat was moving slowly eastwards. Schwieger had arrived at his hunting grounds and his first victim was very much a sprat. The *Earl of Latham*, just ninety-nine tons.

Through the glasses, Ford counted the crew in the ship's boat. A coastguard confirmed that the U-boat had not blown up the schooner until well after the ship's boat had left.

'Have no fear, Bella, my girl!' cried Ford, putting his hand on the girl's shoulder. 'Your father is safe and well and in that boat out there, the one pulling towards that fishing smack. And doesn't that remind you of the gazelles in Africa? The lion makes his kill and once the rest know that he is happy and replete they just get on with their grazing, although their adversary may still be only twenty yards away, tearing their late friend limb from limb.'

One or two of the watchers turned and stared at the deliverer of this piece of philosophy, addressed more to the gulls and rocks than to Bella. As for Bella herself, she just giggled with relief and wondered whether her father had got his feet wet. He hated having wet feet.

Tweedman's visit to Esmond, although apparently successful, had left him drained. On his return to Queenstown he lay for a long time in a deep, hot bath considering his next task, one that was already causing him much anxiety.

Frederick Childs had not booked that passage out of the country and did not seem to have any intention of doing so. The most meticulous examination of his mail had failed to reveal any mention of the information that had fallen into his hands, and but for the fact that Tweedman had had the meeting between Childs and Mortensen watched he might now be thinking that it had never occurred. To all intents and purposes, the papers on 'Tank' had just vanished, leaving a situation that Tweedman could no longer tolerate.

Tweedman dressed slowly and went through the possibilities open to him. He had wanted Childs out of Ireland simply because Childs' presence might increase the threat to

126

the secrecy of the B-12's mission. Yet here they were within forty-eight hours of the operation and so far Childs' presence appeared to be irrelevant. Everything depended, of course, on whether the Sinn Feiners yet knew of the presence of the submarine in Carridleagh and how close Childs' links were with those Sinn Feiners. That sooner or later the local inhabitants were bound to hear of the submarine, Tweedman had no doubt. A fisherman would try and sail in there soon and already there had been that schoolmaster trying to cross the wire. No doubt by now he would have told his story, and the fact that the Army had sealed off the whole area was sure to cause speculation. However, none of that really worried Tweedman now. If he could keep security for just over another twenty-four hours, the B-12 would have left on her final patrol and the whole 'dockyard' could be dismantled. Although, professionally, he would still like Childs out of Ireland, the possibility that the outside world would ever know of the B-12 still seemed slight.

That brought Tweedman to the other and now potentially much more worrying matter, the missing information of the First Lord's pet, the 'Tank'. It was apparently not in Childs' house in Kildare, nor in his lodgings in Queenstown. Tweedman had had both searched. *In extremis*, he did the only thing he could. He neatly forgot his promise to Beresford of MI5 and went to beard Childs himself.

It was Tweedman's habit to reconnoitre whenever and wherever possible. That he had already seen the outside of No. 27 gave him confidence. He was few yards from the door when it was opened from within and a lady shown out. She stood for a moment, looking up and down the street as if not quite sure which of the two possible ways to go, or perhaps it was that she was worried as to who might be about at that time of the evening, then opened her umbrella against the drizzle and turned in Tweedman's direction. Tweedman tried to avoid her but it was too late. The ribs of her umbrella caught his shoulder. Instinctively he felt for his hat but she was already past him, picking up her hobble skirt and quick ening her pace. He watched her for a moment then laughed She posed no threat, for quite evidently Cynthia Maitland did not wish her visit to Childs to be made public anymore than Tweedman wanted his made public. He was thankful that their sentiments were in such close accord. He beat with the door-knocker and waited. This unexpected encounter had certainly heightened his interest in Childs.

Childs' landlady answered Tweedman's knock and, after a short consultation with her lodger, ushered Tweedman into the first room on the right of the narrow corridor. It smelt faintly of cigarette and more strongly of a lady's most expensive scent. On the table was a leather-bound copy of Hardy's *The Woodlanders*. Tweedman would liked to have looked at the fly leaf, but held himself in check.

If Childs did not want Tweedman in his sitting-room that evening he did not show it. He welcomed the auburn-haired stranger with great civility, taking his cape and hanging it on the coat-rack; then, spotting his limp, ensured that the corner of the carpet was quite flat, all without a word of comment. Finally he offered Tweedman the better of his two armchairs and, taking his stick, held the big man's arm while he settled.

This reception, following so closely upon his unexpected sight of Cynthia Maitland, unsettled Tweedman. He had intended a cat-and-mouse start to his encounter with the German, but dropped it.

'I take it the password is Godolphin Arabian?' he asked provocatively.

Childs looked puzzled.

'One of the three sources of all bloodstock, surely?' said Tweedman.

'Ah . . .' said Childs, nodding slightly.

'All right, Mr Childs,' said Tweedman curtly, 'let's come straight to the point. I haven't come here about horses, but about you. You are a German agent.'

Childs still showed no surprise. He remained, as he had first appeared, a perfect gentleman, smiling slightly at the statement as if it had been no more than a comment on the framed sampler that hung above the mantelpiece. Indeed, it was Tweedman who was surprised and not a little angered.

'Perhaps you didn't hear?' he said. 'I know that you are a German agent!'

128

'You gave your name as Gavin Tweedman,' said Childs quietly and with a marked American accent, 'that is all I know about you.'

The man's sangfroid was impressive. As Tweedman had to remind himself, spies were almost always shot.

'Let me explain, Mr Childs. Your position at the moment is, to say the least, extremely precarious. I have only to tell the police or military and you will be apprehended. After that you will be taken to the Tower of London, tried and shot, for the case against you is complete. We have all the facts.'

It was a strange conversation for two grown men, sitting in easy chairs either side of a fire. Yet for the moment, neither seemed to find it so.

'I am an American citizen, sir,' said Childs, 'I have an American passport.'

'You are Hans Frederick Kordt, a reserve korvetten-kapitän in the Imperial German Navy. You were born in 1860 in the small town of Probsteierhagen, first stop on the railway line out of Kiel. Your sister still lives in the same house. In August last year you were recalled to the Navy and joined the battleship *Mecklenburg* at Wilhelmshaven. Before that you spent ten years in America, in Norwich, Connecticut. In November last year you hung up your uniform and went back to America. You took ship from New York on 5 January this year and landed at Cork on the sixteenth under the name Frederick Childs.'

Childs got up and stared into the fire.

'And you are a member of the English counter-espionage?' he asked after a while.

Inwardly Tweedman laughed, for that was exactly what he was not. 'I am a naval officer,' he said.

Childs turned from the fire and his eyes shone. 'We are both sailors?'

Tweedman nodded.

'But why do you tell me all this?' asked Childs. 'If you really think that I am an enemy agent, why not just hand me over to the military you have talked about?'

'I wish to help you.'

Childs smiled. 'And how do you propose to do that, Mr

Tweedman and why? Or do I perhaps call you Commodore or Admiral?'

'I am afraid I never rose to those heights,' said Tweedman, 'just Captain.'

Childs nodded, then delicately indicated Tweedman's leg. 'In the service of His Britannic Majesty, no doubt, Captain? A promising career cut short?'

'An accident . . .'

Childs sighed, then said, 'You have still to answer my other question, Captain. How do you propose to help me, and why?'

'I will ensure you have safe passage out of this country in return for certain papers I believe you to have in your possession.'

Childs looked genuinely puzzled. 'You may search, Captain, but I can assure you, you will find nothing.'

'In the last few weeks you have received information on a device being developed to overcome trenches, barbed wire and machine-guns. It goes under the odd name of "Tank".'

'That!' cried Childs in amusement and relief. 'My dear sir, I thought I was worth more than that!'

'Where is it?' asked Tweedman coldly.

'I am afraid I no longer have it.'

The nerves in Tweedman's amputated foot reacted so violently that his leg jumped from the carpet.

'No longer have it?!' he said in disbelief.

Childs shook his head. 'It is somewhere on the High Seas, Captain. But tell me, why is it so important to you?'

'Merely tidying,' said Tweedman, then added sharply, 'Now tell me. What part of the High Seas?'

'Not quite so fast, Captain,' said Childs. 'This safe passage . .?'

'On the next steamer to call into Cork Harbour bound for America.'

'And what guarantee have I?'

'The best in the world. My word as a British naval officer.'

There was a long pause.

'I will accept that,' said Childs at last, 'but are you not taking a great responsibility upon yourself, allowing someone you believe to be an enemy agent to leave the country?'

'I have to weigh everything in the balance,' said Tweedman, 'and that is the way the scales have tilted. Now, where about on the High Seas is this information?'

'On a Dutch ship, the *Irene*, bound for Rotterdam.'

'In whose hands?'

'The man is an innocent carrier.'

'He will come to no harm. His name?'

Childs hesitated.

'His name?' repeated Tweedman.

'Willem Stöver, the second mate.'

With his heart pounding, Tweedman struggled to his feet.

'I will be back within the hour, Korvetten-Kapitän Kordt. In the meantime, do not leave this house and let no one in. When I come back I will take you to a place of safety. And one other thing. Did you make a copy of the information?'

Childs shook his head. Tweedman had no difficulty in believing him.

Even though the call had the highest priority, it was three-quarters of an hour before Tweedman heard the faint, distorted voice of Stancombe at the other end. During the critical period while Tweedman was in Ireland, he had dragooned Stancombe into using the camp bed in the office. Never in his life had Tweedman been more grateful for his foresight.

'Stancombe!' he roared into the mouthpiece. 'A Dutch steamer, the *Irene*, bound for Rotterdam, should be somewhere in the Channel by now. Get her intercepted bloody quickly, go aboard yourself and search the possessions of the second mate. Our precious bit of information is somewhere on that blasted vessel *and it must not get any further*!'

'Did you say *Irene*, sir?' asked Stancombe from miles away.

'Yes, *Irene*!' and Tweedman spelt out the letters.

'The *Irene* was torpedoed this morning off the Downs . . .'

'The devil she was! Did she sink?'

'Like a stone, sir.'

'And the crew?' breathed Tweedman, and had to repeat it.

'Some lost, sir, some taken aboard a Swedish vessel.'

'Listen, Stancombe,' said Tweedman, 'the man we want is

called Willem Stöver. If he's drowned, then that's it. But if he's aboard that Swede, stop it and stop him! Understand?'

'But, sir,' came back the plaintive cry, 'I am a civilian!'

'Stancombe,' said Tweedman very slowly, 'if that information gets further than the Straits of Dover, I'll escort you to the Tower myself!' Then he slammed down the phone.

For his journeys in Ireland, Tweedman had soon discarded the little bull-nosed Morris for something bigger and more powerful. Inquiries in Cork had produced a Belgian, sixteen-horsepower, 2½-litre Minerva. With its four forward gears and quiet, smooth-running sleeve valves, it was a pleasant car to handle. It could also go fast, as its successes in the pre-war Alpine and Swedish trials had shown. Tweedman now proceeded to drive it in that manner.

He was late getting back to Childs, but fifty-five minutes after he had put the German and his suitcase aboard he was racing up to the house on Compass Hill. Ford, he hoped, could look after Childs until Tweedman had worked out exactly what to do with him.

To Tweedman's dismay there was no one at the house. At that moment Bella was sitting at her father's feet, listening for the third time to the amazing tale of the U-20 and the *Earl of Latham*, while Ford, who had driven back to Mrs Sullivan's, was just uncorking one of his dozen clarets. Tweedman stared at Childs sitting upright in the front of the car, then burst out laughing.

'Why are you laughing, Captain?' asked Childs, looking around and seeing nothing particularly humorous.

'Because I've got to take you with me, Korvetten-Kapitän, that's why. Because for better or for worse, I'm saddled with you, and I cannot leave you here.'

With that, Tweedman climbed back into the Minerva and, turning the car about, headed west towards a sky that was still just light.

When Tweedman and Childs were roughly midway between Kinsale and Carridleagh, the First Lord arrived at the Gare du Nord, Paris, and made for the Place Vendôme. There he checked into the Ritz Hotel.

8

Petty Officer Warren had a liking for delicacies. He was the only non-commissioned crew member of the B-12 to have tasted quail and probably one of the very few to have sampled oysters. Tweedman's largess at lunch had titillated his appetite and reminded him of all the countryside had to offer. Accordingly he dropped the hint to Ordinary Seaman Grant that they ought to be taking more advantage of their situation and how much the petty officers' mess could do with a couple of nice ducks roasted with almonds or cherries. He also mentioned several other possibilities, none of which were to be found in the provisions embarked before leaving Portsmouth.

Warren was an impressive figure at any time; when he talked food he became formidable. So, after thinking the matter over all afternoon, Grant set off with a sack to see what he could find. There was nothing more succulent than rabbits this side of the wire barrier, so he went down to the hollow that had been Mehigan's downfall, and after successfully crawling through the fence set off into the hinterland.

At first, the forces working within Grant were nicely balanced, but quite soon the fear of going too far, getting lost or back to the boat so late that his absence would be discovered proved less than the fear of going back empty-handed and meeting Warren's dark and forbidding gaze. So he pushed on.

Grant's first foray towards habitation set a dog barking and he was forced to run back to the track. The sun had set and the colours had reached a striking brilliance when he made a second attempt, this time on a cottage which stood by a burn that bubbled brown through the boulders. From the distance it looked promising. There were chickens about, and with water the chance of duck seemed high. Grant made a circuit of the building before approaching from the back. He kept low, even taking his cap off, tried hard to steady his breathing and wished he had not worn his leather sea-boots, for they creaked with every step. But his luck seemed to be in. Petty Officer Warren's dinner lay on the grass in the shape of three white ducks roosting, their heads tucked under their wings.

Remembering his short period of rifle training, Grant dropped to his stomach and wriggled. A gap in the broken fence let him through. He was within three yards of his quarries, still and white in the closing darkness, when a hand that could have belonged to a giant grabbed his shoulder, and a soft Irish voice breathed right above his ear.

'Your soul to the devil! I'd a mind to blast your thieving head from your thieving body!'

The nearest duck opened one eye, then deciding that the danger was past, shut it. Grant raised his head fearful of a blow that never came. He tried to get up, but the hand on his shoulder held him down. He could just make out three men standing behind him, and the one holding him had a rifle and a bandoleer of cartridges slung round his body.

'The devil, Con Doyle,' said the second man, 'he must be a sailor from the submarine Párdig talks about, and you're talking to him in English!' Then he turned to a third man who had so far said nothing. 'Faith, Shaun Mehigan, you are a schoolteacher, talk to the man in his native tongue.'

Mehigan bent down and took Grant's cap from his left hand:

'It reads HMS FORTH,' he said. 'That is the cap of an English sailor. His Majesty's Ship . . .'

'Is that so!' cried the man with the rifle, putting his boot none too gently into Grant's side. 'Is it true that you are an English sailor from an English man of war?'

Grant tried to answer but was given no chance. He was hauled upright, shaken, then suddenly let go and all three men stood looking at him as if not quite sure what to do next. Then Mehigan searched the darkness and said, 'Where there is one, there might well be others.'

Doyle, the man with the rifle, laughed. 'Faith man, are we frightened of a few children in fine leather boots!?'

'We must take him to the Captain,' said the second man firmly, 'it is dark enough.'

Doyle spat. 'Is he not a thief, and an English sailor?'

'He is a prisoner,' said the second man.

Mehigan nodded. 'He is a prisoner of war, Michael O'Brien is right. If things are to be asked of this man, then the Captain will know what they should be. Otherwise we should let him go.'

Doyle spat once more, indicated the path to the track, and pushed the muzzle of his rifle into Grant's back.

Matt Kearney had been captain of the newly formed Béal na Liam Company of the South-West Cork Brigade of the Irish Volunteers only a fortnight. He was their first captain and, like all the Volunteers, a greenhorn. His message to go to a house on the outskirts of the village was his first assignment and he set off eagerly. There he found three of his men, Doyle, O'Brien and Mehigan, in the back room guarding a bewildered British sailor of little more than twenty. When Kearney had absorbed the situation, he left O'Brien with the prisoner and took the other two into the front room. Only then did he show his annoyance.

'Have you no more sense than to abduct an English sailor and bring him to Béal na Liam?!' he cried. 'In God's name what is to happen when the military come here searching as they certainly will?! Do we just say we found him walking with his mind gone?!'

Doyle and Mehigan shifted uneasily, and for a moment neither spoke. Then Mehigan said, 'Are we not at war with the British, Captain? Is it not therefore right that we should take prisoners and question them? A good army stands or falls by the quality of its Intelligence.'

Kearney knew the truth of these words; nevertheless he was worried.

'You are certainly right, Shaun,' he said quietly, 'but we

135

have never had a prisoner before. Where are we to keep him after we have questioned him?'

Doyle looked at the whitewashed wall and said, 'Maybe, Captain, after we have questioned him, we do not keep him.'

'Return him to his ship?' asked Kearney, surprised.

'I did not say that, Captain,' said Doyle, fingering his rifle.

They stood for a moment looking at one another, then Kearney said, 'He must not remain here. It is too near the barracks, and the peelers have better eyes than buzzards. Take him to my cousin at Inishslea while it is dark. He has the room to keep him and he is a friend.'

'Faith, Captain,' cried Doyle, 'have you forgotten that your cousin Tom Kearney was a sergeant in the British Army?!'

'Tom Kearney is a friend.'

Doyle shrugged. 'And the questioning, Captain?'

Matt Kearney knew that this was his first big test. He turned without a word and went back into the room where Grant sat dejected at the tiny wooden table.

Doyle, O'Brien and Mehigan leant against the wall behind Grant. Kearney sat on the only other chair.

'You say you were signalling off Ros O Cairbre Bay?' said Kearney.

'I don't know where it was,' said Grant. 'Scott, the signaller, went to the bridge. He told me afterwards.'

'A spy!' said Doyle. 'For sure the man is a spy!'

Kearney waved Doyle down, and turned again to Grant.

'You know how serious this is. A British submarine, lying off the coast, pretending for all the world that it is a German U-boat so as to ensnare the Irish people!'

Grant shrugged. He was tired, frightened and hungry. The evening was not turning out at all the way he had expected. Inwardly he cursed 'Plum' Warren and the whole British Navy.

'I knew nothing about it,' he said at last, 'I only know we came here and the signaller went up with the lamp.'

'You altered the shape of your boat with canvas,' said

136

Kearney severely, 'and you signalled to ordinary houses to trap them.'

Matt Kearney rose, well pleased with the evening. He was quite sure that he had impressed his own men. White ducks in the farmyard had long been forgotten. Under his interrogation, they had got right to the heart of the matter.

'Take him to Inishslea. See that he is well guarded. I will tell the brigade adjutant, and we shall know what to do with him then.'

He picked up his own lantern and strode out into the night.

'Another few miles,' said Tweedman as the Minerva cornered on two wheels, 'ten minutes at the very most. I expect you're getting hungry?'

'I could do with dinner, Captain,' said Childs, his left hand gripping the near-side door.

'I doubt if it will be dinner!' shouted Tweedman over the scream of wind, engine and tyres. 'More a case of left-overs!'

As they took another corner, the beam of the headlights swept across a signpost.

'Carridleagh,' said Childs aloud, as if trying to remember something. Tweedman grunted. A second signpost as they raced through Béal na Liam, and Childs did remember. If he had the name right, a U-boat was supposed to have put in there in the last few days.

'Carridleagh, Captain,' he shouted, 'a nice-sounding name. Have you ever been there?'

Tweedman shook his head. 'A God-forsaken hole, I hear,' he said curtly, then burst out laughing.

'Another joke, Captain?' asked Childs in surprise.

'Nothing really,' replied Tweedman, for how could he possibly explain the irony of the situation. Within five miles of his secret harbour, at the most critical phase of the whole operation, he would be sheltering a German agent. He gave Childs a glance and said, 'Something in confidence between you and me, Herr Korvetten-Kapitän. Plans, however well prepared, can never anticipate the human reaction. That is why the world can never be run properly by England or Germany. A mistake of the Almighty, of course. Should never have given us free will. Bet he's rueing it now!'

Childs smiled and thought of his own roughly formed plan. To reach that U-boat.

'You say we are very near, Captain?'

'Two more miles,' shouted Tweedman, 'then you can stretch your legs!'

Childs nodded and appeared satisfied.

Ford was astounded to see the German agent enter with Tweedman, and Childs was none too happy to see Ford. Tweedman, however, ignored all their feelings.

'We've got to look after this fellow,' he said to Ford, 'he's far too valuable for us to go letting him get picked up by the Special Branch.'

The situation was quite beyond Ford; nevertheless, he joined in the play-acting until he could get Tweedman alone.

'My dear Captain,' he said quietly, 'please forgive me if I'm foolishly missing the point, but why bring the German fellow here?'

'He's no threat. He knows nothing of what's going on.'

'Oh, but he does!'

Tweedman was surprised. 'Childs knows of the submarine in Carridleagh?!'

Ford nodded. 'Only he thinks it's a U-boat.'

Tweedman looked up at the ceiling. He had not expected Childs to know. Indeed, he had decided that Childs could not possibly know so soon.

'How can you be so certain he knows?' he asked sharply.

'My dear Captain,' said Ford, 'your submarine's exploits in signalling off the coast have become famous. The coast-guards saw the lamp and told the peelers and military at Skibbereen and the navy at Queenstown. From there the information went like Jack-o-lantern to the Sinn Feiners!'

'That doesn't necessarily mean that Childs knows.'

'Ah, but you see, Captain, I hastened the process.'

Tweedman glared at Ford, his face growing more the colour of his hair every moment.

'You bloody stupid idiot!' he cried. 'Did I tell you to do that!?'

'I thought it would be helpful,' said Ford. 'My dear fellow, I thought that was what you wanted.'

138

'*I* was looking after Childs, not *you*!'

Tweedman clenched his teeth, trying to hold his fury, then suddenly he shook his head, grinned and relaxed.

'It doesn't matter,' he said, 'of course it doesn't. Except that we must put a guard on him for the night.'

'I'm frightfully sorry,' said Ford, 'I had no idea . . .'

'I said it doesn't matter!' shouted Tweedman.

'The guard,' said Ford nervously, 'I can drive along to the barracks.'

Tweedman shook his head. 'Gossip,' he said, 'more people, more gossip. No, there's only one possible source. Fetch a rating from the submarine and see that he brings his rifle and bayonet. I'll look after Childs.'

Although it was late, and neither his lights nor the roads were too good, Ford was glad to go.

They sat opposite one another by the slowly dying fire. The tall German was erect in his chair, his silver moustache and greying hair making him look more English than Tweedman. Tweedman, his pistol in his pocket, his left leg up on a foot stool, his auburn hair pressed against the wing of the chair, sat slumped in a most un-naval pose.

Childs was puzzled. His captor's attitude to him had suddenly changed. Childs knew from the way the man's right hand strayed to his pocket from time to time that he had a gun. He still did not think that Tweedman intended to kill him, for he had given his word as a British naval officer to get him a passage to America. In his perplexity, Childs was certain of only one thing. Something had passed between Tweedman and the actor after their arrival at the house.

They sat for a long time without speaking, until eventually Tweedman knocked out his pipe and said, 'We've all got to live in this house tonight, Korvetten-Kapitän, and we are all tired. I have sent for a sentry, but it would greatly facilitate matters if I had your word as a German naval officer not to try to communicate with anyone or escape?'

'And where might I escape to?' asked Childs.

'There are German sympathizers amongst the Irish.'

Childs said nothing.

'And if I don't get your word,' continued Tweedman, 'I will have to put a sentry in your room and perhaps restrain you in some way. For a man of your age and rank, that would be neither pleasant nor dignified.'

Childs looked down into the fire. 'I will not try and communicate with anyone tonight, Captain, nor will I try and escape tonight.'

'Good.'

'In return for that pledge I would ask you to confirm your promise to me of a passage out of Ireland?'

Tweedman nodded. 'Given.'

'And I would also ask you to take your hand out of your right-hand pocket. It is not necessary to keep it there.'

Tweedman grinned sheepishly and did as he was asked.

Hans Frederick Kordt, being a man of six foot two, found the small bed in the upstairs back room too short. That, together with the creaking of the landing floorboards under the restricted movements of the armed sentry, made sleep difficult. However, three things did bring Childs some joy that night. The leather-bound book that still carried the lady's scent; the fact that no one had bothered to search his suitcase and he now had the Luger under his pillow; and the small piece of the Fatherland reputed to be not five miles away. Just as the lady's scent warmed his ageing blood, so did the thought of that sheltering U-boat stir his good Schleswig-Holstein soul. Yet even there a small cloud appeared on the horizon and grew with the darkness and the long night hours. He, an officer in the Imperial German Navy, who had worn the crown and three rings of a Korvetten-Kapitän, had failed. Even if the Fatherland could forgive him, he was not sure that he could forgive himself.

'Fog!' said Schwieger in disgust, turning his jacket collar up even higher. 'We have only four or five days here, and there is nothing but fog!'

Rudolf Zentner, the officer of the watch, remembering the steamer that had escaped into a mist bank yesterday evening, nodded. 'It will clear with the sun, Herr Kapitän, fog always does.'

140

'This is Ireland, Zentner,' said Schwieger, 'not Lake Constance!'

They peered together into the white shroud that now engulfed the U-boat. It was a striking contrast to the night when it had been clear and still and they had lain under the stars recharging their batteries. It was only with the dawn that the fog had thickened again.

A foghorn, away to starboard, alerted them both. Schwieger shouted for full speed and gave a new course. The U-20's bow wave rose and the fog seemed to grip them even closer. For five minutes they listened to the deep, rasping note, then suddenly it stopped.

'She has run into a clearing, Herr Kapitän!' cried Zentner, unable to conceal his excitement. Schwieger nodded. His luck could be in after all.

They were eighteen miles south of Waterford and it was 7 am Greenwich Mean Time when the small group on the bridge saw a watery sun and a blue sea. Visibility that had been little more than ten metres was suddenly nearly a mile. Schwieger thumped Zentner on the back, then beat his gloved hands on the bridge rail. At the very limit of their patch of sea, where the fog still swirled in wispish brush-strokes, there was a much darker grey than that provided by nature.

'Smoke bearing green, four-zero!' screamed Zentner.

Schwieger bent over the voice tube. 'Steer one-two-zero! Gun crew on deck!'

The gun crew raced up the hatchway.

'Make tubes ready!'

'Tubes ready, Herr Kapitän!'

'She's turning to port!' screamed Zentner.

'Fire!'

The gun crew got off two shots before the capricious fog took over again. Two minutes after so suddenly appearing, the steamer had completely vanished. On the U-boat's bridge the feeling of anti-climax was as dampening as the water droplets bequeathed by the fog to all it had enfolded.

Zentner looked at the captain, and under the challenge Schwieger rode a hunch. He made a drastic alteration of course and reduced speed. Wherever the steamer had been

141

heading before its evasive action, it would want to get back to that course.

'Cheer up, Zentner,' said Schwieger, 'if my intuition is right we are running parallel with her now. Be patient and wait for the next clearing.'

Schwieger's intuition was right. The skipper of the 6,000-ton *Candidate*, outward bound for the West Indies, did want to get back on course, and at seven thirty-three the steamer appeared from the fog a second time. This time Schwieger made no mistake. Nevertheless, it took a torpedo and a dozen rounds from the 3.4-inch gun to send her to the bottom and that did not happen until nearly midday. When the U-20's boarding-party returned from the *Candidate*, Zentner stood up in the rubber boat and called up to his captain. 'Surface attacks are dangerous, Herr Kapitän. The Tommies' six pounder was mounted in the stern. Had she turned away and we given chase, we would have been a sitting duck!'

Schwieger made a mental note for next time.

In Esmond's case, it was Grant's disappearance and Tweedman's visit of the previous afternoon that had disturbed his sleep. He had lain in his bunk remembering every word that Tweedman had spoken and every second of that torpedo attack in the North Sea. His conviction that Prescott's death and the deaths of the other twenty members of the crew of the D-9 was nothing whatsoever to do with him remained as firm as ever. Whatever Tweedman might say, however much circumstances might appear to be against him, the vessel in Esmond's sights had been a U-boat. None of this, of course, helped him in what he had been ordered to do, but it did bring back some of his self-respect.

Esmond had got a little help too from telling Paynter the bones of their strange mission. Like Esmond, Paynter had reacted badly to the idea, and was only calmed by the news that two torpedo heads were to be replaced with half charges, the effect of which on the mighty *Lusitania* would be no more than to puncture a couple of the longitudinal water-tight compartments that flanked each side of the ship. Indeed, they had discussed the buoyancy of the great liner in

142

detail and made sketches of what they remembered of her structure: the ten transverse bulkheads that gave the eleven great watertight compartments in addition to the longitudinal divisions. That, more than anything, had persuaded them that the risks of the enterprise were, as Tweedman had suggested, virtually nil.

The diversionary run round the shore of Carridleagh was put in hand directly after breakfast. The crew, by now immune to surprises, at first grumbled, then, under Paynter's leadership, began to enter into the spirit of things. They were in the process of being ferried to the Anliem side when Tweedman's odd-looking party arrived in the Minerva. Esmond's first act was to ask that the police be told to search for Grant.

Tweedman shook his head. 'When did he desert?'

'I don't think he did desert, sir,' said Esmond. 'I think, as cook, he went off on a forage.'

Tweedman looked up at the Anliem ridge. 'Fallen down the cliff, no doubt. Bloody dangerous up there.'

'We've looked, sir,'

'You can't look everywhere, man. Not with a shoreline like that.'

Tweedman saw Esmond's face and put his hand on his arm. 'I know how you feel, losing one of your crew. But with an operation like this, we can't go setting up a hue and cry for a British sailor. Let's hope that whatever happened to him, happened damned quickly.'

Esmond was far from happy, but Tweedman brushed further discussion of the subject aside by asking for a fresh guard for the German.

Stoker Thomas was ordered out of his singlet and shorts and back into his white jersey and sea-boots, and given the custody of Frederick Childs.

The German was suffering. Not surprisingly, he too had slept badly. He had been awakened at the moment of his only deep sleep, and although the sentry had done his best with a mug of hot shaving water, breakfast had been rushed; but much worse, they had then set off down the track where the signpost had pointed to Carridleagh. The wire barrier and

143

the Tommies at the neck of Anliem had alarmed him, but the final blow had been the submarine tucked under the abbey ruins. His first thought was that this was to be a sadistic visit to a captured U-boat, but at close quarters the canvas screen behind the conning tower gave it away. It was British, dressed up to look German.

Clutching his suitcase, Childs was ferried over to the island, his guard changed and his dream of returning home on that little piece of the Fatherland he had believed to have been so near faded for ever.

With Paynter leading, three petty officers and nine ratings set off jogging north-east up the long inlet of Carridleagh. As they disappeared, the torpedo-loading hatch of the B-12 was opened and the wherry left the far shore, propelled by Blackmore and Wright and carrying the first of the two warheads. Only Esmond and Tweedman were left on the submarine.

It was warm work. To get at the heads of the two torpedoes already in the tubes, it was necessary to pull back the reloads and winch them up with the derrick until they were at an angle of forty-five degrees. Starboard and port had to be dealt with separately. In the diminutive space in the torpedo flat at the bow of the submarine, amidst a maze of pipes, chains, compressed-air bottles and within the all-pervading aroma of shale oil, Blackmore and Wright worked stripped to the waist. Tweedman watched them and the time. At some point during the attachment of the two new warheads, one other very vital task had to be accomplished. The pistol of one of the reloads had to be changed.

Tweedman saw his chance at mid-morning. The starboard torpedo finished, Blackmore and Wright slid it back into its tube, winched up the port reload, then set off with the captain in the wherry for the second warhead.

For a big man, Tweedman moved quickly. He clamped the propeller and unscrewed the whole pistol with the locking key, the work of no more than a minute. He extracted the pistol and laid it on the mess-room table. From his gladstone he took the new pistol doctored by Petren and laid it alongside the first one, just where a shaft of sunshine came down through the open hatch. He took his watch from his fob pocket and checked the time. It was a quarter to eleven.

144

Thirty-two hours would bring him to six forty-five tomorrow evening. The latest information he had was that the *Lusitania* would round the Fastnet in the night and pass Queenstown about 4 pm. Whatever the outcome, the B-12 should be still submerged at six forty-five.

It was while Tweedman was seated at the mess table setting the timing devices that Childs reached the cliff edge. The German, unsettled, unable to sit on the camp bed in the bell tent any longer, had suggested to Stoker Thomas that they walked through the abbey ruins. Thomas saw no problem and kept a few paces behind, his rifle, with bayonet fixed, in the slung position.

It was from the low wall of the old South Chapel that Childs first saw the submarine below, its hatches open and the sun playing on its rust-streaked casing. It took him some time to focus on the darker interior, and then through the torpedo-loading hatch he saw the great bulk of Tweedman, oblivious to his presence, crouched over a mechanism that lay on the table. Instinctively, as if not wanting to be caught doing something wrong, Childs looked towards his escort, but Thomas's thoughts were miles away.

Childs was not a torpedo expert, but on his recall in August he had spent a week on the latest Schwärzköpfs at the Naval Academy at Flensburg, so the weapon was not unknown to him. He was quite certain that the mechanism in Tweedman's hands was the primer and detonator, and that by his stealthy manner whatever he was doing was without the knowledge of the captain of the vessel, or anyone else for that matter. Childs watched as Tweedman put the pistol to his ear, then apparently satisfied, carefully inserted it into the warhead. Childs moved away just as the wherry left the further shore.

Childs was puzzled. The submarine was quite evidently being prepared for an operation, yet what that operation might be he had no idea. He kept his eyes open for the rest of the morning and saw the old warheads being removed on the wherry. But over and above the changes that were being made to the torpedoes, and of which the captain of the boat was obviously aware, something else was happening that

145

related to the detonator and primer in the port reload torpedo.

There for the moment the matter had to rest, until Tweedman clambered up the rope ladder to the grass and for a second he and Childs were face to face. Tweedman turned quickly away, but in that brief instance when their eyes had met, Childs had had a sudden, deep, instinctive feeling. Tweedman's word as a British naval officer might not be the bond he had imagined.

Childs walked away from the submarine to a quiet part of the ruins and sat in a patch of warm sun. He ran his finger gently over the embossed leather cover of *The Woodlanders*, opened it and tried to read:

> The physiognomy of a deserted highway expresses solitude to a degree that is not reached by mere dales and downs, and bespeaks a tomb-like stillness more emphatic than that of glades and pools . . . .

He knew exactly what the author meant, yet found it difficult to concentrate. He stopped reading and looked at the sky. Only a skylark marked the blue.

It was soon after noon when Schwieger decided to dive. It might bring him better luck. The main vents were opened, the clutches to the diesels let out, the hydroplanes, fore and aft, put to dive, the hatch to the bridge slammed down, and gently the U-20 slid beneath the surface. They levelled out at periscope depth and Schwieger scanned his new, reduced horizon. His luck was in. Half an hour ago he had lost a White Star liner, now he found a replacement. Or was it a ghost ship? He called Lang to the periscope and awaited his reaction.

'A sister to the *Candidate*, Herr Kapitan,' said Lang, and Schwieger took over once again, manoeuvring the U-20 for an attack.

'Keep away from her stern, Herr Kapitän,' called Zentner, but Schwieger had no need of a reminder. He had not forgotten that the *Candidate* had been armed, and had no intention of risking his boat a second time. This time he would stay submerged. There would be no warning. Brief orders to the coxswain, an eye on the depth-gauges, the order to fire, the seemingly endless silence while everyone counted and then the dull boom almost dead ahead.

It was a good shot, the torpedo had struck just below the bridge. Schwieger stayed submerged and watched the crew take to the boats. Although he did not know it then, there was no loss of life. The steamer, however, was a long time sinking. In the end, Schwieger surfaced, closed to point-blank range and fired another torpedo. Even then, the vessel he now identified as the *Centurion*, bound for South Africa, took an hour and twenty minutes to settle slowly within her own whirlpool.

Steering south at slow speed and still on the surface, Schwieger went below. In his log, he summed up his own situation and his reasons for not proceeding towards Liverpool, the intended theatre of operations. In his own order, they were the persistence of the fog, the possibility of being surprised by enemy destroyers in that fog, the difficulty of identifying troopship escorts in unclear weather at night, the heavy consumption of diesel oil due to the long journey around Scotland, and the fact that he had only three torpedoes left, two of which he wanted to keep for the return journey. Finally, in his own neat handwriting, he added his conclusions:

> I have therefore decided to remain to the south of the entrance to the Bristol Channel and attack steamers until two-fifths of the fuel oil is used up. Here there is more opportunity for attack and it is met with less counter-action than in the Irish Sea near Liverpool.

When Schwieger had rationalized his decision, he went back up on the bridge. Earlier he had been able to see the Coningbeg Lightship; now, with the fog closing in again, it was once more invisible. He decided to call it an early night, go further south and recharge his batteries.

Captain Turner did not want to worry his passengers too early, but he had the memorandum of 10 February to think of:

> Vessels navigating in submarine areas should have

their boats turned out and fully provisioned.

At 7.30 am on that Thursday morning, believing that most people should be awake, he gave the necessary orders. In spite of all Turner's consideration for the passengers on the upper decks, the ominous creaking of the davits as the boats were uncovered and swung out was not the most reassuring of sounds. When those who were wondering exactly what was happening quickly dressed and came out on deck to see for themselves, and saw the lifeboats no longer in their usual positions but far over the side, an uneasy feeling swept the vessel.

By noon they had logged 484 nautical miles, driving through the same quiet sea that had been with them all the way, and under the same hazy sunshine. Even with the boats out and the talk of submarines, the war itself still seemed a long way away. Yet for the *Lusitania* it was now little more than twenty-four hours distant. A reminder, if indeed a reminder was really needed, arrived just after noon. It was a radiogram and read:

To all British ships:
Take Liverpool pilot at bar and avoid headlands. Pass harbours at full speed. Steer mid-channel course. Submarines off Fastnet.

Turner did the only thing he could do. He reduced speed to make certain of rounding the Fastnet in the darkness, and steered a new course to pass it by at least twenty-five miles. To be further out might mean missing the *Juno*.

19

The girl looked up and smiled. She had dark brown hair pulled behind her ears, and bright blue eyes. She had the sort of nipped-in waist that Grant had always found pleasing, and when she moved across the yard her feet seemed to glide over the flagstones. He had seen her first last night through a crack in the door, then this morning she had come into the yard with the milk pails. That was when he had first seen the dimples.

Grant wiped the cold water from his face and returned the smile.

'I hope you were not too cold,' she asked, 'and got the blankets?'

Grant nodded and thanked her, never taking his eyes from her. The girl, a little confused, look at the ground.

'You're from a ship?'

'That's right.'

'I didn't know that sailors wore fine boots of leather?'

'Glad you like them,' said Grant, flicking a bit of dirt from one of the toe-caps. 'Mind you, they're a bit hot this weather, but I quite fancy myself in them.'

'And what are they going to do for you, your friends I mean?' asked the girl. 'There's talk of the military being turned out from the barracks to look for you.'

Grant scratched his head. He had been so bewildered by events that he had given very little thought to what the Navy might do. One thing was quite obvious from the first day they had entered Carridleagh. The B-12's operation was so secret, it was most unlikely that the authorities would wish to stir the local countryside looking for an ordinary seaman.

'I honestly don't know. They might do nothing. The Navy's a funny place.'

'They sat up all night arguing about you,' said the girl. 'Shaun Mehigan wants you as a hostage, Michael O'Brien thinks it is safer to send you back to your ship, Uncle Matt is for exchanging you for half a dozen rifles, and Con Doyle . . .'

Grant raised an eyebrow. 'Con Doyle's the one with the rifle?'

The girl nodded, then suddenly said, 'Faith, there's me standing here, talking my head off and you wanting your breakfast!'

Grant grinned and the girl ran off.

Grant looked up from the scrubbed table, the two fried eggs and the thick rasher of bacon. 'What's your name?'

'Bridget. What is yours?'

'Peter.'

'Where do you live?'

'Portsmouth, with my mother.'

'And your father?' asked the girl.

'He was a sailor too,' said Grant thoughtfully, 'never really saw all that much of him. He was drowned when the old *Monmouth* went down.'

The girl had never heard of the Battle of Coronel, let alone the *Monmouth*, but she murmured something about being sorry, then suddenly cried, 'Upon my word, what a funny world it is! Your father a sailor in the British Navy, my father a soldier in the British Army!'

Grant was surprised. The girl ran upstairs to return after a moment with a medal.

'Red, black and orange!' said Grant in amazement. 'That's the South African War Medal! The same as my dad wore. He was on the old *Powerful*. They took their guns across country to Ladysmith.'

'The Queen gave him that,' said the girl proudly. 'Coming from horses, he was in the Cavalry.'

Grant looked round the kitchen. 'And then he became a farmer?'

'When my grandfather died.'

'I wouldn't mind that,' said Grant, 'finishing my time with the Navy and then becoming a farmer.'

The girl asked about his brothers and sisters. When he said he had none, it was her turn to be surprised.

'My dad was away too much!' he said with a laugh, and the girl blushed. He would see her three younger brothers and her sister when school ended.

Grant wiped his plate clean with a piece of coarse brown bread, then took it to the sink. He picked up the frying-pan, wiped it clean with a sheet of newspaper, took the kettle of boiling water from the range and began washing up. Bridget, watching him, suddenly burst out laughing.

Grant stared at her, surprised.

'Anyone would think you'd never seen a man washing up before!'

'I have not!' cried the girl. 'Not only have I never seen a man wash the dishes, I have never seen a sailor standing by a sink with an apron! Do you do that for your sweetheart?'

The question was out, much to Bridget's confusion. Grant shook his head. 'No . . . no, I don't as a matter of fact. Only for my mother.'

'But you have a sweetheart?'

Grant thought for a moment. 'No, not really a sweetheart, if you get my meaning. Just girls I know, sort of thing . . .'

Bridget suddenly felt very excited. She prayed to Mary the Mother of Jesus that she was not showing it too much.

'I'll help you with dinner, if you like,' said Grant, surveying the rows of pans hanging from the beam. 'What's it to be? Roast duck and cherries?' Then he too laughed. 'That's what got me here! "Plum" Warren's insatiable greed.'

There was a long pause, then Grant said, 'Wonder what they're doing now?'

'Do you miss your friends?' asked the girl anxiously.

'Miss them . . .' said Grant vaguely. 'Don't know whether I actually miss them, not like that. But, of course, you get used to living with them, and as mates go they're not a bad lot.'

There was another long pause, then very quietly the girl said, 'You could run away, you know. If you had a mind to do

151

it. Con Doyle's gone. There's no one here but my father and old Dan.'

Grant walked to the door into the yard and stared. Old Dan sat in the morning sun, a shotgun over his knees. He was nearly asleep. With Tom Kearney, the girl's father, up in the fields, a child could have walked free.

'I could, if you really wanted me to, take old Dan out into the orchard?'

Grant shook his head and came back into the kitchen. 'The night's the best, when it's dark. Besides, it's not all that easy. I absconded, didn't I? Went off without permission, so in theory, at least, I'm AWOL.'

'AWOL?' asked the girl puzzled.

'Absent without leave. And on active service that's not a very good thing to be.'

The girl looked worried. 'But you said you were sent to get a pair of Con Doyle's ducks?'

'Not actually sent . . . and then not by an officer. I think I'm what they call a victim of circumstances. What I'm really wondering though is whether I'm also a deserter.'

Four young children burst into the yard: three boys and a girl. They had heard of the English sailor who had arrived late in the night when they had all gone to bed. This morning they had tried to peer into the shed where he had been kept, but the crack wasn't big enough to see inside and Con Doyle had scared them off with his gun. Now they saw the sailor in their kitchen, standing beside their sister. They were surprised at his mild appearance, but liked his fine leather boots.

'By my baptism!' cried Bridget, seeing the four faces looking up at Grant. 'What are you not at school where you belong?!'

'It is the schoolmaster,' said Donal, the eldest. 'Shaun Mehigan has locked the school and gone. They say that he and Con Doyle have taken Michael O'Brien's cart and gone to search for German submarines!'

Bridget laughed. 'And what, in the name of God, are we going to do with the four of you all day?'

Mary, the girl, looked at Grant, then whispered, 'Can't we take the English sailor to St Bridget's Well?'

Bridget looked at the old flagstones and blushed. She found it difficult to explain that he was meant to be a prisoner and an enemy.

'Not now, we've got to put on the dinner.' She looked up at the pots hanging from the beam. 'Now we are eight, Peter,' she said, her eyes sparkling, 'will you be kind enough to get down the biggest?'

20

The three men in the curragh had taken a calculated risk. They had brought the curragh down the south-east side of Anliem, keeping so close to the thin line of breakers that they were invisible to anyone on the ridge. To see them, it was necessary to walk down from the top to where the land suddenly fell away, 300 feet to the Atlantic, and only seabirds, rabbits and a few sure-footed sheep dared to tread.

They did not row as far as the point, or even as far as the rock where Pádrig O'Callaghan had beached his curragh, but pulled into the shore by the cliff they called 'The Cathedral'. Doyle was the first to leap out, and he steadied the boat for the others. They ran the ten yards across the shingle to the sheer face of rock and crouched. Here, in a tiny bay, with a 180-degree arc of cliff, they were visible only to sea and sky.

They stood at the top of the shingle and looked up. A single cloud, like a giant white galloping stallion, appeared over the cliff-edge and raced towards the sea. Mehigan felt intensely giddy watching it. O'Brien turned his head away and stared at the distant Claghan Strand. Neither had climbed here before and, now that they saw the challenge, doubted whether they were capable. Only Doyle seemed unperturbed. He laid the rifle lovingly on a ledge of rock and tightened the bandoleer about his body. Then he slipped a long coil of rope over the bandoleer, slung the rifle and moved quickly towards the north corner. With a nod at the others he began the slow, careful climb. As if reluctant to start, Mehigan took his Webley from his pocket, opened the chamber, spun it, then slipped it back into his shirt. O'Brien tugged at his arm, and they moved together to the rock-face.

Following in the exact steps of Doyle, fingers and toes digging into the same narrow fissures of the ancient strata, the other two Volunteers began their painful, frightening ascent. It took them three-quarters of an hour to reach the top.

They lay on the grass in the sun and rested. Doyle did not secure his rope and throw an end over as he had intended, for he knew now that he was the only one capable of making that same return journey. They would have to go back the long way, by the sheep path much nearer the Point. That would mean at least another half a mile along the shore to reach the curragh.

Lunch was a very tense affair. An elderly ewe that had lived neglected on Anliem for years and had thought to end her days there in peace provided the stew. Tweedman, whose stump had grown inflamed with all the activity of the morning, soon limped away to the privacy of the ruins, and there pulled his left trouser up to the thigh and unstrapped his artificial leg. He felt singularly foolish lying against the wall massaging the shrivelled red point where the sawn-off bone was so painful, and wondered exactly what he, a still serving officer in the British Navy, was doing in such a ludicrous situation. He intended returning to England that night and only hoped that he could make it. He cursed Ireland and prayed he would never see the wretched country again.

Tweedman's irritation affected both Esmond and Paynter. When Tweedman had taken himself away they were relieved, for both were finding the idea of the operation more and more distasteful, and now that everything was ready, bar the refuelling promised for that evening, they wanted to get it over and done with. The abbey ruins that had once been so quaint and amusing had now become sinister, even in the sunlight. Esmond was trying to sort it out in his own mind when Paynter put it into words.

'Do you know, Skipper, I don't think I've ever felt so bloody creepy! First there's that crazy actor, then young Grant disappears into the blue, then this extraordinary Captain Tweedman pops up with his creaking wooden leg when you least expect him, and then there's that German!

It's positively indecent living cheek by jowl with a spy. Why don't they just take him away and shoot him? To be quite honest with you, Skipper, I feel almost sorry for the poor bastard being kept waiting like this.'

'You mustn't let yourself,' said Esmond sharply. 'A spy is not like an ordinary combatant. It's a despicable occupation. This man is as much an enemy as the captain of the *Seydlitz*.' Paynter raised his eyebrows but said nothing more. Esmond turned and walked away.

Esmond had not meant to walk into Childs, it just happened. The German was sitting in the sunshine and Thomas was his usual dozen paces away, his rifle resting across his knees. Childs had his suitcase beside him, a book in his hands, but was not reading. Esmond, embarrassed at suddenly finding himself face to face with the German, was about to turn away when Childs smiled. 'Good afternoon, Lieutenant-Commander. You look very worried for such a beautiful day.'

Esmond had no wish to get into conversation with Childs, but something about the man held him. He found it impossible to move. The German got up from the wall and stood in front of Esmond. He was about to say something more, then turned his head towards Thomas. Esmond instinctively walked away from the sentry. Childs spoke quickly. 'I know you are the captain of the British submarine, I too am a naval officer.'

Esmond stared at Childs but said nothing.

'Oh, I know exactly what you are thinking,' said Childs, 'but there are many ways of serving one's country.'

To his surprise, Esmond found himself nodding. Those were Tweedman's words.

'If I had been an admiral,' said Childs, 'it might have been different, but at my rank I am too old for active service. I suppose', he said, looking up at the sun, 'I might have had a desk job, but that is not the same, as I think you will agree, Lieutenant-Commander?'

'I cannot help you, sir,' said Esmond firmly. 'It is nothing to do with me, I am an operational officer.'

'I have not asked for your help,' said Childs, 'but nevertheless it is nice to talk with you and makes a change from your

156

sailor,' and he indicated Thomas a dozen paces away.

Esmond smiled. 'Perhaps you should talk about football or the girls. That's what Thomas likes.'

Childs shook his head. 'We have little time, you and I, so I will get to the point. You are preparing for some operation, I do not know what.'

Esmond again turned to move away. Childs plucked his sleeve and held him.

'I am not prying,' he said very firmly, 'but as I said, I am a naval officer and I do not like to see one of my own profession, even when he is an enemy, being tricked.'

'Tricked?!' asked Esmond in amazement.

'When you are away from here, and you no longer have Captain Tweedman breathing down your neck, check your ship. And, in particular, check the port reload torpedo.'

Esmond just stared at the man without speaking.

'You are surprised, Lieutenant-Commander, but do as I say. Check the warhead carefully, very carefully, the first moment you can.'

Childs stopped and saluted. Esmond stood for a moment, then returned the salute. Childs about-turned and strode back to his place in the sun. Esmond watched him settle by the wall, as if no word had passed between them, then he too turned away. The sooner they left this blasted abbey the better.

A motorcyclist was coming down the track on the Anliem side. Esmond quickened his pace to the cliff-edge. He was ten yards from it when a single shot rang out across White Sheep Island. The gulls rose shrieking and pigeons fluttered through the trees. For a moment the noise of the motorcycle was drowned, then silence settled on land and sea.

Esmond knew what had happened before he turned to go back. Nevertheless, he broke into a run and was joined by half a dozen of his crew. They rounded the wall of the cloister and stopped. They were all sailors at war but not one had ever seen a man shot before. Thomas was standing on the grass in a daze, looking down at the figure sprawled half across the open suitcase. Childs' face was upwards, the full afternoon sun making the rapid whitening even whiter. His Luger was still firmly grasped in his right hand, and from a

157

neat hole in his right temple a dark stream flowed slowly over the carefully packed clothes. Instinctively, Esmond knelt down and put out a hand to lift the head on to the grass, but the bullet that had gone in so neatly had not come out like that. As Esmond touched the cheeks, the back of the skull fell away. Angry and sickened, he pulled a shirt from the suitcase and threw it over the face.

'The poor bastard,' said Paynter, and crossed himself although he was not a Catholic.

Lying a foot from the suitcase, and apparently untouched by the splatter of blood, was the book. Esmond picked it up and showed Paynter the cover.

'Funny,' said Paynter, 'a German reading that.'

The thoughts of the little group were broken by a voice calling from over in the ruins. A moment later Tweedman limped into sight, moving surprisingly fast, half the weight that would have been on a still tender stump now firmly on his stick.

'What in hell's name is going on?!' he shouted, 'Do you idiots want to attract half of Ireland!?'

No one spoke. They just stood in a half circle around the body, leaving the gap in Tweedman's direction. Tweedman stopped five yards away and stared, then moved closer and with the point of his stick lifted the shirt that Esmond had thrown over the face.

'I didn't know he had a pistol, sir,' said Thomas helplessly.

'A bloody good sentry you make!' shouted Tweedman. 'You were supposed to watch him, not go to sleep. I've a damned good mind to have you clapped in irons for this.'

'Perhaps it was the best way, sir,' said Esmond.

Tweedman did not answer but bent down, and looking like a music-hall comedian getting a laugh by the ungainly use of double-jointed limbs and a walking stick, closed the staring eyes.

An army dispatch rider strode up, gave the body one brief glance, then saluted Esmond. 'Captain Tweedman, Royal Navy?'

Esmond indicated Tweedman, who took the message. It was from Stancombe and read: WILLEM STOVER LOST WITH SHIP STOP.

Tweedman looked at the still body, then up at the trees. All his anger went, and for the first time that day his stump stopped aching. He could leave Ireland now and go back to England. Everything that he had to do had been done.

The sailors stood in a ring watching, the dispatch rider stood waiting. Everyone was expecting Tweedman to erupt again, but when he spoke it was quietly, almost reverently

'I don't suppose you carry a German ensign?'

'No, sir,' said Esmond,

Tweedman bit his lip. 'I don't want a firing-party, we've drawn enough attention to ourselves already, but within that constraint Korvetten-Kapitän Hans Frederick Kordt is to be given a naval funeral.'

'And his belongings, sir?' asked Esmond, indicating the suitcase.

'He has a sister still living in Probsteierhagen, near Kiel. Take them aboard with you when you sail. We'll see that they get to her later.'

None of the crew would want the blood-stained relics of a German agent's suicide on board – submariners were intensely superstitious folk – but Esmond had no option other than to obey.

He held out the book. 'He was reading this, sir. Hardy's *The Woodlanders*. Do you want it to go back with his things?'

Tweedman shook his head. 'I'll return that,' he said, taking the book, 'I happen to know that it was borrowed.'

A flicker of surprise crossed Esmond's face but he said nothing.

The burial arrangements made, Tweedman announced his departure. He asked Esmond to cross to the Anliem side with him, as he had one or two last-minute matters to discuss. Ordinary Seaman Hancock went with them to row the skiff.

When they were midway across 'The Ferries', Tweedman said, 'You will sail as soon as it is dark?'

'Yes, sir.'

'You know your position?'

'Yes, sir.'

'And after your attack you will stay submerged for at least six hours, steering a course south-westerly.'

'Yes, sir.'

'Then I wish you luck.'

'Thank you, sir,' said Esmond without a trace of enthusiasm.

'And don't think that I don't know how you feel,' said Tweedman, 'but as I told you before, there is more than one way of winning a war.'

'That is what Korvetten-Kapitän Kordt said,' murmured Esmond.

'You're not used to it, that's all,' said Tweedman. 'He knew when he took the job on that he had no hope. And as it turned out, it was better than a firing-squad in the Tower and a grave of quicklime.'

'Our refuelling, sir?' said Esmond.

Tweedman consulted his watch. 'You will get six tons this evening. Enough to see you home.'

'And one other thing, sir,' said Esmond quietly. 'Will the *Lusitania* be escorted?'

'No.'

'Not even with U-boats about?'

Tweedman shook his head.

Hancock brought the skiff to the shore and held it while Tweedman struggled over the thwarts. Then he opened the driver's door of the Minerva, helped Tweedman in and cranked the engine. With the motor running, Tweedman shook Esmond warmly by the hand, then pulled the goggles over his eyes, let in the clutch and roared away up the path in a cloud of grey dust. Esmond and Hancock stood watching him go.

'Stoker Thomas never knew the Hun was armed, sir,' said Hancock, the worry still very much in his mind.

Esmond shrugged. 'As Captain Tweedman just said. It was better than a firing-squad in the Tower, and after all, not everyone gets buried in the grounds of a Cistercian abbey.'

'No, sir,' said Hancock, 'I suppose they don't. Not these days,' and he followed Esmond back to the skiff.

The single shot that had rung out across Carridleagh, frightened the gulls and ended the life of Korvetten-Kapitän Kordt, also alerted the three Irish Volunteers. They were resting on the grass at the top of the cliff, but were still on the south side of the ridge. Doyle had intended to lead them not over the ridge, where they would have been silhouetted on the skyline and easily seen by the military, but through a narrow defile much nearer to the neck of Anliem and not all that far from the road block. The single shot confirmed this plan, and at once they set off northwards, taking what cover they could. This meant that they had still not been into Carridleagh or on to the grass of White Sheep Island, and had no idea what might have happened.

They reached the defile and stopped. Doyle, bent double, raced across to the other side of the track, then waved for the next one to follow. It was O'Brien. He too ducked, and was in the process of running across when a car, its motor in low gears and high revs, came roaring up from the shore. O'Brien changed his mind in mid passage, turned and ran back the way he had come. Doyle, seeing that he was now alone, turned to join the other two. Tweedman, swinging the Minerva round the blind corner, saw Doyle's back and the bandoleer as it disappeared behind a rock. He brought the car to a searing stop, staggered out and drew his revolver.

Tweedman made for the side of the track and saw O'Brien twenty yards away, crouched in a hollow on the rim of which the gorse bushes grew ragged and stunted. None of the Volunteers had intended using their weapons, they had been brought simply for self-defence, but when Tweedman fired two shots at the crouching O'Brien, the second of which grazed the flesh of his shoulder, both Doyle and Mehigan returned the fire. Tweedman, realizing that he was out-numbered, ran back to the car and taking up a position behind the engine, fired at the withdrawing Doyle over the bonnet.

Doyle said into the hollow next to O'Brien, and taking aim at the only part of Tweedman visible, fired a single shot. It went more or less where it was intended, under the engine and into Tweedman's left leg. The Director of Naval Intelligence felt a kick like a mule's and his leg taken from under him. He collapsed to the side of the track and had the presence of mind to roll a little way down the slope. There he lay with his revolver in front of him, waiting for the first of the rebels to appear over the skyline.

Esmond and Hancock had just cast the skiff off when they heard the shots. They pulled back to the Anliem shore and raced up the track. Only when they were half-way up and Esmond had shouted at Hancock to go right, up on to the ridge, did Esmond realize that they were both unarmed.

Esmond saw first the car, then Tweedman. The big man was lying flat on the grass, one hand holding the revolver, the other supporting his wrist.

'Are you all right, sir?' called Esmond, and Tweedman waved at him to keep down.

'Three of the bastards. Somewhere over there. One's got a rifle. For God's sake, go and get the Army!'

Esmond ran on up the track, sprinted low past the car and on down towards the road block.

Hancock, in his heavy leather sea-boots, found the going hard. His captain had waved at him to go to the right, to widen their line of search, and this he had done. He had reached the ridge, panting hard, and with considerable relief began running down the other side. But the slope was steep, and hundreds of feet below loomed the still, shining ocean. He had no wish to lose control but the short, dry grass was as slippery as ice. One foot caught a hummock, the other slid forwards, he fell and began to roll. Frantically he tried to dig his fingers into the earth but could get no grip. Sky, sea and green grass flashed before him and he prayed for a thicket before he was dashed to pieces on the rocks below. In the end it wasn't a thicket that saved him from that final plunge to oblivion, but a man who plucked at his flying shoulder and who was dragged several yards down the slope with him.

Hancock focused on the wide open sky, then on the dark silhouette crouched over him.

'God save you, man,' said Doyle, 'you were screaming like a banshee!'

Hancock tried to move but his back hurt. A second man, escorting a third whose arm was covered in blood, ran across the grass towards them.

'The devil, Con Doyle,' he cried, 'one of them is enough! In another minute we shall have all the military about our heads!'

Mehigan grabbed Doyle's arm and pulled him away. All

three ran towards the Point, then down the old sheep track that Pádrig had used, and so to the shore. There, keeping close to the cliff they began the long, difficult trek northwards, back to the curragh.

When Esmond got back to the Minerva with the soldiers, Tweedman was sitting upright on the grass, his left trouser torn apart, surveying his mutilated leg. He looked up at Esmond and laughed.

'They say lightning never strikes twice,' he said. 'Well, I've just proved that it bloody well does!'

Esmond ran on with the soldiers and saw Hancock sitting dazed where Doyle had stopped him from reaching the cliff-edge.

'Did you see anyone, Hancock?' he shouted.

Hancock shook his head. 'Not a soul, sir.'

Esmond was surprised. He looked towards the cliff-edge, decided that no one could have gone that way, then turned back towards the sailor.

'They must have come this way. There is no other.'

'I fell, sir, and stunned myself a bit,' said Hancock, 'but I still didn't see anyone.'

Esmond shouted for the soldiers to search.

At the base of the great cliff called 'The Cathedral', where the shingle reaches its highest, there is an overhang of rock. In there, Mehigan tied up O'Brien's arm with his own shirt, while Doyle crouched ready with the rifle. Wet of feet, cold and exhausted, the three Volunteers could hear the soldiers calling to one another. Sometimes the voices were overhead, sometimes far away, almost drowned by the sound of the sea lapping on the shingle. When darkness came, Doyle and Mehigan took the curragh down to the waters' edge, put O'Brien in, and rowed quietly away.

21

Tweedman had two more matters to see to before leaving Ireland. When he got back to Queenstown he put a phone call through to Guy Carr at the Admiralty. After a surprisingly short wait he heard the cheerful young voice at the other end asking how he was.

'Guy!' shouted Tweedman, cutting him short, 'You know there's a U-boat off here.'

'That's right, sir. The U-20, Kapitän-Leutnant Walter Schwieger. Just sunk the *Candidate* and the *Centurion* south of Waterford.'

'Get operations to order the *Juno* back.'

'But, sir, she's out beyond the Fastnet to escort the *Lucy* tomorrow!'

'If the First Sea Lord knew that she was out there *alone*, without a couple of destroyers, and with a U-boat operating in the same waters, he'd have a heart attack.'

At the other end, Guy was silent. Then he asked, 'And the *Lusitania*, sir?'

'Get her diverted to Queenstown.'

There was another brief pause, then Guy said, 'I understand, sir.'

'Good fellow,' said Tweedman, 'see you tomorrow,' and put the phone down.

Commander and Mrs Maitland had lodgings in the western quarter of Queenstown, on the hill above the station and not far from the small Scots' church. Tweedman, with little time to waste, was fortunate. The Commander was in his ship,

Mrs Maitland alone. She was quite evidently disturbed at seeing Tweedman and he knew then that she had recognised him in the street. When she saw the book in his hand, she blushed. Tweedman placed it on the table and she continued to stare down at the cover.

'I don't understand. . . how did you . . .?' she began in a confused way, then stopped.

'Mr Childs had to go away suddenly and could not return it himself.'

'He gave it to you?' she asked, puzzled.

Tweedman nodded. 'We got to know one another quite well. He asked me to return it to you and say how much he enjoyed reading it.'

'Captain Tweedman . . .' There was a great intensity in the voice and great concern, but Tweedman cut the sentence short by putting his finger to his lips and smiling. A feeling of great relief swept through Cynthia Maitland.

'Thank you,' she cried, clutching the book to her bosom, 'thank you, dear Captain, thank you a million times!'

Before any more could be said, Tweedman picked up his hat and hurried from the room.

The results of Tweedman's phone call reached Rear-Admiral Bone in the early evening. He was thirty miles south-west of the Fastnet Rock when the order came through to return to Queenstown. He had not heard of the sinking of either the *Candidate* or the *Centurion* but he was aware that a U-boat was operating somewhere off the coast.

The Admiral was on the bridge when the radio operator brought the message. He frowned, then passed it to Towers.

'They've gone mad, Brian,' he said, trying to contain his anger, 'they're going to leave the *Lusitania* all alone with a U-boat in her path!'

'Those destroyers from Milford Haven . . .' said Towers, thinking aloud.

'God damn it, man!' cried the Admiral. 'Didn't I ask three days ago for them!' Then he walked to the wing of the bridge and stared towards the western horizon. He had lost the Dover Command because of U-boats, now it looked as if they were going to help him lose command of the

Eleventh Cruiser Squadron.

'Do we put the telescope to our blind eye, sir?' asked Towers.

Henry Bone shook his head. 'The days for those sort of heroics are over, Brian. No, put her about and start praying.'

With her helm thrown over at sixteen knots, the *Juno* heeled like a drunken old lady.

Sunset was 8.16 pm. With the sky cloudless, the light would last well into the night. Esmond decided that he would take the B-12 out of Carridleagh at 11 pm, and expected their only hazard to be fog. Already patches were forming in the sheltered areas of the inlet. He told Paynter his intentions, and Paynter galvanized the crew. Activity around the landing-stage suddenly blossomed. It was good to be going to sea again, for after the disappearance of Grant and the burial of the German everyone felt that a hoodoo hung over White Sheep Island.

For Esmond too the evening could not go fast enough. Everything that had happened had deeply disturbed him, and knowing what lay ahead he felt that the worst might yet be to come. He felt as well the sense of disquiet that hung over the whole crew, and knew how damaging that could be to the submarine. But there still remained one essential task. Before the boat could be called ready, they had to take on fuel.

At seven, two thirty-horsepower, three-ton Thorneycroft subsidy vehicles lumbered down the track, each laden with forty-gallon drums. They passed the small armed post that Esmond had established after the shooting, and drove down to the water's edge. It seemed as if everything had been thought of, for they carried flexible metal tubing and pumps. Cigarettes everywhere were extinguished and a dozen drums loaded on to the wherry and ferried over to the submarine. The cage of white mice was placed on the steel deck above the main forward petrol tank, the inlet cap of the tank unscrewed, and the hose connected. On the wherry, 'Tiffy' Fletcher fitted the pump and broached the first drum. He put his nose to the hole and grimaced, then got one of the ratings to sniff. The rating nodded.

166

'This isn't petrol, sir,' said Fletcher to Paynter, '*it's diesel*.'

Paynter ran over and applied his nose to the open drum.

'They've brought us diesel oil, Skipper!' he shouted up at Esmond, and as Esmond jumped down into the wherry Paynter and Mitchell opened another drum. That too was diesel.

Esmond, sick at heart, put his hand to his forehead and cursed silently. He ordered Fletcher to find out exactly how much petrol they still had in the tanks, then crossed to the Anliem side. The service corps drivers swore that they had taken on the load indicated and blamed the depot. Esmond was standing there helpless when Ford's car clattered down the track, swerving from side to side. As he passed, Ford put his arm over the door and called out:

'Hail, young fellow; as Kipling said, "The barrow and the camp abide, the sunlight and the sward." '

In answer, Esmond grabbed Ford's arm and shouted, 'Who arranged this bloody fuel?'

'Something wrong?' asked Ford in surprise, bringing the car to a halt.

'Everything's wrong! It's diesel oil *and we're a petrol-driven boat*!'

Ford's mouth fell open. 'Petrol driven?' he asked, stupidly.

'*Petrol driven*!'

'But my dear fellow, I thought all submarines were driven by diesel engines?'

'Not an old one like that!' cried Esmond, pointing across at the B-12.

Ford produced a flask from his pocket, wiped the top and offered it to Esmond. Esmond pushed it away.

'You bloody fool, you're drunk!'

'Diesel fuel,' said Ford, taking a swig himself, 'six tons of diesel fuel for a submarine.'

'Are you saying that is what you were told?'

Ford nodded. 'Six tons of the best diesel fuel for a submarine.'

'You really were told that,' asked Esmond, 'you're not just making it up?'

'My dear fellow, why ever should I make up a thing like that?'

There was a long pause.

'What do you know about this operation?'

Ford shrugged. 'It's all over old chap, and a damned good job too! By eleven tonight you'll be on your way back to Portsmouth.'

Esmond was surprised that the man knew nothing of the *Lusitania* project.

'We have one more operation,' said Esmond carefully, 'and by the time we've done that, our tanks will be dry.'

Ford looked at his watch and had a struggle to make out the hands. 'It's nearly eight, old man. The depot shut hours ago. With all the good will in the world we couldn't get petrol here before half-past ten tomorrow morning.'

Esmond shook his head. 'Too late. You must get hold of Captain Tweedman.'

Ford laughed. 'I will, don't you worry. But God only knows when. He's probably on the High Seas himself by now! My dear, young fellow,' added Ford quietly, 'it's been a bloody awful day. Heard about poor old Frederick Childs?'

Esmond nodded.

'Terrible business, blowing his brains out like that,' said Ford, shaking his head then draining the flask. 'Nice fellow . . . charming, old fashioned, a gentleman in the true sense of the word. Not that many left these days. Makes us all feel so damned vulnerable.'

'For Christ's sake stop being so bloody maudlin,' said Esmond. 'Anyway, you're all right, you operate in Ireland.'

Ford gave a cruel laugh. 'My dear fellow, Mistress Sullivan has only to open her mouth and the Sinn Feiners would be knocking at my door.'

'I'm sorry,' said Esmond, 'I didn't realize.'

'Why should you? You've got your own problems. Look,' said Ford coaxingly, putting his hand on Esmond's shoulder, 'now that everything's over, why not be a good fellow and go back to Queenstown? They've got gallons of petrol there and I'll telephone the senior naval stores officer first thing in the morning and tell him to expect you.'

Esmond closed his eyes in anguish. The actor was a

drunken fool. Tweedman a knave, and the island had more than a hoodoo, it was damned.

'I can't go into Queenstown! I have been specifically ordered not to! I shall have to come back to this God-forsaken place!'

Ford shook his head. 'Afraid not, old chap. Everything's got to be dismantled by midnight.' He brought two envelopes out of his pocket. 'Blackmore's and Wright's postings, and the Army have started taking the wire down. By cockcrow tomorrow, no one will ever know that you and your merry men have ever been here. Oh, and that reminds me, do see that your latrines are properly filled. We don't want too many flies here, not with the summer coming on.'

Esmond left Ford sitting disconsolately on the running board of his car, and walked back to the skiff. On the submarine, Fletcher was waiting with the figures. They had approximately three tons of petrol instead of their full load of thirteen. 200-250 miles on the surface, running economically.

'And batteries?' asked Esmond.

The petty officer shrugged. 'They're fully charged, sir, for what that's worth. Maybe thirty miles submerged.'

When they left Carridleagh at eleven, the derrick was already down and the ruins cleared. One of the last items to be embarked was Childs' blood-stained suitcase. A mile outside the entrance they hit fog. They dived to check the trim, then surfaced, but after another two hours' probing for a clearing Esmond took the boat to the bottom so that they wouldn't be rammed. They rested there until dawn.

Ford, Blackmore and Wright watched them go, then the two Navy men sank the wherry in the deepest water and took the skiff to the Anliem side. They loaded it, together with their personal belongings, on to the Crossley and Ford gave them each their postings. Much to Wright's surprise, he was not going back to Sheerness. Instead he was to proceed with the enclosed railway warrant to Lough Swilly and there report to the submarine decoy vessel *Remembrance* bound for the Mediterranean. As Tweedman reasoned, it was a remote and fairly suicidal job and wouldn't last all that long.

Petty Officer Blackmore too was surprised, and wondered exactly what he had done to deserve such a posting. He was to take the Crossley to Kingstown and there proceed to Bristol to join a draft leaving as reinforcements for the Royal Naval Division on Gallipoli.

It was the evening of cocktail parties and the ship's concert. An unreal gaiety embraced the liner. It was almost as if everyone was trying to forget or, at least, not to acknowledge. At 7.50 pm, Captain Turner was called away from the party he had reluctantly attended, and handed a radiogram. It was from the Admiralty, addressed specifically to the *Lusitania*, and read: 'Submarines active off the coast of Ireland.'

Somehow the message seemed incomplete. In view of the contents, Turner expected instructions. It was still not too late for him to divert northwards and enter the Irish Sea through the North Channel. He therefore queried the message and asked for it to be repeated. It still read exactly as before.

Turner stared at the blood-red sun hanging low over the evening sea. He had taken all the precautions he could. The twenty-two lifeboats had been uncovered and swung out; with the exception of essential access way, all watertight doors had been shut; he had doubled the look-outs, both those in the crow's nest and in the bows; doubled the officers on the bridge and ordered the stewards to black out the cabin portholes. He had even requested passengers not to light their after-dinner cigars on the open decks. There was now little more he could do except go below, first to dinner and then to the concert.

It was still light when they reached the dank overhang of the wood. Grant followed the girl along the narrow path. Somewhere above and ahead, a roosting pheasant screamed and flapped its way through the branches. Grant jumped and the girl laughed.

'Anyone would think that you had never been in a wood before!'

'Not sure I have,' said Grant.

170

'Are there no woods in Portsmouth?' asked the girl in surprise.

'Not *in* Portsmouth. Over the hill there's a bit of a forest.'

The girl stopped and pointed. 'That is St Bridget's Well!'

The girl was obviously proud of the local sight. Grant was disappointed. He peered into the gloomy darkness, but could make out little beyond a rough circle of low boulders.

'What's so special about it?' he asked.

The girl did not answer but looked down into the dark waters. Grant slipped his arm round her and although she shuddered she did not move away. He put his hand on the soft skin of her cheek and turned her head towards him.

'I said, what's so special about it?'

'People come here . . .'

'What people?'

'Men and girls . . .'

'You're pretty,' said Grant.

'You can't see me.'

'Oh yes, I can. And anyway, even if I couldn't, I could remember you. I've been looking at you all day. I thought you were pretty the very first time I saw you.'

The girl pulled away:

'When I asked you if you had a sweetheart, you said, "No, not really a sweetheart, if you get my meaning. Just girls I know, sort of thing . . ." '

'Well?'

'Do you know many girls?'

'No, not many . . . not really.'

Bridget turned away and started walking back the way they had come.

'I think we had better be getting back. You are not supposed to go walking and they will wonder where you are.'

She started to run. Grant ran after her.

'But none of them are as pretty as you!' he called.

The girl ran on. Grant caught her at the top of the hill. He took her in his arms and tried to kiss her, but she turned her head aside and struggled free.

'I don't understand,' said Grant, catching her a second time,' you like me, I know you do!'

'This is not Cork!' she cried. 'I am not a Cork girl!'

'Whatever's that got to do with it?!'

'Don't you see, you are English and not even a Catholic! And you have other girls!'

With her white shawl streaming behind her, she ran down towards Inishslea.

In the yard was a strange sight. O'Brien's carrier's cart was drawn up before the door, but he was not in his usual place, the driving seat. He was in the back, under the canvas awning, his right arm wrapped in strips of white cotton through which the blood showed in two dark red patches. Mehigan and Doyle were in the process of helping him out.

'Holy Mother of God!' cried Bridget. 'Has there been an accident?'

'Bestir yourself, Bridget,' shouted Mehigan, 'and fetch your father!'

'He has gone to Béal na Liam!'

'Then prepare a kettle of boiling water and some clean linen.'

'You have no shirt,' said Bridget, pointing.

'Do as I say, girl.'

Bridget ran into the house. Grant, who had entered the yard at that moment, ran to the back of the cart and helped the two men get O'Brien through the door. They laid him on the couch with a rug under his shoulder. Doyle found the whisky, took a mouthful himself, then put the bottle to O'Brien's lips.

'Not that!' said Grant, pushing the bottle away. 'He's suffering from shock and exposure. What he needs is hot tea with plenty of sugar.'

Grant scrubbed his hands with carbolic soap and began unwinding the dirty, makeshift bandages. The others watched as he gently swabbed the dried blood from around the wound.

'It's only a graze,' he said, 'what happened?'

'We were on the ridge at Anliem,' said O'Brien, 'going to look for the submarine, when this car drove up the track. The driver started shooting, then the military arrived.'

'We were all lucky to get away with our lives,' said Mehigan, and Doyle agreed.

Grant and the girl swabbed the wound with iodine, then

wrapped it again in clean linen.

'He ought to see a doctor,' said Grant, 'to make sure it doesn't go septic.'

Mehigan looked at Doyle.

'We will send the doctor . . .' he said, 'but we would like to keep him here for a few days. After all this shooting the place will be buzzing with peelers and the military. A man cannot walk about with a bandage on.'

In the absence of her father, the girl did not know what to say. In the end she looked at Grant and waited for his decision.

'We'll look after him,' said Grant, and the girl nodded.

When they had gone and while O'Brien still sat on the couch, Tom Kearney came back. He had met Doyle and Mehigan and heard of the wound and how O'Brien was to hide for a day or two in his farm. Now he stood looking down at the neatly bandaged arm, an amused smile on his face.

'Upon my word, Michael O'Brien,' he said, 'have you not heard what the Scriptures say: "He that lives by the sword shall perish by the sword"?'

'Faith, man,' cried O'Brien, with more colour in his cheeks than he had had all day, 'and were you not yourself once a soldier and a sergeant? And did you not once live by the sword?'

'Och, man,' cried Kearney, 'but have I not long since given up childish pleasures and beaten my sword into a plough-share?!'

O'Brien forgot his wound and jumped to his feet.

'Did not our captain order us to find out about a sub-marine? And is it not right for soldiers to obey their officers? And did they then not turn a whole regiment of the military upon us? I tell you, Tom Kearney, we were lucky to get back with our skins, any of us!'

'I hear it is only a scratch,' said Kearney, 'and that you will be helping us with the milking in the morning.' Then he gave O'Brien a hearty thump on his good shoulder and went to the table.

Bridget saw to her father and Grant, then sat down herself.

'It was Peter,' she said, 'he knew what to do with the wound.'

'So it is Peter now, is it?' said Kearney, not without humour. 'This morning it was the Englishman!'

Bridget looked down at her plate and tried to hide her blushes. Grant said, 'Did a stint in the sick-bay. Comes in useful sometimes.'

Tom Kearney pushed back his chair and laughed.

'Faith!' he cried. 'Shot by the English and mended by the English! That is what we would call good Irish justice!'

22

Dawn brought the same fog, shrouding the whole southern Irish coast from Mizen Head in the west to Carnsore Point in the east. Turner was on the bridge before five. Ahead of him was an endless grey wall that swirled over the fo'c'sle of the giant vessel, so that at times not just the bow but even the capstans and anchor chains were invisible. Turner was not too sure of his position, but believed he was south-west of Cape Clear and almost due south of the Fastnet Rock. He reduced speed to eighteen knots and ordered the foghorn to be sounded.

Anderson arrived on the bridge at five-ten. Together they listened for the answering sound. Somewhere ahead should be the *Juno*. In spite of his reservations as to the old cruiser's capabilities, Anderson did not wish to miss her any more than Turner, and in spite of his natural inclination to keep everything to himself, Turner found himself telling his aide of his immediate intentions.

'I am going to reduce speed to fifteen knots, Captain Anderson. We do not want to miss her, nor do we want to reach the Liverpool Bar in daylight.'

Anderson nodded. He had been at sea long enough, and knew this route well enough, to know that at the reduced speed it would be about twenty-four hours between the Fastnet Rock and the Liverpool Bar. That would mean that not only would they reach the danger zone of the Bar just before dawn, but they would pass through most of the latter stages of the Irish Sea in darkness.

Turner gave the order and the liner slowed perceptibly. So

175

much, in fact, that it was noticed by all the passengers. Yet a new feeling of apprehension swept the ship, increased by the continual, deep, eerie blasts of the foghorn. After breakfast, many passengers went on deck and peered northwards into the fog, all hoping for the same thing. The first sight of land.

Apprehension gripped the bridge too. In spite of his excellent breakfast, Turner was worried. For what seemed hours now, he and Anderson had been standing in the damp listening for exactly the same thing, the answering call of the *Juno*'s siren.

'We must be well past the Fastnet now,' said Turner, 'and she's not out there.'

The only thought that crossed Anderson's mind at that moment was that the *Juno* herself had been torpedoed. That she had turned about and was now over a hundred miles away, steaming back to the safety of Queenstown Harbour, never entered his head.

At 11.02 am, they received a surprise but not unwelcome radio message. It took some time to decode but eventually proved to be both short and simple. They were to divert to Queenstown. Even though they were unaware that the activities of the U-30, and more recently of Kapitän-Leutnant Walter Schwieger in the U-20, had turned the area through which they were now to pass into a ships' charnel-house, the stark reality of their position was rapidly becoming apparent to both of the *Lusitania*'s captains. They were alone, unescorted on the High Seas, and the danger was sufficient for them to be diverted to the nearest harbour.

A radio message at 11.52 am clinched matters. It was to 'All British ships', and read:

> Submarines active in southern part of Irish Channel.
> Last heard of south of Coningbeg Lighthouse. Make
> certain *Lusitania* gets this.

The fog that persisted with varying degrees of density suddenly lifted to reveal a watery sun and the usual calm sea. Turner wasted no more time. He swung the giant liner towards the coast. Not only was he now heading for Queenstown as instructed and keeping clear of the Coningbeg Light, he would also be able to get an exact fix on the shore.

With his three remaining torpedoes ready in their tubes, Schwieger stood on the bridge of the U-20 and fumed. He had intended taking only two torpedoes back with him in the hope of finding a couple of good targets off the north of Scotland, but that still gave him this single one to use here. Yet would he ever find another target in this dense, swirling fog that at times had visibility down to the length of his own U-boat? Eventually he believed not, for leaving Zentner on watch he went down to his tiny cubicle and wrote in his log, 'Since the fog does not abate, I have now decided upon the return journey. This will allow me to push into the North Channel, should the weather improve.'

That, of course, should have been that, but perhaps like all good U-boat commanders Schiweger, whose 'bag' so far had been little for an ambitious man to boast about, had that instinct that makes the gambler stay for one more throw. In this case, he did not carry out his declared intentions immediately but remained off shore – the hatches open, the batteries on charge and the whole boat wallowing in the fresh damp air. However, when the fog failed to lift the possibility of being rammed in such poor visibility began to worry him, so at mid morning he dived to twenty metres and almost at once heard propellers churning the waters above.

'Up to ten metres! Torpedo tubes stand by!'

The periscope rose above the sea.

'Light cruiser . . . of old type . . . two funnels. I shall follow her in case she turns.'

But the *Juno* did not change her course, except to zig-zag. She steamed as hard as her old boilers would allow for Queenstown. It seemed that the U-20 was never going to fire that spare torpedo.

Schwieger surfaced, and almost at once was rewarded. Not with a ship, but with sun. It suddenly broke through and quickly burned off the mist. Schwieger opened his leather jacket and felt the warmth on his chest. The hatches were thrown wide again, the gramophone started up, the cook prepared their sausage and potato soup, and one of the dogs even came up on deck. After such a dismal start it had suddenly turned into a lovely spring day.

Schwieger turned his gaze from the sea to the shore.

177

Through his powerful Zeiss binoculars he scanned the great promontory of rock with its lighthouse on the tip. Standing 256 feet above the water, he had no difficulty in recognizing the Old Head of Kinsale. To the east was the mouth of the Bandon River; to the west, Courtmacsherry Bay. The sunlight etched the fishermen's cottages and caught a group of sails off Oyster Haven. He must be within a couple of miles of where he had sunk the *Earl of Latham* three days ago. Now that he had an exact bearing, Schwieger turned west and headed towards the Fastnet.

Esmond had planned to get astride the route from Fastnet to Queenstown by ten, and in spite of the fog he was still ahead of schedule. His morning had not been unlike Schwieger's: he had had to contend with the same lack of visibility and the same fear of being rammed. After surfacing he had run south-east at full speed, although it was against all his instincts as a sailor. The fog, however, had provided one benefit. He had been invisible from the land. For Esmond too the fog had suddenly lifted and he had seen the distant smoke that heralded the *Juno*'s return, but in his case the old cruiser had passed too far away to be identified.

With the sun up, Paynter checked their position. Esmond reckoned he still had time in hand, even though his final approach would have to be submerged.

'Steer zero-two-zero!'

The coxswain had just brought the boat round when it slowed. In response to Esmond's shouts into the voice tube, it was evident that Fletcher in the bowels had a struggle on his hands.

'She's overheating, sir!'

'For God's sake, "Tiffy", we need every rev we can get!'

'Two seventy-five, sir, and dropping fast. Looks like a gasket.'

The bow wave slipped down, then the boat seemed to steady at the reduced speed.

'Can you keep her there?!' shouted Esmond anxiously.

'If she doesn't seize up, sir.'

They were down to six knots when Esmond went below. The first thing he noticed as he made his way aft to the

178

Wolseley were the fumes. Although not yet overpowering, even added to the normal stench of oil, bilge water, urine and cooked food, the air was certainly not pleasant.

'Missing, sir!' yelled Fletcher above the uneven hammering of the sixteen pistons.

Esmond could see for himself. They were at 250 rpm, throwing out steam and falling.

'Don't suppose those bloody dagos did much for her, sir!' shouted Fletcher in disgust.

'You stripped her at Portsmouth,' said Esmond, pointing at the engine. 'Why in the bloody hell couldn't you have put her right then?'

'She's old, sir. She's only fit for the knacker's yard.' For want of anything better, Fletcher tapped the rev counter. It was shuddering and falling. 'There's a leak in the air intake . . . we've had to clear the petrol filter already this morning, but they are only flea-bites, sir, mere symptoms. The truth is, the heads need machining.'

'We've got an appointment to keep, so keep her there.'

'Aye, aye, sir.'

Esmond turned back for the control room realizing the uselessness of his order. The revs were down to 235 and if the vibration got worse either the petrol inlet or the exhaust manifold would crack. Esmond looked at the chart. If he could husband what power there was and went to his attack position on the surface, he could still be in time. Everything depended on how long the big Wolseley and its appendages lasted.

'Mice dead!' came the cry from Stoker Thomas.

'Exhaust gone!' shouted Fletcher.

'Can we keep going, "Tiffy"?' Esmond called into the voice tube.

'We'll have to disconnect, sir.'

'Shut engine! Shut all motors! Open hatches!'

The fumes swirled through the boat. One by one the mechanical noises ceased, the lights went out and a strange calm descended throughout the steel hull.

'All motors shut down!'

Those who could, made their way up to the conning tower; others, choking and gasping in the acrid combination of carbon monoxide and petrol vapour, waited beneath the hatches. Suddenly, fore and aft, air and light streamed into the darkened vessel as first the torpedo-loading hatch and then the engine-room hatch were flung open. The scramble for the deck was on.

They stood there gulping the salt sea air as if they would burst their lungs. Esmond, sick and dizzy, was the last to struggle up the ladder to the bridge. There was still a little way on the boat, and the breeze was welcome. When Esmond looked aft he saw the steel rim of the open engine-room hatch shimmering as the petrol vapour rose into the clear air. Nothing but a miracle had saved them from an explosion.

Esmond leant over the bridge rail. His head ached and there was bile in his mouth. When he felt steady enough he went down to the casing where the crew sat about despondently, no one daring to move for fear of causing a spark. The strain of sitting on a bomb told on every face. Esmond knelt and peered down at the offending Wolseley. He couldn't see much, for the engine itself was covered with a catwalk, but he had a feeling that the fumes were clearing. Without a word, 'Tiffy' Fletcher wrapped a wet handkerchief around his face and went down to investigate. After a couple of minutes he came up with the news that, amongst other damage, a petrol-inlet pipe from the main tank under the engine had fractured but was now plugged. Then he retched over the side. It was simply a matter of waiting for the fresh air to take over.

Esmond looked at his watch. Paynter saw the fretful action, and went down the open hatch into the conning tower. Esmond wrapped a wet handkerchief over his mouth, joined his first lieutenant, then lowered himself slowly into the darkened control room. The boat was ominously silent. Forward, in the mess room, the air did not seem bad. But aft, by the engine, the fumes were stronger than he had expected. He saw Fletcher's temporary repair, then climbed back up to the bridge.

'Not too good,' he said, as Paynter put down a hand and hauled him up the last few rungs of the ladder.

Esmond grasped the bridge rails, gulped the fresh air and thought. His orders were to be in position by 10.30 am. If he could take the risk of putting the submarine under way again, he could still be there before 11.30. That might not be too late.

'We can run with the crew on the deck once the motors have started.'

Paynter nodded.

Esmond looked at the empty horizon, then at the little groups fore and aft, and finally at Warren.

' "Tiffy", stand by to start motors!'

'Aye, aye, sir,' cried Warren and disappeared down the engine hatch.

'All other hands take to the boats! All hatches to remain open!' Esmond turned to Paynter, 'I want you in the boats, Hugh. If this thing does go up, one of us must be left. And you can give my love to Elizabeth.'

Only a flicker of Paynter's eyelids showed how much he disliked the order, but he did not question it. He went down on to the casing and organized the inflation of the two rubber dinghies. Then all the crew, except for Esmond on the bridge and Warren in the hull, lay a little way off, watching.

Esmond experienced an odd, uncaring calm and even the irony of the situation appealed to him. Here he was, doing all he could to carry out an order he detested. He almost willed that searing flash and disintegration to make his distasteful task impossible.

'Start up main motors!'

Everyone heard the two 300 BHP electric motors whir into life, and everyone had that moment of scalp-tingling suspense. But there was no explosion. After a couple of minutes, Esmond called the crew back but ordered them to stay on deck.

'Both full ahead!'

Warren put in the clutches, Esmond gave a new course and the B-12 started slowly northwards.

'And when we dive,' said Esmond to Paynter, wiping the sweat from his face, 'we'll stay awash as long as we can and keep the hatches open.'

'God really is on our side,' said Paynter.

'Let's hope he stays there,' said Esmond, grimly.

Tweedman had intended going straight to the Admiralty on his return from Ireland, but decided that he needed a complete change of clothing. He hoped his wife would be out, or at the very least that he might be able to get upstairs without her seeing him. But it was not to be.

Sarah Tweedman was used to her husband's many eccentric ways. In the past he had often returned from Brooklands with his clothes covered with oil. No one in the house begrudged him his boyish interests, even if it did mean extra work for the maids. This morning, however, things were different. Sarah came out of the drawing-room as her husband was creeping up the stairs. She saw his short, borrowed trousers, his unstable gait, and decided that this was something new.

'Gavin, whatever has happened?'

'It's nothing, my dear,' said Tweedman, clutching the banisters and resolutely continuing on his way, 'just a brush with a trio of Irish traitors. Luckily, they knackered the wooden one!'

But Sarah Tweedman was not to be put off so easily. She entered that sanctum, her husband's dressing-room, helped remove the offending trousers, was shocked at the mutilation of the artificial limb, and insisted on contacting the makers and ordering a new one herself.

'I sometimes wish, Gavin,' she said, 'that you were in a ship again. Even with the war on, I think it might be safer. The galling thing is that everyone I know believes that you just sit behind a desk all day, while their husbands are steaming about the North Sea or through those dreadful Dardanelles!'

Tweedman managed a smile. 'Not everyone behaves like the Irish, my dear.'

'Victoria Bone's husband has gone to Ireland,' said Sarah casually, while sorting out the clothes that were to be handed down to the gardener.

Tweedman stiffened. 'Have you been talking to her?'

'Gavin, dear, whatever is wrong? I just happened to bump into her in Harrod's yesterday, and she told me that her husband had gone to Queenstown to take over the Eleventh Cruiser Squadron. Is it that much of a secret?'

'All commands in wartime are secret! You women shouldn't talk like that!'

'I'm surprised you didn't see him if you were in Ireland?'

'Well, I didn't!' snapped Tweedman.

'And their son is doing very well,' said Sarah, oblivious to her husband's ill-humour, 'he's back at sea too.'

Tweedman closed his eyes and prayed for the woman to shut up.

'Look, my dear, I've got a lot to do, so if you'll excuse me . . .?' He held the dressing-room door open for her. She moved towards the door, then stopped and kissed him on the cheek.

'Sorry to bubble on like this when I'm quite sure you've got lots of terribly important things on your mind, but there is one piece of news, family news . . .'

'Yes?' said Tweedman patiently.

'Esmond, that's Victoria's boy, the one that did so well in that submarine, is going to get engaged to my niece Elizabeth.'

Sarah looked up at her husband and beamed. Tweedman, mouth open, gently shook his head.

'It's not official yet,' warned Sarah, 'nothing has been announced and it won't be until next year when the war is over, but they have an understanding.'

Tweedman suddenly felt very tired. He lay back on the bed and closed his eyes.

'Isn't that good news? She's such a nice girl, and doing her bit with the FANY!'

Tweedman nodded.

23

The King lit his inevitable cigarette, then stared through the window across the lawns of the Palace. It was spring in London. The day was fine, warm and very beautiful. At first glance it might have been high summer. In the sunshine, the number of greens was prodigious. The willows by the lake, the first trees out, were now fully draped; the yews had their new tassels; the hawthorns their exploding buds. In the distance a cuckoo gave its ventriloquist call in D sharp, while on the grass in front of the terrace a pair of wagtails fed their young, their crazy tails bobbing as if every bird had St Vitus's dance.

Colonel Ed House, President Wilson's personal representative, stood a little way from the window, thinking of the somewhat harsher spring in his own Texas. All around him the world seemed suddenly dedicated to Nature. Maybe it was just the loveliness of the day, but it all struck him as very incongruous. Already he and the King had talked of bloom and birdsong, while over in France thousands were being killed to the same accompaniment.

Suddenly the King turned from the window and said, 'Tell me, Colonel, what would your country do if the Germans were to sink the *Lusitania* with Americans aboard?'

House was surprised. Not just at the King's question, but because he had already heard it once that morning from the British Foreign Secretary. He thought for a moment, but saw no reason to alter his earlier reply:

'I believe, sir, that such would be the feeling of indignation in my country that it would be swept into this war.'

The King grunted, and tried not to show his satisfaction.

The sight of the soft green land of Ireland, distant though it was, cheered everyone. With the sun unshielded, the sea calm and sparkling with just the gentlest of swells, the fog-horn at last silent, and the liner once again making eighteen knots, it was difficult for passengers and crew to understand how, only an hour ago, they could possibly have been anxious. Certainly, standing on the promenade deck fifty feet above the blue water, or sitting down to luncheon with the band playing, life could not have seemed sweeter or more normal.

Even on the bridge, with the arrival of the sunshine and the distant landmarks it was as if a weight had been lifted. Turner held the latest radiogram, and even that added to the air of relief. Once again it was specifically addressed to the *Lusitania*: 'Submarines five miles south of Cape Clear proceeding west when sighted at 10 am.'

Cape Clear, Turner reckoned, must be at least fifteen miles behind by now. Indeed, the fog that had so worried them, which may well have lost them their rendezvous with the *Juno*, had, in all probability, saved them from the U-boat. For the first time in twenty-four hours, Turner might have been forgiven for feeling that his luck was in. And he would have felt that but for one thing. The whole sea, whichever way he looked from his vantage-point high on the bridge, was too quiet.

They were sailing into Patrol Area XXI. In addition to the Eleventh Cruiser Squadron at Queenstown, there were supposed to be an armed yacht and ten armed trawlers, as well as drifters and motor boats, yet not a vessel of any kind was to be seen. To Turner's mind the ocean was ominously quiet. It was as if everyone had left the world in the week they had taken to cross the Atlantic.

Shortly after 1 pm the watch picked up their first distinct landmark. Turner judged it to be Galley Head. If it was, then he was slightly further east then he had expected.

Now that the fog had gone, Kapitän-Leutnant Schwieger felt almost naked. His small U-boat may have been enjoying the warmth and the sunshine, but it had also suddenly become a very visible object. The only white wake was his and the only craft that the gulls were constantly circling and screaming over was the U-20.

Schwieger took off his leather jacket and stood in cap and shirt-sleeves, his hand on his binoculars. Although he was still disappointed with the patrol – after all, his single schooner and two small steamers were nothing compared with the results poor Weddigen had got, or Hersing before he had left for the Mediterranean – the weather was fine, his boat was a happy one, and they still had the homeward voyage to complete. There could be fine pickings up north. That was where the larger British warships were to be found.

Schwieger's reverie was interrupted by a smudge of smoke ahead and to starboard. Through the binoculars he saw what looked like a forest of masts and funnels appearing rapidly over the horizon. At first he thought that they belonged to a group of ships, or, more probably from their speed, to two destroyers. But even while he looked the specks increased in size so quickly that he soon knew it was a single ship, and a very big one at that. Schwieger glanced at his watch. It was 2.20 pm his time, 1.20 pm Greenwich Mean Time when he pressed the alarm bell.

Quickly and smoothly the crew of the U-20 moved to their diving stations. Schwieger grabbed his leather jacket, then followed the watch down from the bridge. He slammed the hatch shut behind him, clipped it and ran down the ladder.

'Stand by to dive!'

The petty officer engineer had his hand on the clutches ready to disengage the diesels.

'Clutches out!' called Schwieger.

'Clutches out!'

'Both full ahead!'

The ammeter needles of both electric motors swung into the red discharge area.

'All hands at diving stations?'

'All clear for diving!' called Zentner.

'Open main vents!'

Two petty officers spun the wheels that controlled the vents, the ballast tanks filled with sea-water, the forward hydroplanes drove the bow under, and the rear hydroplanes, tilted in the opposite direction and acting like an aeroplane's elevators, brought the stern up. The U-20 slipped below the surface.

At the periscope Schwieger watched a sight he sometimes saw in his dreams. The turbulence as the bow of the U-boat disappeared, the net-cutter slicing its way into that turbulence, the spray coming up over the periscope lens, then the ocean suddenly calming as he levelled the boat at eleven metres.

'Steer two-seven-four!'

The U-boat turned to starboard. Schwieger wrote in his log, '1.25 pm. Submerged to eleven metres and travelled at high speed on course converging towards steamer, hoping she will change course to starboard along Irish coast.'

Schwieger put his eye back to the periscope and corrected the trim. 'Up . . . up . . . level at that . . . down . . .' Then came another slight adjustment of course. Out of the corner of his eye, he saw Lang watching him.

'Got your *Jane's Fighting Ships*, Lang?'

'Yes, Herr Kapitän.'

'Then let's see what you make of her. Large, upwards of 30,000 tons, fast, twenty knots or more, four funnels, square bow, schooner stern . . .'

'Either the *Mauritania* or *Lusitania*, Herr Kapitän. Both now armed merchant cruisers and used for trooping. How about ventilators, are they very evident?'

'Not particularly,' said Schwieger.

'Then she might be the *Lusitania*, Herr Kapitän,' said Lang, controlling his excitement.

'In that case,' said Schwieger, 'if she turns to starboard we'll get her, and your wish comes true. Remind me, Lang, to take you on every patrol we go on.'

Lang was pleased, not just with his captain's words, but for the captain himself. After all the frustrations of the fog, the young kapitän-leutnant deserved his break.

'Beware of her guns, Herr Kapitän!' called Zentner.

Schwieger could see no guns, but with many steamers carrying stern guns and with this one listed in *Jane's Fighting*

Ships, he was taking no chances. This would be an underwater attack.

Captain Turner raised his hand to shield his eyes, then pointed into the distance: 'The Old Head of Kinsale.'

It was unmistakable twenty miles away. He knew it and so did Anderson beside him. Turner had taken bearing on the great hunched headland that stood out to sea just beyond the wide expanse of Courtmacsherry Bay many times. So had every sea captain who had ever navigated those waters. With Mizen Head, Cape Clear and Galley Head to the west, it was one of the four great landmarks of southern Ireland, and on the eastwards passage a welcoming sight to mariners over many centuries. From there to the safety of Cork Harbour and Queenstown was barely fifteen miles.

Turner now had to make a series of decisions that only he as captain of the *Lusitania* could make. One of the Admiralty memoranda had told him to avoid headlands. On the other hand, he was making for Queenstown and he had to know his own position with absolute accuracy if he was to enter the only channel swept daily for mines. None of the searching through his binoculars showed a single escort vessel to guide him in, and the entrances were narrow. After the doubts he had had of his exact position earlier in the day, when coming up from the Fastnet in the fog, Turner opted for caution and the routine he knew. He changed course to eighty-seven degrees and called for a four-point bearing to be taken on the Old Head. For the next forty minutes, the speed and course of the giant liner must be kept absolutely constant. If Anderson had any doubts he did not express them. But then the decision was not his.

As the liner swung to starboard, Turner went to the wing of the bridge and stared at the distant land. He had no doubts as to the correctness of his action. The U-boat he had been warned about must be miles to the west of them by now. He saw no need to zig-zag, believing that such action was only necessary after a submarine had been spotted. But perhaps his strongest reason for taking that straight course for so long was the knowledge that he could never have dared take his charge through the narrow mine-swept defile into Cork

Harbour without first taking a precise bearing. As the miles to safety apparently grew less, the *Lusitania* set rigidly on her new course.

'My God, Lang!' shouted Schwieger, his face pressed to the rubber shield of the periscope, 'I do believe she is changing course!'

'Our way, Herr Kapitän?'

'Perfect!' said Schwieger, 'Take this down, Lang. 2.35 pm: the steamer turns to starboard, taking a course towards Queenstown and thereby allows us to close for a shot.'

He swung the periscope. To his amazement, there was still no other vessel to be seen. The great steamer was unescorted.

'Make tubes ready!'

In the control room, men stiffened in anticipation. The only sounds were the whir of the electric motors and the orders.

'Torpedoes cleared for firing, Herr Kapitän.'

Schwieger adjusted trim and course while keeping his sights on the target. He could still hardly believe his luck. If the steamer continued on its present bearing it would be a textbook operation. When the time came to fire, the range would be between 600 and 800 metres, and with a target of 240 metres he could not possibly miss. His only concern was that his bronze torpedoes, old and obsolescent, might run badly or misfire.

'Take this down, Lang. Ran at high speed right up to 3 pm to get into a position directly ahead.'

Esmond could see the land and knew that he must dive soon. Tweedman, who had had the *Lusitania*'s previous noon position, had given Esmond a probable range of interception times between noon and 4 pm, but had ordered him to be in position by 10.30 am. From his limited height on the bridge, Esmond scanned the horizon. Not even a fishing-boat was to be seen. Although it was now 11.30 am, and he had several more miles to go, Esmond was quite certain that he had not missed the liner. If she was to appear over the horizon now, there was a fair chance that even the antiquated B-12 with her limited speed and torpedo range could still carry

189

out her bizarre mission.

With the promontory of the Old Head of Kinsale to the west, and the Daunt Lightship just to the east, Esmond took the old submarine down to an awash position and moved slowly towards the apex of all the likely courses from the Fastnet to Queenstown. With both motors running at maximum revs they could just make six knots.

Schwieger was now so near the steamer that he brought the periscope down for a few minutes, believing that the feather of water on the still ocean was bound to be seen. In complete silence he watched the boat's chronometer.

'Up periscope! Stand by number one tube!'

To Schwieger's relief, the steamer was exactly where he had expected. Still dead on course. Schwieger adjusted his sights. He estimated the target speed at twenty-two knots, and did a rapid computation of angles, speeds and deflections. He glanced again at the chronometer. It was 3.08 pm. His hands gripped the periscope handles so tightly that the knuckles were white.

'Fire number one tube!'

There was a hiss of air from the torpedo room, and the boat lifted a little with the loss of weight.

'Down . . . steady . . .'

Although only their captain had seen the target, all thirty-five men in the U-20 held their breath as they automatically counted.

A scenic artist from Covent Garden, having finished luncheon, left the dining-room and went on deck. He was leaning against the starboard rail when he saw something sticking out of the sea only a few hundred yards away. It was moving slowly and he decided almost nonchalantly that it was a submarine's periscope. Then he noticed a long streak of white foam. He watched fascinated and sickened as it headed towards the ship.

Seaman Leslie Morton, extra bow look-out on the fo'c'sle of the *Lusitania*, saw the same ominous white streak.

'Torpedoes coming to starboard!'

Seaman Thomas Quinn in the crow's nest added his voice.

On the bridge, the second officer echoed Morton's cry.

'Torpedo, sir!'

Turner, on the port side looking towards the shore, turned quickly. He saw the streak across the ocean but the missile itself was hidden from him. Of all the people on the sea off the Old Head of Kinsale that day, Kapitän-Leutnant Walter Schwieger, from his vantage-point 700 metres away, saw the explosion best, and the results were far beyond his expectations.

In the stalking period, Schwieger had fired a torpedo that had caused him considerable anixety, for its efficacy had been a matter of some doubt. Knowing that the steamer coming towards him would have a draught of about ten metres, he had set the torpedo to run at a depth of three metres, so that it would hit the boiler-room about half-way up. His crew had been waiting and counting, but through his periscope Schwieger saw the eruption he had caused well before the huge double boom hit the U-boat's hull and reverberated through the machinery. Twenty-six seconds after firing the torpedo, Schwieger began shouting to Lang, Zentner and the petty officers in the control room.

'We've hit her right behind the bridge! My God, what an explosion! It's ripped right through her!'

Schwieger kept his eyes to the Zeiss lenses, turning the periscope a little either way as he surveyed the doomed vessel before him. Lang sat, the log-book in front of him, taking everything down.

'Shot hit starboard side right behind the bridge. There was an unusually strong explosion with smoke and debris hurled well above the funnels. In addition to the torpedo, a second explosion must have taken place. It might be boilers or coal or powder. The superstructure above the point of torpedo impact and the bridge are torn asunder. Fire breaks out. The ship stops immediately and heels over to starboard, at the same time sinking quickly by the bow. It appears as if she is going to capsize. There is great confusion on deck. The boats are prepared and some lowered into the water. There is much panic on deck for many of the boats are coming down full, bow first or stern first and sinking immediately.'

Schwieger gave a new course and speed to the helmsman.

The U-20 came in closer to her victim and circled slowly.

'Port boats are not being lowered due to the list,' Schwieger called, then stood aside and let Lang, the old merchant skipper, have the periscope.

'My God, it *is* the *Lusitania*!' cried Lang. 'That great black stern, those propellers!'

'A unique sight,' said Schwieger quietly, then took the periscope back. He glanced up at the chronometer. By his time it was 3.25 pm.

'Fifteen minutes, and she won't stay afloat much longer. What is the depth here, Zentner?'

'One hundred metres, Herr Kapitän.'

'Then her bow must already be on the bottom. My God!' shouted Schwieger, 'she's blown off her third funnel!'

Schwieger turned to Lang. 'The cruiser will be back soon, with destroyers.'

Lang nodded.

'Down to twenty-four metres! Steer two-one-zero!'

The U-boat, set for the open sea, slid deeper into the ocean. Again Schwieger spoke to Lang.

'They are struggling for their lives out there. I couldn't have sent another torpedo into that throng.'

'Of course not, Herr Kapitän.'

Three minutes later, some strange urge brought Schwieger to eleven metres again. Through the periscope he took an all-round look.

'Lifeboats and flotsam, Lang, that's all. No sign of the *Lusitania*.'

'Eighteen minutes at the most, Herr Kapitän, that is very quick for a ship of that size.'

'That explosion, Lang, it was huge. I've never seen anything like it before.'

When a cup of coffee appeared miraculously in front of him, Schwieger took it gratefully. Now it was all over he felt very little emotion, just tired. After all the frustrations of the fog, it had been amazingly easy. On the credit side there was the 30,000 tons added to his tally, on the debit side − but Schwieger shrugged. He was not a vicious man nor a particularly cruel one, but simply a U-boat captain fighting for his country. It was as uncomplicated as that.

What Schwieger had been spared were the noises and the close-ups. he had seen that great explosion and, indeed, felt its shock wave. He had seen the huge rudder and the four giant propellers rise from the waters like a vision of Jules Verne, and was not surprised at Lang's exclamation on seeing the same awesome sight; but cocooned beneath the sea, he had not heard the human cries. Even that more terrible cacophony as the guts of the Atlantic giant had wrenched themselves free from their steel beds and torn through the hull like a horrific cataract had been heavily muted.

Schwieger had seen much but not all. The boiling surface of the ocean as the stricken liner had taken its final plunge, when those hundreds who were not sucked down in the turmoil or trapped in the hull could only imagine that a great underwater volcano had erupted, Schwieger had missed, for he had been submerged. When he talked of lifeboats and flotsam, it was a distant impression. He had been spared the thick scum of clotted wreckage that rose and fell with the turbulence, the obscene blanket of planks, boxes, chairs, furniture, garments and human heads on which the gulls were so soon to descend. But even had Schwieger seen all this, it would not have disturbed him as much as the knowledge that amongst the thousand or more to drown were three of his own countrymen, still locked in the *Lusitania*'s cells 300 feet down.

24

For more than two hours Esmond had been expecting smoke over the western horizon, but none had appeared. Fifty minutes ago they had heard a large explosion away to the west. In the submarine, speculation had ranged from the detonation of a floating mine to a U-boat at work. Esmond took yet one more look through the periscope.

'I don't understand it, unless she's increased speed in the night.' He breathed the words just loud enough for Paynter to hear.

'Not in that fog, Skipper.'

'She hasn't come between us and Queenstown. We'd have seen her.'

'In that case, maybe she got diverted to the North Channel at the last moment?'

Somehow, Esmond knew that she had not.

It was hard communicating with Paynter in the tiny, congested control room yet keep the subject from all other ears. Ostensibly, they were waiting for a U-boat, but the *sotto voce* conversations between the two officers had done little to reassure the rest of the crew. Esmond had known from the very start that this would be a problem, but by now it was only one of many.

The long run in on the motors after the Wolseley had failed had taken its toll of the batteries. Now, to conserve what little energy they had left, the propeller was turning just enough to keep the boat on station. Esmond now knew that when this was all over, and however it might turn out, he would have to put into Queenstown in spite of his orders.

'How much in the batteries, "Tiffy"?' he called into the voice tube.

'Maybe twenty miles, sir, maybe less.'

Things were getting perilously near their limit. Soon they really would be wallowing helplessly on the surface.

'I thought the Almighty was with us,' said Paynter, 'when "Tiffy" Warren started up the motors, now I'm beginning to wonder.'

'It's that damned suitcase, sir,' said Phillips at the wheel, 'the one that belonged to that Hun.'

Esmond had forgotten about the German and his words. Now he handed the periscope to Paynter, told him to keep the boat steady as she was, and ducking through the bulkhead, crossed the battery tank to the tiny mess-room that doubled as home for the reloads.

Esmond stared at the warhead of the port reload torpedo. To the eye, everything seemed to be in order. Leading Seaman Prentice, wearing on his arm the star and torpedo insignia of a seaman torpedoman third class watched Esmond respectfully. Next to Prentice stood his mate, Ordinary Seaman Hancock.

Esmond gently touched the propeller of the detonator and asked Prentice if he had noticed anything wrong.

Prentice looked carefully. 'Can't say I have, sir.'

'Take the pistol out, but do it very, very carefully.'

'Aye, aye, sir.'

Prentice fixed the propeller and unlocked the head of the pistol with the key.

'Excuse me, sir,' said Hancock, 'but what exactly are we doing here? I mean, what are we waiting for off Ireland?'

It was a cheeky sort of challenge, and Esmond hated deceiving his crew. But he had been doing it for hours and had no choice.

'A U-boat. Set a submarine to catch a submarine.'

'And that explosion, sir? It was two-eleven exactly and sounded pretty big. Do you reckon that was a U-boat?'

'Could have been,' said Esmond, 'or a drifter detonating a loose mine.'

'Captain to control room!' rang down the boat. Esmond's pulse quickened, was this his target at last? He went back

195

amidships. Paynter, his head bent over the eyepiece, was searching to stern.

'I don't know what you make of it, Skipper, but there's a flotilla of small craft coming out of Queenstown and Kinsale.'

Esmond took the periscope. Fishing smacks, a ketch, several long boats, a harbour ferry, a trawler and a couple of drifters were all heading towards the open sea. Esmond swung the periscope ahead and to westwards. There was still no sign of the *Lusitania*. He held on to the periscope handles, rested his forehead on the padding of the eyepiece and tried to think.

Paynter was watching him, so was Phillips at the wheel. That they each saw the problem quite differently was not important. What was important was that a procession of small craft was putting to sea; the liner he had been sent to attack, a strange enough task in itself, was nowhere to be seen; his own boat's capability was rapidly running down; and he did not know what to do.

Esmond put his eye back to the scope. The procession was there, as ragged and slow as before, and he still hadn't answered Paynter's question as to what he made of it all. The truth was that he made very little of it. Indeed, almost nothing. Nevertheless, his position as captain demanded that he did make something of it. With motors about to die, and a useless petrol engine, his choice of action was limited. He could surface, increase their field of visibility, but he was too near land. He could stay as he was, at periscope depth, and continue the vigil while he had air and power. That was probably the most prudent thing to do. On the other hand, that meant inaction and in their present state inaction seemed inadvisable. For a short while he could dive deeper and listen. The *Lusitania* was a four-screw vessel. Under water, her turbines and propellers should be audible over a considerable range.

'Full ahead! Down periscope!'

Warren gave the tired motors their maximum revs; Mills winched the periscope into its well.

'Keep sixty feet!'

The hydroplanes turned to dive, the main vents were

opened, Paynter watched the gauges and the B-12 settled to her new depth.

'Stop together!'

They listened in silence. A slowly turning propeller moved overhead, probably a trawler. In the torpedo bay, Prentice began the careful extraction of the pistol. Hancock looked at the emerging metal mushroom.

'If you ask me, something bloody funny's going on.'

'Bloody funny?' said Prentice absently, all his concentration on the delicate job in front of him.

'Yes, bloody funny,' repeated Hancock. 'When have you ever been told to do that before on a patrol?'

'Can't say I ever have.'

'That's what I mean, and I reckon it all ties up with this bloody dago writing everywhere, us keeping FORTH on our caps when we commissioned at *Dolphin*, all that whispering between the Skipper and Jimmy the One, and Grant . . .'

'Grant?' said Prentice, pulling the pistol towards him, 'What's he got to do with it all?'

'He was picked up by the Paddies,' said Hancock, watching Prentice's mouth fall open. 'Remember when me and the captain chased up that track yesterday, and they took a pot-shot at that mad chap with the wooden leg?'

Prentice nodded.

'I nearly fell down the bloody cliff! Would have if one of the Paddies hadn't grabbed me! The bastard actually saved me from going right over the edge, and one of his mates said, "One of them's enough!" '

Hancock was pleased with the effect of his words. Just for the moment, Prentice had forgotten the almost completely extracted pistol.

'They've probably killed the poor bastard by now!'

'Killed him? Killed Grant?! Why kill Grant?!'

'They're rebels, aren't they? They were trying to kill some-one, otherwise why lay an ambush? Anyway, I saw them, I know what they were like.'

Prentice thought about the matter for a while, then said, 'I don't see what it's got to do with this?' and very gently extracted the complete pistol.

'I'll tell you,' said Hancock, 'nothing in this bloody boat is

197

straightforward, and you know what's under the Skipper's bunk, don't you? That Hun's suitcase!'

Prentice took the mechanism under the bulkhead light and examined it carefully. There appeared to be nothing abnormal about the outside. On the inside of the cone, however, there were several alterations to the original, the most evident where two holes had been drilled in the metal and two dials, like clockfaces, inserted into the base. Both dials were identical, and the face of each was divided into sixty-four segments. Each dial had two hands, a red one and a black one. In each case the red hands were at thirty-two, the black ones just beyond twenty-nine, the angle between them, looking alarmingly narrow, was about seventeen degrees.

Automatically, Prentice put the head of the pistol to his ear. The faint ticking was just audible. Then he put the mechanism to Hancock's ear.

'Just like I said,' said Hancock, 'something bloody funny is going on!'

Prentice stood, nursing the pistol like a new-born baby.

'What are you waiting for?' cried Hancock. 'Take the bloody thing to the Captain!'

Prentice turned and set off towards the control room.

It was not in Rear-Admiral Henry Bone's nature to give up, nor was it a characteristic of his to believe that the whole world was against him. He had grown to accept the loss of the Dover Command, fortifying himself with the knowledge that the First Sea Lord had been wrong in believing that the U-boats were still coming through the Straits, and that his demotion, although palpably unfair, was the sort of thing that happened to senior officers of his age, particularly in the stress of war.

Henry Bone had even accepted that when his flagship the *Juno* had been ordered back to Queenstown from its patrolling position to the south-west of the Fastnet, and the *Lusitania* left to fend for itself through the submarine-infested waters off southern Ireland, that their Lordships might have reasons he did not know of. But when he got back to Queenstown and learned of the sinking of both the *Candidate* and *Centurion,* his doubts as to the wisdom of orders emanating from Whitehall increased considerably. He had been alongside but a short while when the most horrifying news of all reached him. A signal from the coast-guard at the Old Head of Kinsale reported that the *Lusitania* had been torpedoed at 2.10 pm and had sunk within eighteen minutes, going down about twelve miles due south of the promontory.

Bone stormed on to the bridge.

'By God, Brian!' he shouted to Towers, 'They've got her! The *Lusitania*! Steam up at once, we're going back out there. We'll pick up every man Jack of them, and I'll get that bloody U-boat if it's the last thing I ever do!'

Despite all the haste by the bewildered crew, it still took what seemed an astonishingly long time to cast off the moorings and get the old cruiser moving again. In the meantime, Rear-Admiral Bone could only gaze at the spire of St Colman's Cathedral and swear.

Everyone in the control room saw the pistol, everyone knew that there was something wrong. Most were simply puzzled, but to Esmond it was as if a shaft of light had suddenly flooded upon him. Knowledge was his. All the mystery of the operation was falling away, yet the full enormity had still to sink in. As it did so, he found it so horrifying that at first he tried to reject it.

'Ever seen anything like it before, Hugh?' he asked quietly.

Paynter fingered the pistol and shook his head.

'Can't say I have, Skipper, but it looks like a couple of timing devices.'

'You, Chief?'

'No, sir.'

Esmond looked round the tiny control room at the faces of his crew. Paynter, scratching his chin, working out the rest of the story; Phillips, sitting at the wheel, frowning in genuine bewilderment; Warren, shaking his head; Prentice, who had brought the rogue pistol, puzzled, his mouth open; and Esmond's anger boiled. He wanted to tell them everything. The way he had been duped over the D-9, why they had been sent diesel instead of petrol, what their target was supposed to be, and how they were to have been disposed of.

'This was the one in the port reload?' he asked, knowing the answer perfectly well but gaining time to think.

'Yes, sir,' said Prentice.

'240 pounds of amatol . . .'

It would have been like hitting a mine. The B-12 would have gone to the bottom in seconds with all hands and all evidence. Esmond held the pistol up.

'It's not quite what you thought, Chief,' he said. 'We can thank Korvetten-Kapitän Kordt for this, and at least repay him by seeing that that suitcase does get back to his sister in Probsteierhagen.'

'Yes, sir,' said Phillips without understanding.

Esmond closed his eyes. Imprinted on his retina were the green rectangles left by the glare of the bulkhead lights: half a dozen Tweedman faces, evil, grinning, like nautical warlocks. No more treachery, no more deceit. He would surface, disobey all his orders and limp into Queenstown with what was left in the batteries. Let someone else get America into the war.

'Half ahead! Up to twenty feet!'

The motor whir increased, the bow rose a little, then stopped. It was obvious that the submarine was not rising.

'Stern hydroplane jammed!' came the cry.

'Blow all tanks!'

Compressed air hissed through the tiny hull, and the bow began to rise alarmingly. Soon they were at sixty degrees.

'All hands forward!' shouted Esmond in a frantic effort to level the trim. In their heavy sea-boots, a dozen sailors scrambled forward, hauling themselves up the decking, grabbing anything they could to lift themselves past the next bulkhead, sliding back, pushing, shoving, swearing and sweating, until eventually they were crowded body to body in the torpedo flat. The bow hung at the same angle for what seemed an hour, then slowly began to fall.

'Stop blowing tanks!'

The fall grew faster. The bow was heading for the sea-bed 170 feet beneath.

'All hands aft!'

Again there came that mad scramble through the narrow companionway, this time for the engine and motor room.

200

'40 metres . . . 131 feet!' called Paynter, translating the dial of the depth-gauge.

'Revs dropping, sir!' cried Warren.

There was a flash from the after of the two motors. A stream of sparks ran up the wiring on the inside of the hull, looking with the curvature like an immense Catherine-wheel, and the stern was filled with choking, acrid smoke. The crew instinctively reeled back down the sloping decking, crawling over the Wolseley catwalk – shaken, bruised, groggy from the fumes, yet all the time trying to grab something, anything, to steady themselves.

'Fire!' cried Warren, and staggered back towards the control room with the last of the ratings that had been used to trim the boat. He had the presence of mind to slam shut the bulkhead door between the Wolseley and the bilge-pump motors, and so for the moment trapped much of the asphyxiating gases in the stern compartment. Devoid of power, plunged into darkness, the submarine went out of control.

'Emergency lighting!'

A dull glow lit the interior.

'Blow all tanks! All hands forward!'

Above the coughing and the clopping of boots came the hiss of compressed air. The boat shook, slowly levelled, then began to rise. The smoke that had reached the torpedo tubes rolled back to swirl in white streaks in the control room.

'Seventy feet . . .' chanted Paynter, his eyes fixed on the depth-gauge, '. . . sixty . . . fifty-five . . .'

Air! When would they reach it? With eyes and throats burning, lungs bursting, they waited for the call to open the hatch, but the B-12 was reluctant to break the surface.

'. . . Forty . . . thirty-five . . . thirty . . . twenty-five . . .'

The intervals between calls became longer.

'Up periscope! Stand by to open hatch!'

Esmond braced himself to see the world above. Through the periscope he saw the sky and the top of the dripping net-cutter emerge from the sea. Everywhere else there was a glassy calm. Just a few more seconds. He pivoted the periscope to starboard. The great ram bow of a warship, twenty-five feet high, cutting through the water at high speed, was fifty yards away. The B-12 was directly in its path.

'*Flood all tanks!*'

It was an academic order. Even with the poor definition given by the lenses of that obsolescent periscope, and through the distortion of size and the blurring of the image, Esmond had no difficulty in seeing the sun sparkling on the immense bow wave, the anchor hawses peering cruelly down like hawks' eyes, every link in the chain across the bows, and every streak of blood-red rust on the giant, bulbous ram.

Esmond laughed. He had seen death many times but never quite like this. The door of a torpedo tube left open, a mine scraping along the hull until one of the horns reached a hydroplane, a destroyer dragging its explosive charge over them while they hid on the bottom of the Bight, a net enfolding them like a doomed gladiator, or the greatest horror of all, a long lingering death on the sea-bed while the salt water slowly released the chlorine from the batteries. But never from the ram of an old British cruiser tearing through his control room.

'The stupid bastards!' he screamed as the world was obliterated from his vision for ever and the submarine lurched violently to port, at the same time heeling right over and sending everyone inside flying against the sharp edges of its steel intestines.

The stern of the submarine dropped and they slid down in cold, clammy darkness. They all knew what had happened for they had heard the ship pass over them. They had heard the thunder of her two triple-expansion engines and the deafening churning of her propellers. There was no panic and very little sound, except that of the boat itself. Shaken from the impact, old, tired and mortally wounded, the submarine went deeper, its steel hull groaning with its last breath. Water poured through the periscope packing and spouted from the valves in the control room.

Esmond, flung against the aft bulkhead door, held out his arms in a futile embrace as if to keep the door closed or enfold his crew in one final act of love. But the moment needed more than flesh and blood. When the bulkhead door to the engine room gave way and sixty-six tons of battery broke loose from below the deck, the dark merciless sea took over. Those still alive died, drenched to the skin, trembling, in a

202

stench of sea-water, petrol, oil, chlorine and urine.

No one on the bridge of the *Juno* saw the disabled submarine struggling to rise. The moment the periscope broke surface it was already in the dead ground immediately beneath the bow. Nor would it have mattered had the distance been greater and the officer of the watch or look-outs seen the boat fighting to reach the sunlight a few points to port or starboard. The wheel would have been thrown over and the ram directed towards the deadly shape. It would have been taken for what it was supposed to be, a U-boat, and the desire to revenge the *Lusitania* was strong.

As it was, the *Juno*'s ram passed over the stern of the B-12 and the underside of the cruiser's hull, where it levelled out at the No. 2 bulkhead and caught the submarine forty feet aft of the conning tower, ripping the exhaust away and tearing a hole in the pressure hull directly over the burnt-out motors. For the *Juno*, travelling near to her top speed at eighteen knots, the collision was so slight that no one on the bridge even turned to see if there was any debris in their wake. The scraping heard in the forward magazine and boiler room was thought to be no more than passing flotsam. Indeed, at the moment of impact, both Henry Bone and Towers had their glasses firmly on the horizon to the south of the Old Head. Towers, the younger, with the better eyesight, saw them first.

'Lifeboats, sir . . . five or six . . .'

Henry Bone saw them too and nodded. 'Three-quarters of an hour, Brian? We shall be there then, eh?'

In spite of the captain's optimism, it was not to be. 400 miles away in Whitehall, the First Sea Lord too had heard of the loss of the *Lusitania*, and of the hurried departure of the *Juno* on her mission of mercy. With a U-boat about he decided, in a moment of great lucidity, not to risk the old cruiser further. So once again a message of recall was brought to the bridge of the flagship of the Eleventh Cruiser Squadron.

As the ship turned about, Rear-Admiral Bone gripped the bridge rails and watched the half a dozen white lifeboats, all that was left of a once great ocean liner, disappear into the afternoon haze. Broken, he went below. He knew now that this must be the end of his career. Everything that could go wrong had gone wrong, yet none of it seemed to be his fault. He felt immensely old and tired and lowered himself on to his cot. He lay there for a while staring at the steel stanchion that ended in the girder above his head, then raised himself up and stared instead at the element he had known and loved for so long, the sea.

Henry Bone was distressed that over forty years of service in Her and His Majesty's Ships was coming to an end in such an inglorious way. He was distressed too, and not a little ashamed, that his colleagues would think that the task he had been given was too great. He should, of course, have made Vice-Admiral four years ago, then matters would have been different. Only one thing gave the Rear-Admiral any solace at that moment, the thought that his son Esmond, who had already made such a fine start in the waters of the North Sea, would be able to carry on the family tradition. He was immensely grateful to Gavin Tweedman for getting his son another command, and as he gazed at the calm sea he wondered just where Esmond was. He did not notice the patch of petrol from the old *Admirante Miranda* bursting into rainbows on the glassy surface after its long journey from the sand 170 feet below. Even if he had noticed that pool of refraction, he would never have connected it with anyone he had ever known.

25

Grant would like to have walked up to St Bridget's Well with her, but the girl's father had kept an eye on them, so Grant took up the broom and went back to sweeping the yard. Already it seemed as if he had been at Inishslea a month; in fact it was still not two whole days. In that time he had done what he could to be helpful, and his white woollen submariner's jersey was not just stained with oil, it was now stained with dung as well. He had exchanged the galley of the B-12 for the kitchen, yard and sties of Inishslea with ease. Tom Kearney had every reason to be pleased with his new help, as long as he kept his Protestant hands off his daughter.

Grant heard the hoofbeats of Matt Kearney's cob while it was still a hundred yards down the lane. The man was evidently in a hurry. When he rode into the yard, his face was aglow and the cob sweating. Grant looked up and smiled. Matt, surprised to find the English sailor working and apparently unguarded, was not quite sure what to say or how to return the smile. Fortunately, at that moment, his cousin appeared at the farm door.

'Faith!' cried Tom, 'what brings you here at this time of the afternoon?'

Matt leapt down from the cob, tied her reins round the pump handle, and with a glance at Grant took his cousin into his own kitchen.

'They've gone,' he said, with another glance over his shoulder at Grant in the yard, 'the English submarine has gone. Flown like a fledgling in June.'

'Is that so bad?' asked Tom.

Matt lowered his voice. 'Upon my word, cousin, does it not mean that we can never return him? And if we do not, then what are we going to do with him?' He dropped his voice even lower. 'Unless you are one who thinks as Con Doyle?'

'I do not!' said Tom firmly.

'Then what if he should escape and lead the military here?'

Tom shook his head. 'He will not try and escape.'

'Wist, man,' said Matt, 'how can you be so sure?'

'Did not my own daughter ask me only yesterday what a deserter was? And where else could she have got that but from the Englishman? Does that not tell you the state of his mind? Besides, you forget, cousin, that I myself was ten years in the British Army. I know what they do to deserters. I have seen them, and it is not a pretty sight!' He put his hand on his cousin's arm. 'But if you do not believe me, come outside and tell this young man what you have told me, then see his face for yourself.'

They went out into the yard and told Grant that the submarine had gone. To Matt's surprise, the English sailor did indeed seem relieved.

'When did they go?' asked Grant.

'At sometime in the night,' said Matt, 'there was nothing there this morning. The military had gone too, and all their wire.'

Grant grinned and went back to sweeping the yard.

'See, cousin,' said Tom, 'he will never run away. No sane soldier or sailor wants to stay in His Majesty's forces if they have the chance to get out.'

Bridget came down from the spring carrying a posy of wild spring flowers, germander speedwell, buttercups and blue-bells. She looked very pretty in a simple white lawn dress with lace cuffs, her hair brushed back behind her ears, her blue eyes shining in the late sunlight. Grant watched her, and Matt Kearney scuffed his feet on the cobbles of the yard. The girl picked a handful of grass by the fence, and placing it on the palm of her hand, offered it to the cob.

'The English submarine has gone,' said her father.

The girl glanced at Grant and smiled.

'I thought there was more than that,' she said, pointing

away down the hill, 'with Con Doyle driving up here as fast as Michael O'Brien's cart will go!'

The two cousins hurried to the yard gate. Con Doyle drove in, breathless and excited.

'My heart to the devil!' he cried, above the clatter of the wheels, 'Have you not heard the news?!'

'The English submarine has gone,' said Matt.

'That may be so,' said Doyle, stopping the cart, 'but I have better news than that. A great steamer has been sunk off the Old Head and they say the sea is full of the finest pickings you ever did see. And they are there just for the taking!'

'God and Mary save you!' said Matt, 'but is that true?'

'Has not Pádrig O'Callaghan gone for his curragh?' cried Doyle. 'And do they not say that the steamer was full of Americans, all with their pockets rattling with gold dollars?'

O'Brien, brought to the door by the grinding of his own cart-wheels, inquired exactly what had happened. Doyle repeated the story.

'Great God of virtues!' cried O'Brien. 'The ocean is at its most bountiful and here we are dribbling away the day at Inishslea!' And quite forgetting his wounded shoulder, he jumped up beside Doyle, seized the reins, and lashed at the nag between the shafts.

'Goodbye to you, cousin,' said Matt, as he too mounted the cob and turned her head back towards the lane. 'And if we find a bale of fine Indian silks, I will send them for your Bridget!'

Tom Kearney watched them go, then went back into the farmhouse. Bridget came back to Grant standing in the middle of the yard, his hands clasped round the top of the broom handle, his eyes towards the invisible sea.

'They've gone,' she said, 'your friends have gone.'

Grant nodded.

'They're not going to look for you now.'

'No . . .'

'Why do you stare so?'

'They've gone back to the war . . .'

'Do you want to go back to the war too?'

'Not really. It's just . . . well, it's funny to be out of it.'

The girl put her hand on Grant's.

'Come, I'll take you up to St Bridget's Well —' she pointed up towards the frowning hill, beyond the rock that sheltered the little spring, ' — we'll see it in daylight, no one will mind now.'

Grant threw down the broom and followed her. When they crossed the spring and jumped on to the small stepping-stones, he took her hand. She made no effort to take it away.

'You can have three wishes,' she said. 'The first one can be for your friends. What the others are you must not tell me or they will not come true!'

26

The sight that met the caller who opened the door of the office of the Director of Naval Intelligence was bizarre indeed. Tweedman sat askew to his desk, his left trouser-leg pulled up beyond the knee, the pathetic withered stump, red and raw, sticking over the edge of his chair; while his artificial leg, with a neat entry-hole and a splintered exit-hole, lay across his writing-pad. Kneeling at his feet was a small man in a white apron taking measurements and jotting the results in a black notebook. All this went on while an avalanche of signals poured between the Admiralty and southern Ireland, Tweedman watching every one like an enormous spider observing each thread of its web.

The *Lusitania*'s shocking demise seemed to have alerted every branch of the Navy. In addition, newspaper reporters, the embassies, the Cunard Company, the Board of Trade and even the Solicitor-General were all asking questions or giving answers. Tweedman had not been naïve enough to believe that he wouldn't create a stir, but even in his most extravagant moments he had not believed that it could be as hectic as this. What he was waiting for more than anything, of course, were the American reactions. After all, that was what the whole affair had been about. Everything else, so far as the Director of Naval Intelligence was concerned, was peripheral.

Stancombe kept up a steady progress in and out of the office with the latest signals, but usually said nothing. He simply laid the batch of papers on the pad to Tweedman's left and withdrew those that had been read and thrust on to the right. With one, however, although he had not meant to say a word, he found himself uttering, in a sepulchral voice, the figures on the paper.

'The latest count, sir, is coming up towards 1,200 lives lost.'

Tweedman said nothing until the man in the white apron had left the room and he himself was strapping back the mutilated limb. Then he snapped out the single word, 'Americans?'

'Looks like being a little over 120, sir.'

Tweedman grunted, looked up and said, 'I don't mind admitting, Stancombe, that the whole thing is more than I would have expected, much more . . .'

'She sank very quickly, sir. Eighteen minutes is not long for a ship of that size.'

Tweedman leaned back in the chair.

'Two things puzzle me. It was west of the position we had agreed, and Lieutenant-Commander Bone's orders were to aim for the No. 4 boiler-room. The effect should have been, well, at least containable, and certainly nothing like this.'

'I understand that the Mark V GS torpedo isn't all that accurate, sir,' volunteered Stancombe.

Tweedman shook his head. 'It was nothing to do with the torpedo, it was that damned cargo! But thank God the Huns have taken the blame!'

In the afternoon, Stancombe brought in several more pieces of information. The first was an intercept of a message from a U-boat of the Third Emden Half Flotilla actually claiming the *Lusitania* sinking.

'Can we identify the boat?' asked Tweedman quickly.

'The U-20. Kapitän-Leutnant Walter Schwieger.'

Tweedman gave a great sigh of relief.

'Thank God,' he said quietly.

'Do you think she really did sink the *Lusitania*, sir?'

'She is the correct boat and she was certainly down there. And U-boat captains still tend, on the whole, to tell the truth. Besides, as I said, it was further west than we might have expected. Yes. I see no reason whatsoever to doubt the good kapitän-leutnant's claim. Indeed, we must promote it!'

'And the *Admirante Miranda*, sir?'

Tweedman struggled up from his desk and hobbled to the window. The London of St James's Park looked particularly beautiful.

'None of that was in vain . . .'

'No, sir.'

'We could never be sure the Germans would sink her. We had to have a fall-back. Lieutenant-Commander Esmond Bone and his crew died as much in the service of their country as if they had gone down in the Sea of Marmara, the Heligoland Bight or the Skagerrak.' Tweedman turned and stared at Stancombe. 'But I will admit, Stancombe, that I'm damned glad for all our sakes that in the end it was the Hun that did it and not us!'

Tweedman held out his hand for the next message.

'More intercepts, sir. The American ambassador in Berlin has made arrangements to close down the embassy there.'

Tweedman spun round on his right leg. 'Has he, by God!'

'And Mr Page, the American ambassador at the Court of St James, has cabled President Wilson saying, and I quote his words, sir, "The United States must declare war or forfeit all European respect." '

'And Washington's reply?' asked Tweedman eagerly.

'We've heard nothing yet, sir, but I have a telegram with the headlines of this morning's *New York Tribune*.'

'Read them, go on, man, read them!'

' "900 Die as *Lusitania* Goes to Bottom: 400 Americans on Board Torpedoed Ship; Washington Stirred as when *Maine* Sank. Capital Aroused, Situation Gravest yet Faced in War." '

'No mention of German guilt?' asked Tweedman anxiously.

'Yes, sir, next paragraph. "Washington Determined that Germany shall not be Allowed to Shirk Responsibility for Deaths." '

'Give it to me!' cried Tweedman, and seizing the signal read it again himself. Suddenly he started to laugh, great gusts that filled the room and made his face crack and his eyes weep.

'We've done it, Stancombe! America will come in now! If

211

not this week, then next! And the Huns have helped us magnificently with all this glory they're making out of it!'

'Casualties, sir?' said Stancombe quietly. 'Two officers and fourteen ratings. They will have to be announced in due course.'

Tweedman nodded. 'In the performance of special duties while on active service ...' Suddenly he noticed Stancombe's arm. Barely visible on the dark suit was an even darker band. Tweedman pointed, stupidly. 'Stancombe ... God, damn it man ... I didn't know! Why in hell's name didn't you tell me?!'

'You had great things on your mind, sir ...'

'Where? How? When?'

'At a wood named after Lord Kitchener, sir. We believe it to have been machine-gun fire. It happened on the twenty-fourth of last month but we only heard this morning. His platoon officer wrote to say that John died bravely.'

'Take the rest of the day off, Stancombe.'

'But, sir, with all this ...' began Stancombe, when Tweedman waved him down.

'Take the day off and give my deepest sympathy to Mrs Stancombe. Assure her from me that final victory will certainly now be ours and that her son's sacrifice will not have been in vain.'

'Thank you, sir,' said Stancombe, 'and may I say how much Mrs Stancombe will appreciate your remarks.'

Tweedman nodded and went back to his desk. As Stancombe left the room, a worried-looking Guy Carr entered. Tweedman had no wish to see Carr at that moment, but he remained perfectly civil.

'What is it, Guy?'

'The *Lusitania*, sir. I've been thinking about that paper you asked me to draft, and your phone call from Queenstown about the *Juno* ...'

'Regarding the *Juno*,' said Tweedman, 'that was a normal tactical decision not to hazard a cruiser, confirmed later by the First Sea Lord when he ordered her to turn about. As for the *Lusitania*, from what I have heard, the master was not zig-zagging, although he had been specifically warned on no less than three occasions that U-boats were operating in his area. You know as well as I do, Guy, that had he been zig-zagging and at full speed, no U-boat could ever have got into a firing position.'

'That may be true, sir,' said Carr, still unconvinced, 'nevertheless, some people may think that we've been a bit negligent.'

'There is to be a full inquiry,' said Tweedman, 'the facts will all come out. The inquiry will certainly show that the master's actions were not above criticism. However, that is not our main concern at the moment. Our task is to make the greatest use we can of an outrage that will go down in our history alongside the Black Hole of Calcutta and the Cawn-pore Massacre, an outrage that has cost the lives of over 750 innocent passengers, nearly 100 of whom were children! For-tunately the task will not be difficult. Schwieger of the U-20 is already a popular hero in the Fatherland.'

'That doesn't mean, sir, that we might not have done more to protect her,' said Carr. 'There are already quite bitter criti-cisms on that score from American survivors.'

'For God's sake, Guy, we can't escort every ship! What with the Dardanelles, the North Sea and the Med, the Navy's overstretched as it is.'

'But the *Lucy*, sir, she was special. And we did recall the *Juno*.'

'That's not our weak point,' said Tweedman. 'Our weak point is that she blew her bottom out. *That it wasn't the torpedo that sank her, but that blasted cargo!* That's what we've got to work on, and you'd better start right away.'

'You mean, sir, that she carried nothing that wasn't on the declared manifest?'

'Exactly. And there was *no* secondary explosion, and if there was, then it was another torpedo. Now, be a good fellow, will you,' said Tweedman, 'I've got a couple of rather difficult letters to write.'

Carr left the room. Tweedman took two sheets of note-paper from the drawer of his desk and began the easier letter first, the one to Rear-Admiral Henry Augustus Ewing Bone MVO, RN. He would see how this one went before tackling the other, to Nurse Elizabeth Brett.

Epilogue

Although the sinking of the *Lusitania* shocked the United States and profoundly affected sentiment there, it did not bring America into the war. It was almost another two years, on Good Friday, 6 April 1917, before President Wilson signed the Declaration of War upon Germany.

Not unexpectedly, both sides dragged the maximum propaganda out of the *Lusitania* tragedy. Either the sinking was an outrage against humanity, or an example of British and American perfidy in shipping armaments upon a passenger-carrying vessel. In Germany, Kapitän-Leutnant Schwieger was, for a brief while, a hero. A few medals were struck, perhaps satirically, depicting the deck of the sunken liner crowded with munitions of every kind, below the words *Keine Bannware* (no contraband). The British copied the medal as an example of Hun frightfulness, and circulated it, with a suitable cover-note, in hundreds of thousands around the world. In the summer of 1915, the Board of Trade, at the Admiralty's request, held an inquiry into the sinking. To our 1970 minds, the cover-ups and omissions appear to be of almost Watergate proportions.

There have been more than sixty springs since that exceptionally fine one of 1915. Each of the next three years brought their particular holocaust: Verdun, the Somme, Passchendaele, and the great German breakthroughs of St Quentin and Chemin-des-Dames in 1918. Yet the sinking of the *Lusitania* still remains one of the most vivid and traumatic events of the Great War. Indeed, the name *Lusitania* has been engraved into the English language, not as a Roman province in Iberia – barely one in a hundred thousand ever knew it as that – but as a ship that died in strange and shocking circumstances. Only the *Titanic* can vie with her.

The aura the *Lusitania* had in life and at death has never diminished. Even her last resting-place could hardly be more dramatic. The Old Head of Kinsale has need of neither history nor legend. It is already a most awe-inspiring site. The walk to the lighthouse, nearly a mile and a half along road and track, is bounded by treeless grass eaten smooth by sheep, and precipitous cliffs. The *Lusitania* lies just west of south, twelve miles out, in 315 feet of water. She was located in 1935 by a Captain Henry Russell, and to tread on her plates a diver has to descend about 240 feet into the dark and often angry waters.

Now she is no more than an 800-foot reef. Giant congers swim through the once majestic dining-room; mussels adorn those early turbines. She is broken just forward of the bridge, and divers assert that the bottom of her hull, in the area of the bows, has been blown clean away. Many plates, lying scattered at a distance, bear witness to a huge internal explosion.

The *Lusitania* is more than remembered, she has become a legend, and nowhere is that legend and the speculation that lies behind it stronger than in southern Ireland. There is the evident: 'The Lusitania Grill', a kiosk in Kinsale, and the somewhat crude yet arresting painting of the liner in the nearest inn to the Old Head. There are also the inferences, the innuendoes. These mainly centre around the cargo, the British veto on survivors and bodies being landed at Kinsale – all had to be channelled through the Royal Navy at Queenstown, now Cobh – and activity over the wreck in the past sixty years, including allegations that explosives have been dropped.

The Royal Navy salvage vessel *Reclaim* appears to have been over the wreck, although for some reason this is denied; and Messrs Risdon Beazley, the marine salvage experts from Southampton, have also visited the site, apparently without diving. Here and there, though, along that coast, there are more concrete items to satisfy the pilgrim.

In the churchyard of the twelfth-century church of St Multose, Kinsale, there are the three '*Lusitania* outrage'

215

graves. In the square at Cobh there is the *Lusitania* Peace Memorial, with its dominant angel surmounting the two bronze figures that one takes to be sodden, ragged survivors until the somewhat enigmatic inscription is read: 'They helped in the rescue, gave aid and comfort to the survivors and buried the dead.'

In all, about 280 bodies were recovered, the great majority being landed at Queenstown. Some however, came ashore as far distant as Bantry and the Blasket Islands. About 900 were washed out into the Atlantic or trapped within the liner.

A mile to the north of Cobh, at the west end of Old Clonmel Cemetery, beyond the tombs of two IRA Volunteers, lie the three low mounds of the great common graves. Each has its thuyas, privets and yews, and its small whitened tablet, broken in two cases, reading simply, '*Lusitania*, 7 May 1915.'

For Kapitän-Leutnant Walter Schwieger, the end came on 5 September 1917, when his new command the U-88 was mined off the Dutch coast. For the old U-20, stranded off Denmark in fog, it was two of her own torpedoes, deliberately detonated, that immolated her. However, it was not until 25 August 1925 that the wreck was finally destroyed by the Danish Navy.

Admiral of the Fleet Lord Fisher resigned as First Sea Lord on 15 May 1915 – according to Churchill, in a state of 'mental distress and wild excitement' as a result of war strain. His departure precipitated the fall of the Government, with the First Lord the main casualty. Churchill himself left the Admiralty eleven days later.

Only the obsolescent B-12, the one-time *Admirante Miranda*, and the grave of Ordinary Seaman P. Grant, killed in the 'Troubles', have yet to be found.

WAR STORY

BY GORDON McGILL

Berlin, April 1945.

The city – and Germany – is only hours away from final
defeat. Deep in the underground passages of the burning
city a four-man British unit is fighting a desperate battle
against time. Its top-secret mission: to bring a German
general back alive, whatever the cost. And to keep one
step ahead of the advancing Russian army.

But why?

Find out in WAR STORY

IT'S THE WAR STORY TO END ALL WAR
STORIES

WAR FICTION   0 7221 5901 3   £1.00

A selection of bestsellers from SPHERE

FICTION

INNOCENT BLOOD	P. D. James	£1.50 ☐
HOLLYWOOD GOTHIC	Thomas Gifford	£1.50 ☐
STEPPING	Nancy Thayer	£1.25 ☐
UNHOLY CHILD	Catherine Breslin	£1.75 ☐
TO LOVE AGAIN	Danielle Steel	£1.25 ☐
THE ELDORADO NETWORK	Derek Robinson	£1.50 ☐

FILM & TV TIE-INS

RAISE THE TITANIC	Clive Cussler	£1.50 ☐
CLOSE ENCOUNTERS OF THE THIRD KIND	Steven Spielberg	85p ☐
LLOYD GEORGE	David Benedictus	£1.25 ☐
SOMEWHERE IN TIME	Richard Matheson	£1.25 ☐
THE GENTLE TOUCH	Terence Feely	£1.10 ☐

NON FICTION

WAR IN 2080	David Langford	£1.50 ☐
A MATTER OF LIFE	R. Edwards & P. Steptoe	£1.50 ☐
WORLD OF SALADS	Rosalie Swedlin	£2.75 ☐
SUPERLEARNING	S. Ostrander & L. Schroeder with N. Ostrander	£1.75 ☐

All Sphere books are available at your local bookshop or newsagent, or can be ordered direct from the publisher. Just tick the titles you want and fill in the form below.

Name ....

Address ....

....

Write to Sphere Books, Cash Sales Department, P.O. Box 11, Falmouth, Cornwall TR10 9EN.

Please enclose cheque or postal order to the value of the cover price plus:

UK: 40p for the first book, 18p for the second and 13p per copy for each additional book ordered to a maximum charge of £1.49.

OVERSEAS: 60p for the first book and 18p for each additional book.

BFPO & EIRE: 40p for the first book, 18p for the second book plus 13p per copy for the next 7 books, thereafter 7p per book.

Sphere Books reserve the right to show new retail prices on covers which may differ from those previously advertised in the text or elsewhere, and to increase postal rates in accordance with the P.O.